BOUQUET

A PRICE FAMILY ROMANCE

LUCINDA RACE

MC TWO PRESS

A PRICE FAMILY ROMANCE

Bouquet
Crescent Lake Winery Series
Book 6
By
Lucinda Race

Editor Susan of West of Mars
Proofreader Kimberly Dawn

Cover design by Jade Webb www.meetcutecreative.com

Manufactured in the United States of America
First Edition May 2022
Print Edition ISBN 978-1-954520-08-0
E-book ISBN 978-1-954520-07-3

INSPIRATION

For My Dear Rick
Love never dies, it endures forever...

Your words are my food, your breath my wine. You are
everything to me.
Sarah Bernhardt

THANK YOU...

Thank you for purchasing Bouquet. I hope you enjoy reading Liza and Drew's story. I love writing characters who are a bit older and deserve a second chance at happiness. So, turn the page and fall in love in with the Price Family.

If you'd like to stay in touch, consider joining my Newsletter. I release it twice per month with tidbits, recipes and an occasional a special gift just for my readers. Just click this link

https://lucindarace.com/newsletter/

and there is a free book when you join! Happy reading...

---

*L*iza couldn't believe what she was seeing as her boys raced around Anna's house into her sister's backyard. Even though she had just gotten done telling them she needed help unloading the van.

"George. Johnny!"

She contained the frustration that threatened to bubble up and over and at the same time hoped someone would think to come and help her. If they did, they could make one trip instead of three with the jugs of lemonade and iced tea and, of course, the cake. It was Memorial Day and this family liked every reason to get together. As the family grew, there were more and more celebrations.

It would have been so much easier to have it at her place, but it was Anna's turn to host and she and her husband Colin wanted to show off their backyard, complete with an inground pool that had been finished just in time for the holiday weekend. She smiled to herself. That also explained why the boys had taken off like a shot from a cannon. It was hot.

She pushed her blond bangs from her forehead and tapped the button to ease open the hatch on her minivan. She grabbed the sweat-covered tea jug and struggled to hold on to it before it slipped and crashed to the ground. The plastic top popped off, drenching her pale-blue capris with the caramel-colored liquid.

"Damn it." She tried to whisk the tea from her pants in vain.

"Hey, Liza, can I help?"

A deep male voice interrupted her next slew of profanity. Heat flushed her cheeks as she noticed Drew Cameron's concerned face.

"Hi. Are you here for the party?" She propped one hand on the side of the van in a poor attempt to look casual.

"I am." He bent over, straightened the gallon-sized plastic jug, and then reached under the van to retrieve the lid. He handed it to her. "I guess no tea today."

She glanced down and inwardly groaned. What a way to make a good impression on the man she had a tiny crush on for the last year or so. "Except on my clothes and it's okay; it was just for a couple people who love my sweet tea."

He handed her a pure-white linen handkerchief from his back pocket. "Here. Use this."

What guy carried around a fancy handkerchief anymore? Her late husband, Steve, never had anything this fancy. She accepted it since it was better to try and blot the spots than let them stain her new outfit.

"Thanks." She gave him a smile so as not to appear ungrateful.

"Colin invited me to stop over and see the new landscaping, and he mentioned the family was getting together. Since I happen to know some of the best cooks in the valley would be here, I took him up on the offer."

She held out the now-stained cloth and quickly withdrew it. "I'll wash this and get it back to you."

"No need." He took it from her. "Give me a sec to toss this in the car and I'll help you get the rest of the stuff into the house."

She watched as he jogged to the sleek BMW. His long legs and backside looked pretty good in dark cargo shorts. He also wore an untucked pale-yellow short-sleeve button-down shirt and deck shoes. Classic preppy look. She had to admit Drew was easy to look at with his intense green eyes, dark-brown hair, and the scar just off from the center of his chin. He had well-toned arms that she guessed could hold a woman all night and make her sigh.

She tore her eyes away lest he saw her ogling him. She felt an odd twinge in her stomach as she reminded herself it had been a long time since Steve died and there were *things* she missed.

"I'll take the cake if you can handle the jug of lemonade without turning yourself into an Arnold Palmer; you're good the way you are." The corners of his mouth quirked up and a deep dimple appeared in his cheek. It just enhanced his smoldering appeal.

"We've moved on to beverage jokes now." She bobbed her head. "Tea and lemonade. That would have been delicious on this hot day." She fanned herself, but not from the actual temperature in the air. Rather, the way he looked at her made her internal temp spike. What was she thinking? He was her brother-in-law's best friend. Not someone she was going to date.

"Be careful with the cake; it's got four layers and it's heavier than it looks."

"Not to worry. I can deal with the cake-carrying job as long as you've got the jug."

She gave him a little shove in jest. "If you drop it—" Her voice held a playful warning tone.

"What will happen?" He gave her an easy grin.

"Um, you'll have to arrange for a new cake." Jeez, that sounded lame to her ears. What would he think?

"Not to worry, dear Liza. If I drop the cake, it'll give me a chance to ask you where it came from, and maybe you'll take pity and help me find a new one?"

She gave him a sharp look. *Is he clueless about where to buy a cake or is he flirting with me?* With a quick double-check of the lid before she picked up the jug of lemonade, Drew slid the cake from the back of the van.

"Are we going in the house or out back?"

Before she could answer, the front door opened. Anna hovered in the doorway. "Hey, you two. What's going on? The party is this way."

Liza pushed the button on the van and the hatch shut with a soft clunk. She and Drew walked up the wide front porch steps.

"I had a minor mishap. What iced tea isn't on my clothes is puddled in the driveway."

Anna took the lemonade and stepped to one side so Drew could walk through the door.

"Would you set the cake on the kitchen counter? It's too hot out. I don't want the frosting to melt off."

Liza looked down at her capris. "I'm going to run home and change. Can you keep an eye on the boys for me?"

"There's no reason to drive back to your place." Anna

pulled her into the house and closed the screen door. "Go upstairs and dig through my closet. I have something that will match your top. You might as well wear my clothes. I won't be wearing any of those until next summer." She rubbed her slight baby bump. "Things are getting a little snug."

"Thanks, sis. But are you sure?"

"Don't be ridiculous. We're the same size; you're just a little shorter."

Liza didn't need to be told twice. Anna had developed a new appreciation for clothes after living in France for over a year and her closet was a dream come true.

*D*rew watched as Liza zipped up the stairs. It was nice the sisters were so close they shared clothes; he'd never experienced that kind of a relationship as an only child. Inwardly, he groaned. Every time he saw her, he was struck not only by her beauty, with those golden hazel eyes, long blond hair, and the curvy, petite figure, but it was her mind with the quick, snappy retorts that was the most attractive part about her. She didn't seem to care one iota about who he was or his bank account.

Colin walked out of the kitchen and glanced curiously at Drew as he stood there, staring.

"Hi. I heard you were here."

"Just. I met up with Liza in the driveway and carried the cake in."

Colin clapped him on the back. "From what I heard, if you had been one minute earlier, she wouldn't have dropped the tea."

Drew gave him a sidelong look. "Timing is everything."

"Hmm. Not sure if you think your timing is good or bad." He walked to the kitchen. "I'm bringing out some trays for Anna. If you think you can spare a few minutes from guarding the stairwell, wanna give me a hand?"

"Yeah, sure." Drew took one last look at the stairs before joining Colin.

*N*o one seemed to miss the iced tea, and Liza's nephew Ben announced her lemonade was the best ever, so despite walking around in a borrowed skirt, which happened to match her top perfectly, things hadn't turned out too badly after all.

She noticed Drew was tossing the ball around with the kids, and her oldest brother, Don, was keeping a close eye on Jack's youngest, Hannah, and his twins, Spencer and Madison. She leaned back in a chair and observed the controlled chaos. Funny how the first four grandsons were about the same age, and then the next three were a year apart. She and Steve had talked about having more kids. She had always wanted to have four, but after George was born, there had seemed to be plenty of time. She swallowed the lump in her throat and sighed heavily.

"Penny for your thoughts." Tessa bumped her chair. "You seemed a million miles away just now."

"Just a little trip to what might have been." She gave her older sister a look. "What are you up to? Checking on me?'

"You looked like you were sinking into a sad place, and this is a party." Tessa handed her a glass of sangria and

Anna leaned back in the deck chair facing the boys, who were running after a soccer ball around the yard.

She gestured toward Don, who was chasing the little girls. "I was remembering that Steve and I talked about having more kids." She looked at Tessa. "I liked growing up in a big family—well, most of the time. You have to get along with different personalities, and that's a good life skill."

Tessa sipped her lemonade. "There were some days I'm sure Mom regretted having six kids, but since you and Leo were the babies, you probably never saw that side of things. It would be nuts around the house, especially on a rainy day when she couldn't shoo us outside. I swear that's why they kept adding on to the house."

With a laugh, Liza said, "To be able to send us to different corners?"

"Something like that." Tessa gave her a probing look. "How old are you?"

"Mid-thirties." Tessa knew exactly how old she was. "What's with the question?"

"You're not ancient, and you can still have a couple more rug rats."

Liza followed her gaze. Tessa was looking at her husband. "What about you and Max? Will you have more than one?"

She shrugged. "We're not sure yet, but we'll be happy with one if that's all that's in the cards for us." She wagged a finger in Liza's direction. "Stop changing the subject."

A stab of longing hit Liza like a ton of bricks. "I'm missing a crucial element to have a baby."

"Are you lonely?"

With a snort, Liza shook her head. "I'm so busy and

don't have time to be lonely. The boys' schedules are nuts, then there's the house, and my event planning business has taken off much faster than I thought it would."

"What about at night when you go to bed? Wouldn't you like someone to hold you, talk about the day's ups and downs, you know, share the load?"

Anna flicked the beads of moisture from the side of her glass. Sure she would, but Steve had been a special man. It would be hard to find another guy who was that amazing, and then she had the boys to consider. "I've thought about it, but I wouldn't know how to go about dating. It's been a long time, and what about my sons? How would they feel about me dating? Of course, there's another unknown. Would this imaginary guy understand the boys have to come first?" She sipped her drink. "It's overwhelming, so for now, it's easier to be the enigmatic widow."

"Would you consider dating a friend of the family?"

Tessa was looking at Drew. "I appreciate your concern but"—Liza gave her a forced smile—"the boys and I are just fine as we are."

"But"—Tessa's eyebrow arched, which always meant she was up to something—"if there was a nice guy that was single and you found him interesting and easy on the eyes, would you consider going on a date?"

Liza had to chuckle at the way Tessa drawled out the word *consider*. "I'll tell you what. If the stars line up and someone drops into my life whom I like and who understands about the boys, then yes. I'd consider a casual date." She set her glass down and stood up. "But since the stars will never align in perfect harmony, we don't need to keep talking about it." She crossed the short distance to the kitchen door and turned back around to her sister. "Thanks for worrying about me."

Tessa grinned. "That's what big sisters are for, to butt in when we're not asked."

Liza caught Drew looking at her and his smile caused her pulse to quicken.

Too bad I don't have time.

*J*ohnny and George bounded into the kitchen where Liza was sipping her morning coffee. The sun streamed in the bay windows by the table. School had been out for two weeks and summer camp started today.

"Pour your cereal and milk. We need to leave in thirty minutes."

They plunked down in their chairs. Milk glugged from the carton over George's bowl and onto the table.

He gave her a grin. "Sorry, Mom."

She handed him a couple paper napkins. There was one thing she wasn't going to do, and that was flip out over spilled milk. "Wipe it up, please."

He placed the napkins over the spill and began to shovel cereal in his mouth. Between bites, he mumbled, "Will Johnny be in the same group?"

At eleven, Johnny was the older of the two and always paved the way for his somewhat shy ten-year-old brother, but it was time George broadened his comfort zone.

"No," she began carefully. "You're going to be with

kids in your grade. That's how the camp breaks everyone up, but there will be some group activities when you can hang out."

George said, "Why can't it be like last year? We got to be together all the time."

She looked between the boys. "You said you wanted to do sports camp, and this is the best one. It'll be fun and just think. When I pick you up every afternoon, you can swap stories about all the fun things you did."

Johnny came to the rescue. It had been that way since their dad died. "George, I'll bet we can eat lunch together and if anyone is mean to you, just let me know. I'll punch their lights out."

"John Bradford. You will do no such thing. If either of you have any trouble, you'll tell your counselor and they'll take care of it." She gave him the all-powerful mom stare and her sternest voice. "Do I make myself perfectly clear?"

"Yeah, but—"

"No ifs, ands, or buts. You will not, under any circumstances, give the staff a reason to call me."

George kept his eyes downcast and pushed his cereal around in the bowl of milk. "It's okay, Johnny."

She knew he was nervous without Johnny around, but they'd be going to different schools in the fall. It was time to create some healthy distance between them.

"What kind of sports are at camp?" George lifted the bowl to his mouth and drank the last of the milk. When he was finished, he sported a fine-looking milk mustache.

Choosing to ignore the obvious, she said, "There's soccer, basketball, archery, boating, swimming, and hiking trails. I'm not sure what else." She had their attention now. "And every other Friday, there is the option if you want to stay over and sleep in tents."

"Like real camping?"

She suppressed a laugh. "Is there fake camping?"

"Mom," Johnny groaned, "it's not like sleeping in a tent in the backyard, where we can come inside if it rains."

"Oh, I didn't know that tenting in the backyard wasn't camping. I'll remember that the next time you ask." She wanted to laugh, but seeing her son starting to think bigger than their backyard was gratifying.

With their dishes in the sink, Johnny tossed the soggy napkins in the garbage.

"Wash your face, brush your teeth, and grab your backpacks. Make sure you have your swim trunks, a towel, and a sweatshirt."

They thumped up the stairs. Despite George's reticence about being separated from Johnny, she knew it was absolutely the best thing for both of them.

She savored the last swallow of lukewarm coffee and wiped the table with a dish towel. After loading the dishwasher, she rinsed her mug for another cup when she worked from home later today. She had a mountain of phone calls to make for three upcoming weddings and she still needed to get several quotes out to more. Coffee was essential for this working woman.

*L*iza slowed the minivan and joined the long line of cars in what appeared to be the drop-off lane. The boys unbuckled and, since they were barely moving, she decided to not harp on them about seat belt safety.

"Wow, look at all the kids." George's face was within a fraction of an inch of the window. "I don't know anybody." He swiveled in his seat. "Do you know anyone, Johnny?"

"Nope, but that's cool. It means nobody knows us either."

She had to wonder what he meant by that but filed it away to ask later. She inched closer, moving up by a car length, waiting their turn.

"Mom, what's taking so long? Can't we get out here?"

"Johnny, there is a drop-off process. You're met by counselors who put you in a group first, and then you'll go into the main building."

"How do you know that?" Johnny thrust his chin out.

Teenage years were going to be tough with this one. "I read it in the paperwork they sent."

George peered out the window. "Only three more cars are in front of us."

Johnny grabbed his backpack and adjusted his ballcap. "You don't have to get out of the car, Mom."

"I need to introduce myself to the counselor and make sure they have my cell phone in case of an emergency."

"Mom." There was that preteen groan again. "You're gonna make us look like babies."

"If I didn't check in, they'd wonder what kind of a mother you have. So be polite while I speak to the person in charge of your groups."

Finally, it was their turn. She set the emergency brake and left the van running. The boys tumbled out the passenger side. George waited for his brother to lead the way.

A young woman with a clipboard hurried in their direction. "Hi, I'm Sandy." She gave the boys a perky smile. "And you are?"

"I'm Johnny Bradford and this is my brother, George."

She scanned her list and, with that huge welcoming smile, pointed over her shoulder. "George, you're with the group behind the green line, and Johnny, you're in the yellow group."

Liza took a step forward. "Hi, I'm Liza Bradford and I wanted to make sure you have my cell number." A wave of nerves raced through her. It was like that each time she left them.

"Hello, Ms. Bradford. I don't have that information here but if you want"—she handed her a card—"call the office when you get to work and you can double-check."

"Thank you. I'll do that." She went to give the boys each a kiss goodbye, but from the look on Johnny's face, she held back and gave them a wave. Somedays she just didn't want them to grow up. "See you at four."

Sandy gave her a reassuring smile. "A few nerves are normal, but the boys will have a great time."

She gave them one last look. Johnny was talking to the girl next to him and George was looking at her, his huge brown eyes almost imploring her not to leave. She gave him one last wave and walked with purpose toward the van. Looking at him made her heart sink, as if she were abandoning him. It had been like this since Steve died. George seemed to be the most vulnerable.

Liza pulled away from the curb and looked in the rearview mirror. The boy next to George was showing him something inside his backpack. Reassured, she concentrated on the road in front of her. She went over the mental checklist for the upcoming wedding at the winery and decided to make a stop to check on things with Peyton and Kate before going home. Her sisters-in-law had become like sisters, more than just her brothers' wives. They each had their own unique ideas about how the upcoming wedding would work best. Chuckling, she guessed it would be a lively conversation. Since everyone seemed to work better over coffee and pastries, she'd stop at the coffee shop.

She loved the painted white walls and bright-yellow-checked curtains that graced the front windows of the small cozy café. The display cases were yellow with a dash here and there of a bright sky blue. Small tables and chairs for two and four people were scattered around the room. The eclectic mix worked perfectly. In the middle of each table was one fresh daisy, the owner's signature flower. In fact, the café was called Daisy's Bakery. Sue Mallery had been open two years and business was brisk.

Approaching the counter, Liza smiled at Sue. "Hello there."

"Morning. Where are the boys this morning?"

"I dropped them off at Cam's Sports Camp."

"Are they going for the summer?" She opened a small white cardboard box and waited. She wasn't being presumptuous; she knew her customers' routines.

"Yes. I've heard really good things about it. Low camper to counselor ratio and lots of activities, so hopefully at the end of the day, they'll be tired and want to go to bed." She laughed. "They have too much energy."

"Don't all kids." Sue gestured to the case. "What can I get for you?"

"I have a meeting with Kate and Peyton. I was thinking it would be nice to have some refreshments while we work." She looked at the handwritten menu on the chalkboard. "Could I order three iced cold brews with cream and sugar on the side." She studied the case, noting the variety to choose from. "How about four scones and four fruit Danish."

Sue put them in the box and then added two oversized sugar cookies before taping the top securely in place. "For the boys after they've had dinner." She placed the box next to the cash register and took three large plastic cups and quickly filled them with ice and cold brew.

"That's so sweet of you. Thanks." Sue was a thoughtful woman, one of the reasons her customers kept coming back.

She secured them in a carboard tray and balanced the pastry box on the top. "Can I get you anything else?"

"That'll be it." She handed Sue her credit card. "Wait. Can you add one more cookie to the box?"

Sue gave her a wink. "They're irresistible."

As she was on her way out the door, Stella Maxwell, Tessa's sister-in-law, held it open.

"Stella, this is a nice surprise." Liza grinned.

"I'm sorry I didn't get much of a chance to talk with you at Anna's picnic. I was on a deadline for the book I've been editing and wasn't able to stay long."

Stella was related to the Price family through her brother Max, Tessa's husband.

"That's fine. We should get together for lunch or something. Give me a call when things ease up." Liza smiled.

"Sounds like a plan." Stella held the door for Liza with a promise to talk soon.

*G*rapevines lined both sides of the road. They were loaded with tiny fruit and from Liza's observation, it should be a good harvest, barring any weather issues for the remainder of the season. If there was one thing that was in her blood, it was wine.

She drove between two massive stone pillars and

under a large purple carved wooden sign. Crescent Lake Winery, established 1942. As always when she thought of it, a thrill raced through her. Her great-grandfather worked this land for his family's future. He did his best to ensure the winery would provide for future generations. Well, however secure a farm of any kind could be. She remembered her grandfather saying people will always want to drink wine, in good times or bad.

With a twinge of regret for not going into the family business, she reminded herself how nicely her event planning dovetailed with the winery. Things had worked out for the best. She brought clients to the winery and Kate referred clients to her as an event planner. Not that she didn't use other venues when the client or occasion warranted it, but this was her favorite, and then Tessa's winery, Sand Creek, was a close second. The Prices had become a family of business owners.

She turned down the road that led to the tasting room, bypassing the main house for now. She'd swing by and see Mom later; it had been a couple of days since they'd chatted.

She thought about how far she had come in the last few years. It was never her plan to start a business, but as an event planner, she was in demand and had begun thinking about hiring someone to be ready for the busy season next year. This year, she had to decline two events that had overlapped.

Thank heavens Leo and his fiancée, Stephanie, took the boys overnight from time to time. Her brother had been amazing with the boys when Steve died. Even now, with Leo and Steph working to combine their two vintage car restoration businesses, they still made time to pitch in. Not that the rest of the family wouldn't, but her twin, Leo, and the boys had a special relationship, and her other brothers had their hands full with their own expanding families.

She parked outside the tasting room, noting Kate's and Peyton's SUVs. Maybe she should trade in the minivan for something like Kate had. It was roomy and she'd still have plenty of space to lug the boys' stuff around, along with anything she might need for work. And some of the looks she got when she showed up to a job in the mommy van were downright insulting. *It's just transportation.*

Peyton stood in the open doorway. "Hey. It's about time you got here."

She held up the carboard tray and box. "Provisions." She nodded to Peyton's hair. "Love the blond highlights." Normally Peyton's dark hair was in a short bob but recently she had grown it a little longer and the new style framed her light-brown eyes and pixie face perfectly.

"Thanks. Trying something different." Peyton held out her hands to take the coffees while Liza retrieved her laptop bag from the passenger side.

She glanced over her shoulder. "What's Kate doing?"

"Tweaking the menu for the wedding. I gave her my suggestions for the wines. The groom only likes white sweet wines and the bride isn't a fan."

Liza and Peyton went inside. The tasting room wasn't open yet, so there were few lights on, which allowed the natural light to stream in from the windows overlooking the vineyard, creating a relaxing and comfortable environment.

"Do you want to meet in the gazebo or inside?"

"It'll be hard to see my screen outside, so let's pull a couple of tables together. I have samples to show you both."

Peyton set the refreshments aside and pulled two square tables together. "Better?"

"Perfect." Liza began to set out file folders and her laptop. She glanced up. "How are Hannah and Owen?"

Her sister-in-law's eyes lit up. "Owen is such a good kid. He asked if he could go to camp with the boys, but only for a couple of weeks; he wants to be able to play with his little sister too. Hannah is an absolute joy, so easygoing, smart as a whip, and follows her brother everywhere. Those two make quite a pair."

"Jack's good too? I know this time of year requires long days."

"He's hired two new guys and hopefully they'll work out. He loves running the vineyard and tending to the vines; it's managing people that's harder for him. Anna's better with the workers but she has her hands full with morning sickness."

Liza sat down and grinned. "I'm waiting for Tessa to announce she's pregnant."

"In due time. I think they're trying." Peyton handed her an iced coffee and a couple of creamer packets before fixing one for herself. "All the Price kids will have kids soon except for Leo and Steph."

"He's old-fashioned. Marriage first and then babies."

"Do you think they'll have any?"

As she asked the question, Kate walked in, tall and curvy with long, dark hair, emerald-green eyes, and an easy smile. Liza marveled at how she really was the perfect match for Don, not just that they made a striking couple but in temperament too.

"Are we talking about Leo and Stephanie?" She spotted the white pastry box and untouched iced coffee.

She pointed to the cup and to herself and grinned. "For me?"

Liza chuckled. "Of course. I got scones and Danish, but leave the cookies. They're for the boys later."

"I whipped up cupcakes. You both have a small tray waiting for you to take home." Kate added sugar and then a splash of cream to her coffee before sitting down. "And to get back to your earlier question, Steph wants kids."

That made Liza smile. "Leo will be a great dad." She tapped her pen on the pink legal pad sitting in front of her. "Let's get down to business."

With a twinkle in her eye, Kate said, "Peyton, the mini mogul, has spoken. She's softened us with snacks and no more time for small talk."

Liza shrugged. "What can I say? I'm my father's daughter and I intend to conquer the event planning world."

The balance of the day flew by, and at four o'clock, Liza was in line waiting to pick up the boys. Mentally, she had her fingers and toes crossed that they both had a good day.

She inched forward and thought she saw the top of Johnny's ballcap among a group of kids. But where was George? Shouldn't they be together by now? Concern wrapped around her heart.

Another car pulled away from the curb and she slid the passenger window down to speak with a guy dressed in baggy shorts, a camp logo tee, and sneakers.

"I'm Johnny and George Bradford's mom."

"Hold on." He turned and called their names. Johnny stepped forward. No George. He called out louder, "George Bradford."

From the back of the group, she could see kids moving aside as he wove his way through. "Here I am."

She let out a stilted breath. He looked okay. No, he looked happy.

The boys ran over, smiles plastered on their faces. The

counselor opened the van door for them and Johnny jumped in and George plopped down next to him.

"See ya tomorrow, Todd." George waved before he closed the door.

She watched them in the mirror as they buckled up before she pulled onto the main road. "Did you have fun today?"

They nodded like bobbleheads. "George made a bunch of friends and I knew a couple of kids from school that are in my group."

George said, "It was awesome, Mom. We did bows and arrows, went swimming, and played kickball and a bunch of other stuff."

"Johnny, what did you do?"

"Some of the same, but we also had an assessment of soccer skills. Tomorrow we're going to meet some guy who'll be our coach for the summer. He's gonna break us into teams and part of the day we'll do drills and then a scrimmage."

She caught his eye in the rearview. "Does that mean you don't get to do other things?"

"No. Todd said soccer was a two-hour block for our age group. Younger kids only have an hour. By the end of the summer, I'm gonna be super good. Just wait and see."

She focused on the road. He was good on the soccer field and his coach said he was a natural.

"Mom." George could barely contain his excitement. "Did you know that I'm tall for my age?"

She felt the corners of her mouth pull upward. "Really? What makes you say that?"

"Well, ya see, there's this other coach. Her name is, um —" He tapped his chin and said, "I forget."

"It's Faith, dummy."

"Johnny, don't call your brother names."

George stuck his tongue out. "Faith said I could play center on our basketball team cuz I'm so tall."

"Your uncles and Dad are all tall, so you must take after them and not me."

"Yeah, maybe I do." He sat up a little straighter in the back seat for the rest of the drive home and told her every detail about the day.

Johnny interjected about the soccer coach, and it made Liza wonder if he'd be able to live up to John's expectations.

"As long as you boys had fun. That's all that matters."

"It's great, Mom."

She pulled the van into the driveway and stopped in front of the garage door. Before they could bolt from the van, she said, "Take your bags in the house and drop your swim trunks and wet towels in the laundry room."

"But Mom, we want to ride our bikes."

"It'll take you three minutes and you can still ride." She pointed to the back door. "Go."

They grumbled as they got out. She was grateful they wanted to be outside and not like some kids who plopped in front of a screen, playing video games all day. She wished she had a fraction of their energy. There was dinner to make, dishes, showers, a couple of new proposals, and then she could crash.

I want to be a successful businesswoman, and that takes work and more hard work. She lingered in the van, watching the boys race from the house to take care of their swimsuits and toward the now open garage bay that used to hold Steve's car. Now it was filled with bikes and other sports equipment. Shelves filled the rest of the space and didn't serve as a constant reminder of what was missing.

The boys were tugging on a small wooden bike ramp Leo had built for them to use for tricks.

"Guys, what do you say about packing up some sandwiches, loading the bikes, and taking them to the rail trail? We can go for a ride and have a picnic." It had been a while since they'd done anything spontaneous and she could use some exercise to boot.

"Can we go all the way to the ice cream stand?" Johnny's eyes grew wide.

She leaned against the open doorway. "Sure. Come help me make sandwiches and I'll change. Then we'll hit the road."

"Come on, George. Let's park the bikes next to the van. Mom's too."

She pointed to the shelf where the helmets were stored. "Toss those in the front seat and I'll see you inside."

As she veered to the back door, she overheard Johnny say, "Mom is so cool." She couldn't help but smile. It wouldn't be long before they'd think the opposite.

"Let's hurry up so we can leave."

"Someone grab the insulated backpack," she called out and heard a muffled *okay*. Sometimes it was good to shake things up. She hurried off to change into shorts and a t-shirt.

"George, tighten the strap on your helmet." She adjusted the weight of the pack over her shoulders. Along with sandwiches, she had bottles of water and a couple of apples.

"Oh, Mom, it's fine."

"We are not moving until you do." Her voice held firm and kept her feet planted on the asphalt.

"Come on, George. Hurry up. I wanna ride." Johnny was balanced on his bike, using one foot and then the other to steady himself as he played with an empty water bottle. Which was odd since he finished one on the way over. Maybe he was a bit dehydrated from camp.

With a tug, George tightened the strap and secured it under his chin. "Ready."

"Alright, as a reminder, bikers need to watch out for everyone else so make sure you be respectful to others on the trail."

Johnny rolled his eyes. "Yeah, okay, Mom. You say the same thing every time."

She suppressed a smile. "Just reminding you." She nodded in the direction of the trail. "Go on. I'm right behind you."

They set an easy pace. From time to time, they'd pass people walking but for the most part, they had the trail to themselves.

After about a half hour, Johnny pulled to the side. "Hey, Mom? Can we stop and eat? I'm starving."

She glanced at her fitness watch to check the time. "There should be picnic tables just a short way up the path. We'll stop there and then change direction and head for ice cream."

The boys set off once again, with her bringing up the rear. In less than five minutes, she could see tables in the distance. With the bikes in a rack, the boys picked out a table. She slipped the pack from her back and from the pocket pulled out wet wipes for them to use on their hands. She gave them the mom look—no arguing. Then she pulled out a small bag to use for garbage. As she removed the drinks, sandwiches, and apples, she asked, "Are you guys tired?"

"Nah." Johnny took a big bite from his sandwich. "This is good." Jelly was smeared on his cheeks.

She laughed and took a bite of hers. He was right. It was.

It didn't take long for the sandwiches and apples to be devoured. After a long drink of water, she said, "We need to bear left at the fork ahead to find the ice cream truck."

"Do you think it'll be there tonight?" Johnny's hazel eyes were filled with concern.

She tweaked his nose. "If it's not, we'll ride back to the car and go someplace else."

He grinned.

They cruised around the corner and before Liza could shout a warning, a runner appeared out of nowhere. Johnny and George tried to swerve around him. The runner stumbled and fell. Liza locked up her brakes and jumped off her bike and the boys did the same.

She dropped to her knees next to the man lying motionless in the grass. "Hey, are you okay?"

He groaned, rolled over, and pulled earbuds from his ears.

Deep-green eyes met hers. Drew Cameron. A pleasurable zing rippled through her system. She helped him sit up. The boys watched quietly.

"Mom, is he okay?" Johnny asked. "We didn't mean to run him off the road."

He half turned. "Boys, I wasn't paying attention." He gave Liza a lazy smile. "Any chance you'd help up an injured runner?"

She slipped her arm under his and said, "Johnny, stand in front of Mr. Cameron in case he falls forward."

"Ready?" She tightened her arm. "Give me your weight. I've got you."

What would Liza Price think if she knew he was okay other than the wind being knocked out of him, but he liked her hovering? Her hair caressed his cheek.

Her voice was slightly breathless. "I've got you."

Yes, she did—from the first time he had lain eyes on her. *Goner* hadn't begun to describe it.

"Oh, gosh. Your knee is bleeding."

He didn't feel the sting. "It's fine. I just had the wind knocked out of me." He held her arm close, not ready to let go.

"Are you feeling better?" Her eyes were filled with concern. "I have a first aid kit in my pack."

"Thanks." He allowed her to steer him to a weathered stone bench. Lame way to see her again, but he'd take it.

"Easy now."

He caught the fresh lemony scent in her hair. "You're very kind, but I'm fine. Really." Everything about her was perfect.

"Drew, it's our fault you got hurt."

"I should have been paying attention instead of listening to an audiobook."

"Hopefully it's a good one." Her smile reached her eyes. "I prefer to hold a book in my hands."

"Running gives me time to catch up on the classics."

"What are you listening to now?" She dug out the first aid kit and ripped open an antiseptic wipe.

"You'll laugh if I tell you."

Intent on cleaning his cut, she didn't look up. "Try me." She wiped an antiseptic pad over the wound.

"*Pride and Prejudice*. The narrator is English and she tells the story perfectly." He winced as the moist pad hit his knee. "Careful there."

"It's okay, Mr. Cameron. Mom will blow on it so it won't hurt."

He wasn't sure if it was Johnny or George—but he was pretty sure they were joking.

"George, I only did that for you and your brother when you were younger." Color flushed her cheeks.

He smiled at George. "Your mom's a good nurse."

His smile faded. "She's not a nurse. She plans weddings and stuff." George looked at his mother.

She lifted a shoulder and smiled. "He's very literal."

"Good to know."

She handed him a Band-Aid and stuffed the first aid kit back in her bag. "There you go."

He placed the Band-Aid over the cut and flexed his leg. "Thanks."

"Boys, we should let Mr. Cameron get back to his run."

"Wanna come for ice cream with us?"

He would have liked to say yes but he held back. "No, thank you." He looked between the kids. Noting Johnny had hazel eyes and George had brown eyes, he said, "Johnny, maybe some other time." Did he see a look of relief flash across Liza's face, or was it his imagination? "Enjoy your ice cream."

They climbed onto their bikes and Liza's smile was guarded as they pushed off. He watched as they rode down the path and took the final turn where the ice cream truck would be parked. He ran in the opposite direction.

He was losing track of how many times he had seen Liza Bradford, and each time, he felt the inexplicable pull. He couldn't wait until they bumped into each other again.

George peered over his shoulder. "Mom, why do you think Mr. C didn't come with us? Do you think he's mad?"

Johnny said, "It was an accident."

They slowed to a stop and the boys stashed their bikes in the rack and hurried to the truck to study the menu. Not that it would make a difference what they ordered; it was always the same, a Nutty Buddy cone for Johnny and a Chipwich sandwich for George. She liked the raspberry frozen yogurt pop.

When she reached the truck, George was pointing out what he was going to order, and then he stepped up to the counter and ordered the Chipwich anyway. They soon had ice cream dripping down the front of their t-shirts. She paid and took her pop to the picnic table.

Mid-lick, Johnny said, "This is fun, Mom."

"We have a long ride back to the van. Are you two going to make it?"

"Yeah, easy-peasy." George pulled the bottom of his shirt up to wipe his chin.

Her laugh ended with a sigh. "I would prefer you use a napkin." She passed one to him. "Good thing you're washable."

As they finished up, she dug out a couple of wet wipes and said, "Wipe."

She knew their half-hearted attempt was only to placate her. Boys weren't concerned about being sticky-free.

The ride back was uneventful, with the boys swapping stories about camp. She was happy they had a strong connection and hoped it would last well into adulthood. As they approached the parking lot, she was surprised to see Drew bent down next to her van. What the hell was he doing?

He stood as they got closer. He had changed his t-shirt and held up his hand in greeting. The boys hopped off their bikes.

"How was your ice cream?"

"Good, but what are you doing here?" Johnny had a wary edge to his voice.

Liza parked at the back of her van. Johnny and George were standing between the cars.

"This is a surprise." What was he doing, hanging around? Was he waiting for them to get back?

"I noticed you had a flat tire and I hung around in case you needed some help changing it."

She looked down. "Shoot." She dug her keys out of her pocket. The door eased up and she took out the plastic box that held work items and set it on the ground. Changing a tire was a pain.

"Let me help."

"Thanks, but I know how to change a tire." That sounded bitchy. "Dad made sure all his girls could change tires and jump-start a car."

"I'm not doubting your ability but just offering to lend a hand"—he gave a low laugh—"or two."

She flipped up the tire well cover and took a step back, shocked to see it was empty. Not even the little donut was in the space.

"When was the last time you had to change the tire?"

"On the van, never." She flipped the lid back down

with a thud. "I'll call my brother Leo and see if he has a spare I can use."

"I could drive you home."

"That's very nice of you, but I'll need my van tomorrow."

She walked to her backpack, which she had dropped at the van, and retrieved her phone. Leo picked up right away. After she explained the situation and tire size, he said he'd be over. She stuffed the phone in her shorts pocket. "He's on his way."

Shadows were lengthening across the parking lot as dusk fell. "Boys, let's stash your bikes and get in the van until Uncle Leo gets here."

"Do we have to?" The whine in George's voice reminded her they'd had a full day and he must be tired.

"He'll be here soon."

Drew had already taken her bike and secured it to the rack. He waited while the boys put their kickstands up and he picked up the first one.

Liza said, "I'll take care of those." She was far from helpless, and the last few years had made her even stronger.

He stepped back from the car, still holding the bike off the ground. "I'm sorry. I was just trying to help."

Flustered, she jammed her hands in her pockets. "No, I'm sorry. I'm used to doing most things on my own." She looked at the boys chasing each other in the grass next to the parked cars. So much for being tired. "They help, but as you can see, they get distracted easily."

"They're kids." He nodded toward the rack and secured the bikes on it as she handed them up to him.

She smiled at him and hoped this time it was friendly. "Thanks."

"Just returning the kindness you gave to me earlier."

She furrowed her brow.

He held up the Band-Aid-covered knee. "I can hang out until your brother gets here if you'd like."

Her heart fluttered and she smiled. "That would be nice."

4

------

*D*rew sat with Liza on a bench while she kept an eye on the boys as they played tag around her van and his Chevelle.

She stood up as George slipped between two parked cars in an attempt to get away from Johnny. "Boys, stay out of the parking area."

"They're high energy." He remembered always being on the go when he was a kid too.

She sat down and crossed her legs. "Actually, they're winding down. They went to camp today and now the bike ride, so they should hit the beds and be out."

"Where are they going to camp?"

"A sports camp. They're doing the day program and a couple of times per month, they'll spend a Friday night. I wasn't sure how they'd like it, to be honest"—she dropped her voice—"first-time campers and George is a little too reliant on his older brother."

He propped an ankle on his knee, very relaxed and enjoying their conversation. "They should have a lot of fun."

"I was worried about George. He relies heavily on his brother, but if today was an indication of how he's going to adjust when they go to different schools in the fall, he'll be fine." She gave him a sidelong look. "Do you have children?"

"Not yet. I haven't met anyone I'd like to take that step with."

She gave him a quick look of doubt before turning back to the boys. "I was lucky. Steve—that's my late husband—was a wonderful man and a great dad. He took the boys tent camping, taught them to ride bikes, and couldn't wait until they started playing sports. He would have attended every game and been their biggest fans."

"He sounds like a good dad." He was sorry she had lost him so young. "It must have left a huge hole in your lives."

"He was and it did."

The question on his lips was left unasked. Would she say yes if he asked her out?

"So what did you think of Anna and Colin's pool?" she asked.

Although he had been acutely aware of her at the party, he hadn't talked with her again after the tea incident. That might have been a little too obvious to Colin, who seemed to be able to pick up on the subtleties of his actions. He was never the kind of guy to spend too much time with any one woman. He never wanted to lead anyone on and besides, he knew who he wanted to get to know. Until Liza gave him a sign she was interested, he'd keep a respectful distance. Before he had the chance to answer her, a late model black pickup truck rumbled into the parking lot.

"There's Leo." She stood up and Drew fell in step beside her.

"He got here fast."

She replied, "Their place is on this side of town."

Leo parked the truck next to the van. His fiancée was in the passenger seat. They both got out.

"Hey, sis." He flashed her a questioning look before he looked at Drew. "Hi, Drew. This is a surprise."

"I was out for a run and when I got back, I noticed Liza's van had a flat. Then she discovered the spare was missing so I thought I'd hang out until you got here."

He scanned the darkening parking lot. "I appreciate that."

"Hello," Liza interjected. "I can take care of me and my kids, thank you very much, and I always carry mace with me too."

Stephanie slipped an arm around Liza's shoulders. In an exaggerated Southern drawl, she said, "I do declare. We are such delicate little flowers."

Leo chuckled. "Alright, I get your point." He called for the boys to help him. "When I get the spare out of the truck, you can change it, Liza."

She lifted her chin. A haughty glare burned in her eyes. "Since you're here, you might as well take care of it for me. You can show the boys how to do it."

The boys kept pace with Leo's long strides as they reached the back of the truck. Johnny carried a toolbox and George was rolling the tire across the parking lot. Both of them were wearing their game face; it was all business.

Drew knew this was the cue for him to leave. His reason for hanging around wasn't valid any longer.

"Liza, it was nice bumping into you tonight."

She smiled at him. "It was. Have a good night." She pointed to the bandage. "Sorry again about the mishap."

"Not a big deal." He waved to the boys. "See ya later, guys."

Leo said, "Thanks again." And Stephanie waved.

He jogged across the parking lot and before he got in his car he looked back at Liza, who was watching her sons change the tire under the watchful eye of their uncle.

Liza lifted her head and looked in his direction. Their eyes locked for one ice-melting moment. He'd see those golden-hazel eyes in his dreams.

*L*iza watched Drew leave. She had talked more about herself than she normally did with someone who was a casual acquaintance.

She pulled her gaze from his taillights when Steph said, "He's kind of cute."

Looking at her kids, she said, "Who?"

"Drew. Was there another man sitting next to you when we pulled up?"

Offhanded, she said, "I guess he's good-looking. I hadn't really noticed."

"Yeah, right." With a snort, she asked, "What's going on between the two of you?"

Liza took a step away from the van and Steph followed her.

"Nothing. We ran him down on the trail, and then we got back here and found the flat. He offered to drive us home. But I told him I needed my van and he hung around until you two got here."

"Hmm. That's all?" A slow smile spread over her mouth. "It might be more than that. I saw how he was looking at you and the protective air was obvious—a knight driving a Chevelle."

She pressed her lips together. "He's not going to be interested in a single mother of two Energizer Bunny-charged boys when he could have a beautiful woman on his arm."

Stephanie poked Liza's arm. "You're a beautiful woman. Don't sell yourself short. Besides, did he say that?"

"No."

George let out a whoop. Liza swiveled to see her son standing with his arms held up in a victory stance.

"Mom, come look. Johnny and I did it." He beamed, and the smile on his face was contagious.

Leo pivoted on the ball of his foot. "Sis, it's all tightened down and you're in good shape for tonight, but make an appointment at the tire shop. Don't forget to ask them to get a new spare for you too. You shouldn't be riding around without one."

"I've never had to change the tire, so I have no idea why it wasn't there. Maybe it got overlooked when I bought it."

Leo stood and wiped his hands on a rag from his back pocket. He instructed the boys to replace the tools in the box and together, they carried it to the truck.

Before her eyes, the boys seemed to wilt after the excitement evaporated from fixing the flat.

"I really appreciate your help." She slid open the back door on the van. "Boys, hop in."

Without a protest, they got in and buckled up. She closed the door.

He nodded to the van. "I looked at the other three tires and you need to get a complete new set."

"Well, I was thinking of trading it in for an SUV. What do you think?"

"The mileage is high on this. It might be a good idea. Want me to go with you?"

"That's not necessary. When I get some time, I'll check out what I might want. Either way, I'll get tires."

Steph touched her arm. "We need to finish our conversation."

Leo shifted from foot to foot. "I'll take care of the tools." Liza appreciated the consideration so she and Steph could talk. She watched as her twin loaded the toolbox and shut the tailgate.

"He's a good man."

Steph also watched as Leo finished stowing the tools. "He is. I'm lucky to have him in my life. If you met me a year ago, you'd know I would never interfere in matters of the heart, but becoming a part of this family has allowed me the opportunity to know when someone good comes around, you take a chance to see what might develop."

With a small shake of her head, Liza said, "I appreciate your intention, but Drew Cameron is not interested in me."

"I saw the way he was looking at you, and that's a man who likes what he sees."

"I don't know if I want to go down that path again. It still hurts. Losing Steve was excruciating, and I have my sons to think about."

"I know it's not the same as losing your husband, but when I lost Dad, I didn't think I'd ever have someone who'd love and understand me." Her gaze returned to the truck. "Not only does Leo love me for exactly who I am, but he understands where I'm coming from. I needed time to get used to the huge family events, and I'm getting there."

"Are you saying there's hope for me?" Liza glanced

inside the van. The boys were zonked. It had been a big day.

"Of course there is. What harm would it do to think about dating again? We'll keep the kids for you so you never have to worry about hiring a babysitter. We love having them. And if for any reason we can't, there are five other sets of aunts and uncles they could crash with for a night."

Liza snickered. "I don't need them to have sleepovers if I decide to date. I'd start slow, meet for coffee or maybe a drink, and progress to a meal. I'll be moving at a sloth's pace."

"You do whatever you're comfortable with." Steph cocked her head. "What's your closet looking like these days?"

Liza waved a hand down her outfit. "Kind of like this. With the exception of the dresses I have for work events."

A gleam sparked in Steph's eye. "I love shopping. What do you say we have Leo keep the boys on Saturday and we'll pick up some outfits that will be perfect for dating?"

"I think you're rushing things. I haven't been asked, so therefore, I don't need new clothes."

"Oh, Liza. You have been out of the game much too long. To be prepared for being asked out is just opening the door to fate. And for the record, you can ask him too." She tapped her fingertip to her nose. "Actually," she drawled, "that might be an interesting idea. If you were to ask Drew out for coffee, then you control the date. It might make it a smooth transition from a non-dater to a woman dating."

With a quick stomach clench, Liza said, "I've never asked a man out before."

Stephanie placed her hands on Liza's shoulders and looked her square in the eye. "Then it's about time you stuck your toe in the pond and tested the water. You might just be surprised how warm it really is."

"Is that what you did with Leo?"

Stephanie threw her head back and laughed. "I thought I was so smooth. I actually went to his shop on the guise of checking out the quality of his work, and I also thought he was"—she pointed to the van—"their father."

Liza snorted. "I never knew that."

"Like I said, take control of your destiny and ask the handsome Drew Cameron out for coffee, but not until we go shopping for new clothes."

"He's already seen me dressed like this. Would it make that much of a difference?"

"When was the last time you had a date?"

"Fifteen years ago."

"You're not waiting fifteen days for your next one." Steph laughed. "Stop looking like a deer in headlights. We're talking about sharing a beverage with a good-looking man, nothing more." She winked. "Unless, of course, you'd like more."

"You're incorrigible, so stop pushing, Steph." She opened the driver's door and cocked her head. "But thanks."

5

or George and Johnny, the days at camp had been action-packed and by the end of the first week, they were ready to spend time with family. A toot came from the driveway and Liza glanced out the kitchen window.

"Boys, Uncle Jack is here." Jack, Peyton, and the kids were going fishing and Owen wanted his cousins to go with them.

They raced into the kitchen.

"Did you make your beds and brush your teeth?"

"Yup, and I even used toothpaste," George announced proudly.

She shook her head. "The dentist will be happy." She pointed to their fishing poles and tackle boxes next to the door. "Make sure you follow all of your aunt and uncle's rules on the boat." They nodded. "And wear your life jackets the entire time. Understood?"

Johnny groaned. "Mom, we know all this stuff. We've been boating forever."

She ruffled their hair and kissed their cheeks. "One last thing. Have fun."

She opened the door and they hurried out with their poles bouncing off the driveway as they went.

George said, "Uncle Jack, Aunt Peyton, we're ready."

Liza followed at a more sedate pace.

Peyton leaned out the window. "Did you remember bathing suits?"

They both nodded. Jack came around the side and took their poles and tackle boxes from them to stow in the back of the truck.

"Who wants to ride up front between me and Peyton?" He flashed George an encouraging smile. "What do you think, buddy?"

"Uncle Jack, I wanna sit in the back."

He put a hand on George's shoulder and didn't look at Liza to get any guidance. His adopted son Owen was almost twelve and he was good with the boys.

"Hannah's car seat takes up a lot of room, which gives me two seat belts on either side of her and since you're the smallest, you will be the most comfortable up front."

He dropped his head and stared at the ground. In a small voice, he said, "Okay."

"Thank you, George."

Jack opened the driver's door and George climbed inside. Peyton had pulled out the ends of the seat belt for him.

Peyton said, "We'll have the kids back around four. Is that okay?"

"Sure. You're welcome to stay for dinner. I'll burn some burgers and dogs."

Jack gave a shake of his head. "Thanks, sis, but another

time. A day on the water makes Hannah very tired and she'll be cranky. So, we'll pass on tonight."

With a pang of nostalgia, thinking about when the boys were small and life was almost perfect, Liza said, "I remember those days." She waved to the boys. "Have fun."

"Bye, Mom," George called out.

Peyton said to Liza, "Do something fun today."

"I will."

Liza stood in the driveway until the truck turned the corner. More and more, she was spending time alone while the boys were off with friends. Their social life was more active than hers. Was Stephanie right? Should she bite the bullet and ask Drew out? Well, she couldn't even if she wanted to. She didn't have his number.

She kicked the gravel driveway. But she could call Anna, if she really wanted to talk to him. She dismissed the idea and went to tidy the kitchen before Steph arrived. It hadn't taken long for the family grapevine to spread that Liza had free time. Steph followed up about the shopping trip they'd discussed. She was looking forward to spending time with her future sister-in-law. Maybe she and Steph could talk about the wedding, especially if they had set a date.

*L*iza shifted several oversized shopping bags to her left arm as she paid for a pair of pink strappy sandals she'd found on a clearance rack. She glanced at the bags Steph was carrying. "You made quite a dent today for new outfits."

"Honeymoon clothes." She had finally shared they

were going someplace tropical, but that was all she'd divulge.

Liza stashed her credit card in her wallet and said, "I'm starved. Lunch?"

"Sawyers?" Steph asked.

"That sounds good." They were strolling in the direction of the mall exit when Liza saw Drew coming out of the sporting goods store.

Liza pointed to Drew's retreating back. "Look who's over there in the dark-green polo shirt and khaki shorts. Walking away from us."

Steph gave her a playful push. "We should see if he wants to join us for lunch." With a laugh, Steph pulled her into the corridor. "Come on. Maybe with some luck, we can still catch up to him."

Since that was a slim chance, she fell in step alongside Steph. "He's so tall."

"Just like all the men in our lives."

"I'll bet that green shirt looks good on him with those eyes."

"Hmm," was all Steph said.

One of Liza's bags began to tear away from the handles. She put everything on the bench before it hit the floor and said to Steph, "I'll be right back."

Her heart skipped a couple of beats and she called out, "Drew." He turned and even from this distance, she couldn't help but notice his twinkling green eyes.

ell, this was a lucky break. If Drew had left the mall a few minutes earlier, he would never have seen Liza. The best-laid plans were meant to be altered. "Hi, how've you been?"

"Busy. You know the boys and camp. New tires for the van and"—she pointed to her shopping bags—"some retail therapy." Her smile looked strained. "How's the knee?"

"Like it never happened." He flexed his knee and pointed to where she had placed the Band-Aid. "Must have been the excellent assistance I had."

Color rose in her cheeks.

"Good. Good." She glanced toward the shop that Steph had disappeared into.

"Boys still having fun at camp?"

She looked into his eyes and blurted out, "Do you want to have a drink with me sometime?"

Had he heard right? "A drink?"

She shook her head and mumbled, "Never mind. It was a dumb idea."

"No. Liza. I'd love to. Name the place and time and I'll be there."

At that moment, Steph walked up. "How about tomorrow at two? You could meet at Sawyers."

He thought that was an awesome idea. But did Liza?

"Sure, tomorrow would be okay. But I need someone to watch the boys."

Steph gave her a grin. "Leo and I have been wanting to hang out with our nephews, so the timing is perfect." She looked between Drew and Liza. "Oh, I see one more thing I need."

She walked away again. Drew had her number; she was attempting to play matchmaker, and he liked it. With a smile, he said, "If you want to meet tomorrow, I'm free."

She picked up her bags and looked at the floor before

lifting her eyes to meet his. "I don't want you to feel like you've been coerced. Steph can be a little pushy."

"I'm happy you asked and I'm glad she suggested tomorrow." Even if he had plans he'd change them. With any luck this would be the first of many dates with the lovely Liza.

"Maybe you should take my number, just in case you change your mind or something comes up." Her voice cracked and she shifted her bags again.

There was no way he wouldn't be at Sawyers tomorrow. Heck, he'd get there early just to make sure he wasn't late.

He pulled his cell from his shorts pocket and flashed her a wide smile. "What's your number?"

She rattled off the digits, and then her cell rang. She fumbled in her purse to answer it.

"It's just me. I wanted you to have my number too."

She tipped her head and gave him a shy smile. "Well, now that we've exchanged numbers, I guess I'll see you tomorrow."

"It's a date." He touched her arm. "I'm looking forward to it."

The gold flecks in her wide eyes were more pronounced. "Me too."

"See you tomorrow at two."

Now she gave him a heartwarming smile and not that he wanted to rush her, but he wished she had asked him what he was doing later today. He couldn't wait to see her again.

• • •

*L*iza watched Drew walk out the exit with a quick look over his shoulder. He flashed her a sexy smile. Her knees grew weak. He was as nice as he was handsome and she couldn't believe she asked him out and he said yes.

"Timing is everything." Liza smiled at Steph's comment. "How did I do?"

Steph squealed. "Like a champ." She hurried Liza toward the exit. "Over lunch, we'll decide what you're wearing."

"And we're going to discuss the theme for your wedding and, even more important, the date."

*I*t didn't take long for Liza to drive to Sawyers. The minute they walked in, Alan, the owner and longtime family friend, greeted them with hugs and a smile.

"Hello, ladies. A table for two?"

"Hi, Alan. And yes, please."

Steph walked ahead of her. With a sharp eye, Liza looked around the room. There weren't many diners since the lunch rush was over. She wondered if she could ask Alan to reserve a table for tomorrow that was out of the way of eavesdroppers.

He pulled out two chairs. "Would you have rather been on the patio?"

"This is fine." Liza said. "Alan, would it be possible to reserve a table outside for tomorrow at two?"

"For you, of course. How many people?"

She hesitated and then met his eyes. "Two."

His eyebrow arched and a smile graced his face. "I'll have the perfect table ready for you."

"I appreciate that."

He placed a card on the table. "Here are today's specials, and what can I bring you to drink?"

"Sparkling water for me."

Steph said, "I'll have the same."

Once Alan had moved away, the girls looked at the menus and set them aside. Liza was anxious to hear about the wedding.

"Spill it." She leaned forward. "I want to know what you're currently mulling over. You're toying with your wedding planner and that's just not nice." She forced her lower lip out in a small pout.

Steph laughed. She twirled her finger around Liza's face. "Your brother tried that look once and it got him nowhere."

"He has other tools in his arsenal to get his way." She pointed at her face. "This is all I've got."

Alan delivered their drinks and moved away.

"True." Stephanie sipped her water. "If I tell you our ideas, you have to promise you'll act surprised when we make our announcement to the family."

"I can do that."

"We're planning to elope."

Liza's mouth dropped open. What? That was unthinkable. "You're going to run off and get married. By yourselves?"

Steph's eyes were bright. "Doesn't that sound so romantic?"

Before she could think of a tactful answer, she responded, "No. It doesn't."

6

"Steph, you don't have to have a big wedding like Anna," Liza said. "We could do an intimate family wedding, elegant, but relaxed, that would suit you and Leo."

She watched as Steph's face fell and her heart broke a little. Something was weighing heavily on Stephanie's heart. Before she could ask what the real issue was, the waitress took their lunch order. She waited for Steph to say something, but it seemed like an eternity. "Talk to me; tell me what's going on. You're marrying my twin and I want to be supportive."

Steph's voice broke. "I don't have any family. Dad's gone, so he can't walk me down the aisle. My mom isn't here to help me shop for my dress and primp with me before the ceremony. When we started talking about what kind of wedding we wanted, it made me realize how many holes I have in my life." She lifted her eyes to Liza's. "Don't get me wrong. Your family has welcomed me right from the very beginning. When I was having problems at the shop with Val stealing from me, your dad was great.

He supported me, like my dad would have done. But even thinking about a traditional wedding made me sad."

Softly, Liza said, "Leo suggested you elope, didn't he?" That would be just like her brother to do anything to make the woman he loves happy.

She sniffed. "The most important thing, to both of us, is that we're married. Does it really make that big of a difference where it happens?"

"No, of course not." Liza's mind raced. Why couldn't she help them plan a small, intimate wedding that would be special and family-centric while still not causing Steph any additional sadness?

Lunch was delivered and Steph toyed with her quiche.

Liza said, "I've got an idea."

Her tone lighter, Steph tipped her head and said, "I'm not sure if I should be excited or nervous based on that gleam in your eye."

"Definitely excited. What if Tessa and Max hosted a small wedding at Sand Creek Winery? It was where you went after going to Leo's shop that first time, right?"

She nodded. "But I'm still going to have all the same problems."

"I hear you, but what if you look at this a little differently." Liza was warming to the idea. "The day you met Leo, who did he have with him?"

"The boys."

"That's our starting point. Your new life began in that moment."

"I see where you're going with this. We create the wedding about everything and everyone who supported us while we were falling in love." Steph's smile grew.

Liza exhaled, relieved that Stephanie could see what she meant. "Exactly. What if we found you a wedding dress that had pockets? You could carry a picture of your parents with you as you walk down the aisle. That way, they're with you."

"I can take that one step further." A sparkle lit up her eyes. "Do you think if I asked George and Johnny, they'd give me away? They're a huge part of our love story."

Liza felt a tug to her heart and placed her hand over her chest. "They'd be thrilled."

"Maybe Tessa could get one of those one-day marriage officiant licenses and would marry us."

"Now you're talking."

"And on our first dinner date, Kate made us an amazing meal that we had in the gazebo at CLW. Maybe we could replicate that menu. And if Sam still has some of my favorite wine, we could serve that along with Fuse from Sand Creek." She sat up straighter as her words tumbled out. "I could carry a bouquet of wildflowers like Leo picked for me when we first started dating."

"And it could be just the family. My parents, our brothers and sisters, and their kids or whoever you want to add."

She placed her hand on Liza's. "If Leo agrees, you'll still plan it for us? Just like we talked about?"

"I'd be hurt if you didn't let me do this for you."

Steph's glow dimmed. "But what about dress shopping? Will you go with me?"

Her breath caught in her chest, Stephanie would come to realize she had a big, crazy but loving family and that would come in time. "You're kidding, right? Off the top of my head, I can think of six women who would be honored to go with you. All you have to do is let them know when."

Steph's smile went from ear to ear. "I'm going to talk to

Leo tonight and when you come by tomorrow with the boys, we'll have a definite answer."

Relieved, Liza squeezed her hand and smiled. "Just do me one favor?"

"Anything."

Liza squeezed Stephanie's hand. "I don't know when you planned on eloping, but could you give me more than a couple of weeks to plan it?"

"No worries. We were thinking after the crush, so maybe early to mid-November."

"That gives us almost five months to plan. More than enough time to give you a day you'll always remember."

Steph tipped her head to the side and gave Liza a long look. "If you're dating someone seriously by then, I expect you to bring him to the wedding."

With a laugh, Liza said, "Now who's pushing?" She jabbed her fork in the direction of Steph's plate. "Eat up before it's ice-cold."

"Now we're changing the topic to what you're wearing tomorrow for your first date with the handsome hunk."

Liza could feel her cheeks flush, and her heart ticked up with anticipation. "I'll wear the blue floral print sundress I bought and new sandals. Comfy and casual but still look nice."

"Hair up or down?"

"Since it'll be warm on the patio, I'll wear it up. Keep it off the back of my neck so I don't sweat like I'm working out."

"That's quite the visual." Stephanie was making short work of her lunch. "But I see your point. I do like that dress." With a wink, she said, "It shows off your curves perfectly."

"Stephanie James. You're going to make me reconsider this date."

Steph shrugged. "Why? You're a beautiful woman and should be proud of exactly who you are and how you look. It's not a crime to be comfortable in your own skin."

"I know that, but the way you say it, I need to make sure I don't give him the wrong impression."

Steph looked up, her eyes wide. "What's the wrong idea? That you are interested in him? That you find him attractive? That you like who you are?"

She groaned. "Yes. No. I don't know." She set her fork down; her appetite vanished. "Maybe he said yes because he didn't have a way to give me a polite no."

Steph shook her head and frowned. "What do you see when you look in the mirror?"

"A tired single mom who has no idea some days if she's coming or going and who is worried about raising my sons to be good men. A woman who usually doesn't remember to get her hair trimmed or her eyebrows waxed until the last minute when I realize I need to present myself to clients." She looked out the window. "And I wonder how I got so unlucky to become a widow."

"Hey, I get it. You're looking at the princess of loss. But we keep moving forward and like you reminded me today, we're in this together. We're family, Liza."

"We are. I'm so happy you and Leo found each other."

"You're going to find someone amazing too. If it's not Drew, then it might be the next guy. And the next time you walk past a mirror, try to see what we all see in you. A woman who is kindhearted, strong, funny, beautiful, and a person who does deserve her happy ending."

"I appreciate that." She felt the tears well up, and they

weren't sad for a change. Having Steph as a good friend was a stroke of luck and Liza was grateful.

The waitress appeared with two servings of lemon tart with a raspberry sauce. "Compliments of Alan."

Liza looked over. He was standing behind the entrance podium. She smiled and mouthed thanks.

He gave her a tiny salute like he had when they were kids.

"Dig in, Steph. This is one of the best lemon tarts you'll ever eat. But promise you'll never tell Kate I said that."

*L*iza pulled into Leo's driveway the next day. She had been practicing her deep breathing to quell her nerves. The boys were looking forward to hanging out at Leo and Steph's inground pool.

Before she could remove the keys from the ignition, the boys had seat belts off and were jumping out and racing in the side door. Did those two ever even think about walking? More than likely not. She got out and smoothed down the front of her floral sundress, hoping to wipe away the nerves she was feeling. If Steph thought it wasn't the right outfit, she had two others in the van.

The slider to the deck was standing open when she stepped inside. The kitchen was cool despite the afternoon heat. The boys were on the deck, begging Leo to let them jump in.

"Don't you look pretty." Steph breezed down the hall in her bathing suit and matching cover-up. Her blond hair was in a messy bun that highlighted her prominent cheekbones and soft-gray eyes.

Liza looked down. "Are you sure this dress is alright? I have two others with me so I can still change."

Steph gave her a quick hug. "You look great."

Liza licked her lips. The boost of moral support didn't do much to quell the butterflies in her stomach. "If you and Leo changed your mind, you don't need to keep the boys this afternoon."

"Nope, you're not canceling." She pointed to the boys and Leo. "Say goodbye and go. You have exactly twenty minutes to get there."

Liza pressed her hand against her stomach and whispered, "I don't think I can do this."

"Nerves are a good sign. It means this date matters to you."

"What if once we start talking, I don't like him after all? Can I leave?"

Steph laughed softly. "Would you like me to call you in about an hour to let you know how the boys are doing?"

"No. I know he's not a creeper, so I'll be fine. I can have one drink and then leave, right?"

"Absolutely."

Liza found solace in the way Steph put extra emphasis on each syllable. "What if I like him and he doesn't like me and he leaves? I'll be so embarrassed."

"Relax. The man has manners. He's not going to act like a jerk. Besides, he's been to countless family functions. And I've seen how he looks at you when you're not looking. The man is interested." She urged Liza to the back door.

Sticking her head outside, Liza saw the boys were already in their swimsuits and goggles. "Guys, make sure you listen to your aunt and uncle. They're in charge." She gave them each an extra stern mom stare. "Do you hear me?"

"We got it. Right, George?"

"Yup. Bye, Mom. Have fun." Johnny picked up the squirt gun and shot George, who grabbed the water hose and soaked his brother.

Liza jumped back before they drenched her. "Boys!"

Leo was chuckling when he came around the corner of the house, carrying a couple of water cannons. "You should take off and stop worrying." He winked at Steph and jerked his thumb in her direction. "She'll keep us in line."

With a shake of her head, Liza turned to Steph. "You have your hands full today."

"I know. Aren't I the lucky one?" The smile on Stephanie's face revealed her happiness.

Liza was quick to say, "Leo's pretty lucky too."

Stephanie gave her a hard hug. "Have fun and don't rush back. If things are going well and you want to go for dinner, the boys can eat with us. We're cooking burgers on the grill."

"I'm sure it won't, but I appreciate the thought." She waved to the boys one last time.

She sat in Leo's driveway with the air conditioner in the minivan on high, taking a few deep cleansing breaths like she practiced in yoga. With a small measure of luck, she wouldn't spill anything down the front of her dress. She flipped the visor mirror down and checked her makeup. Her eyes had a touch of blue shadow and brown liner, but the dark mascara made her eyes appear larger than they were, and she had applied a light coating of raspberry lipstick.

"This is as good as it gets." She snapped the mirror up and backed out of the driveway.

Instead of putting so much pressure on herself, she needed to stop and think. This was Drew, Colin's best friend. If it didn't work out, it would be fine and a good practice run to build on for her next first date. But if it did, well, he was still Colin's friend. She exhaled her anxiety and drove to Sawyers.

7

---

*D*rew strode into Sawyers. It was ten till two and he couldn't wait to see Liza again. She had surprised him when she'd asked if he'd have a drink with her. Hopefully jumping at the chance didn't make him seem overeager. He had wanted to ask her out the last time he saw her at Colin's but hadn't been sure if the timing was right.

A young lady wearing a white blouse, black pants, and a dark-green apron approached him.

"May I help you?"

"I'm meeting a friend here at two."

"You must be looking for Liza. Please follow me."

She led the way to the patio. Sitting at a table with her back toward him was Liza. She must have heard them approach because she turned in her chair. He felt weak in the knees. She was gorgeous, with her blond hair swept away from her heart-shaped face.

She gave him a welcoming smile. "Drew."

The way she said his name was like silk rippling on the breeze.

Would it be inappropriate to kiss her cheek? Yes. He touched her arm as he walked by and took the chair across from her.

"Liza, you look beautiful."

She actually blushed. "Thank you."

The waitress said, "Would you like to order something now or should I come back?"

Liza looked up. "A glass of white wine, please, something from either Sand Creek or Crescent Lake Winery, whichever is open." She turned to Drew and grinned. "I need to support the home teams."

Drew smiled at the waitress. "I'll have the same." He looked around the patio and noticed they had it all to themselves. "This is nice out here."

"I'm inside so much of the day that I like to be out when I can." She folded her hands in her lap.

"I like to spend as much time as possible outdoors too." *Gosh, that was lame. It's like my brain has taken a vacation now that I'm on a date with Liza.*

She bobbed her head and gave him a smile.

Drew leaned forward. "I was glad when you asked me to meet you."

Her eyes grew wide. "You were?"

"Yes." He was charmed. "I've wanted to ask you to have coffee or something, but I wasn't sure if you'd say yes."

She averted her gaze. "It's been a while since I've dated."

"Well, you're doing great so far."

She looked him directly in the eyes and arched an eyebrow. "Thanks."

He needed to fess up. "I asked Colin if you were dating anyone, and he said no."

She seemed confused and pleased at the same time. "You did?"

He leaned forward. "From the first time I was invited to your home for the pre-wedding barbeque for Anna and Colin, I wanted to get to know you better." Should he tell her that he remembered what she was wearing and doing the first time they were introduced or would she find that weird? He thought better of saying anything.

She glanced up at the waitress, who set down two glasses of wine and a small plate of cheese and charcuterie and sliced rounds of baguettes. "Alan thought you'd enjoy this with your wine."

Liza smiled at her. "Please tell him thank you for us."

She tapped her glass to Drew's and smiled over the rim. Now her face relaxed and the smile that graced her full mouth was warm and enticing. With a musical laugh, she said, "My family is a bit overwhelming at parties. I'm surprised you keep coming back."

"I think they're great. Everyone welcomed Colin and his sister Marie into the fold so easily. It's like they were always a part of the group and I trailed in behind them."

She set her glass down and he pushed the plate closer to her. She picked up a slice of prosciutto and nibbled on it. "This is good. You should try some."

He took a thin wedge of blue cheese and slice of apple.

"It's funny, really. We've always collected people into our family fold. Take Max, for example. His sister Stella is like one of us. Jack adopted Owen, and Peyton's parents are at every family event."

"Did Owen's dad pass away and that's how Jack came about adopting him?"

Her smile sagged at the edges.

He had overstepped now and tried to backpedal. "If it's too personal, just forget I asked."

She seemed to weigh her response. "Owen's biological father was never in the picture. She's a strong woman and has a wonderful family with Jack, Owen, and Hannah."

"That's nice." He was impressed by the depth of caring this family seemed to have and whatever had happened, Drew was content to let it rest. Some skeletons belonged firmly in the past.

"Do you have any brothers or sisters?" she asked.

"The closest I have to siblings are Colin and Marie. We've been friends since we were in college together."

"You must have had a quiet childhood."

Was that sadness in her voice?

"I was a pretty lucky kid. I played sports and understand Johnny and George's energy. Every summer, I went to camp and loved it. My parents took me to interesting places all over the world and I never really felt like I missed out on anything." He finished his cheese. "Until I met your family. That's when I discovered how a large group of people, related or not, can have a blast together."

"It's not all fun and games. We get mad at each other and fight."

"I've seen the bond you have with your twin, Leo, and the rest of your family. It's special."

"Yeah, I guess we are a little unique. Working together, having fun together, and choosing to spend time with each other. I think that's why when we bring others in, like Stella, Marie, and you, it adds a new dimension to the dynamic. And of course, our friends from school, like Alan, who owns this place, are around when they can be too." She sipped her wine. "What do you do for work? I don't think Colin has ever said."

It was a little intimidating when Liza put it like that, but he had seen some of what she talked about in action when Colin started inviting Drew to parties. "My father has a line of car dealerships, and my mother has her own publishing company. They both decided to retire and hand the reins of each company over to me. But I prefer to be hands off. I have excellent people who run the day-to-day operations. I visit them on a regular basis, but my passion is giving kids experiences like I had as a child, so I own a summer camp—well, actually, several summer camps around the country but I spend most of my time here, only traveling to the other locations occasionally."

"That sounds like a fun job."

"There's nothing like walking through one of the camps and seeing kids having fun, running and being outside and not tethered to a screen."

She arched an eyebrow. "Do you have a camp locally?"

"I do." He leaned back in the chair and chuckled. "Let me guess. Are the boys going to Cam's this summer?"

She grinned. "It just dawned on me. Cam's stands for Cameron."

"That's one of my locations. I have one in Colorado that focuses on hiking and climbing and one in Maine that features lake water sports."

"My kids are having a blast and thankfully they come home exhausted every day."

He grinned. "Good to know the team is doing their job and tiring kids out with lots of activities."

"They are. In fact, the night we saw you on the trail was their first day."

"I'm surprised they had energy to burn."

With a grin, she said, "That was the last time we've gone biking after camp. Now we leave it for the weekend."

He noticed their glasses were empty and pointed to hers. "Would you care for another?"

"I'll have lemonade. I have to pick up the boys from Leo's in a while and one is my limit when I'm driving."

He smiled to the waitress. "Two lemonades, please?"

"Drew, go ahead and have another glass if you'd like."

"I happen to love lemonade." He was having a great time and had never been much of a drinker anyway.

"Thank you."

"For what?" He held up the plate and she took some cheese and a baguette round.

"I'm having a really nice time."

"Does this mean you'd like to have dinner with me?" He held his breath, praying she'd say yes.

id he really just ask her out for dinner? Without hesitation, she said, "I'd like that. Yes."

He beamed. "When?"

Oh, shoot. Now what should she say? "Next Sunday?" Was that too much time in between? How was she supposed to know? "With the boys' schedule during the week, it's hard for me to break away and I'll need to ask someone in the family to take them for me."

She knew it would be one phone call and she'd have lots of volunteers, but she didn't want to wear out her welcome by giving her family short notice.

"We could do something with your sons if you'd like."

With a firm shake of her head, she said, "No."

His eyes seemed to dim.

"You're a very nice man, but I want to keep dating and my sons separate for the time being." She realized how that sounded. "Not that I'm looking for a relationship or something." She was digging a deeper hole for herself. It was time she was completely honest.

"Drew, thank you for the offer, but you are the first man I've gone on a date with since my husband died. I don't have any idea how my boys will take the news that I'm dating. For now, I'd like to keep them out of it. Can you understand?"

"Liza." He placed a hand over hers for a brief moment and the warmth of his hand lingered after he pulled it away. "I don't want you to do anything that you're not comfortable with. I'm happy you agreed to dinner, and the timing is up to you too."

Her shoulders released the tension they had been holding. He didn't seem to mind the caveat she had placed on their next date. "Then I'll look forward to Sunday. We can touch base during the week, and you can let me know what time and where you'd like to go."

He arched a brow. "Is that your way of telling me this date is over?"

Once again, she could feel heat flush her cheeks. "No. I was just confirming our other plans."

"Oh, good, because I'm enjoying our conversation. Tell me about the wine business and why are you an event planner instead of making your mark at Crescent Lake Winery?"

Over lemonade, Liza explained. "Dad's dream was for all of us to go into the family business. We're the fourth generation of vintners. But our father had already figured out who was going to do what jobs while we were kids. As the oldest, Don would run the company. Jack and Tessa would be in sales and marketing. Anna is our quiet brainiac, so she was the logical choice for the enologist.

Leo was going to be in charge of the warehouse, and I had the tasting room."

"He got one pegged, but what happened with Jack, Tessa, you, and Leo?"

"I'll save that story until Sunday. Just in case I run out of things to talk about."

"You have nothing to worry about. I have a million questions I want to ask. That way conversation will not dry up."

She smiled. It was odd, but trusting him came easy.

8

*L*ater that afternoon, wearing a smile on her face, Liza lightly ran up the front steps at Leo's house. She had another date planned with a great guy and she couldn't wait.

"Hello?" She closed the door behind her.

"We're out back," Leo called.

She slipped out of her sandals and padded barefoot to the deck.

"Hi there." She smiled at Steph and Leo.

The boys were still in the pool and barely looked up when she sat down on a lounge chair. "Hi, boys."

They shot their hands up from the water in a quick greeting and went back to playing Marco Polo.

"Have they been out of the water since I left?"

"Um, they got out long enough to have a burger and then got right back in." Steph's grin held a wicked little look. "Did you have fun?"

"I did. I was wondering if you guys were free next Sunday, would you like to come to the house, have dinner with the boys, and put them to bed for me?"

Steph rubbed her hands together, beaming. "Does this mean what I hope it does?"

A slow, easy grin slid across Liza's face, excited to share her news. "I have a dinner date."

Steph clapped her hands together. "Yes!"

Leo was keeping a close eye on her. "Was he a gentleman?"

"You're kidding, right?" She gave him her stink eye. "You're only two minutes older than me and I don't need you checking up on me."

"I'm your brother and your twin. It's my job to look out for you."

"Hon." Steph reached out and rested her hand on his leg. "We know Drew, and I'm sure Colin would have his head if he was anything less than a gentleman with Liza. Besides, she can take care of herself."

He grumbled and got up. "Sis, want a burger?"

"That sounds good, but I'll fix it. You don't need to wait on me."

She went to stand when Leo said, "Give Steph the details and I'll fix you a plate."

Liza settled back on the chair and tucked her feet under the skirt of her dress.

"So, was it all you hoped for?"

"He's nice and conversation flowed and when I talked, he was genuinely interested in what I had to say." She took her hair down and massaged her scalp.

"Did the time fly or was it just average kind of time drifting by?"

"We were sitting there and the next thing I knew, they were seating people for dinner."

"Why didn't you just stay and eat? The boys were fine here."

"He asked, but I thought it was better to just keep with a shorter date to start with."

Steph let out a hoot. "Liza, a short date is two hours. When it crossed into four, well, let's just say you must have captured his attention, and likewise for you."

"All I can say is it was a good thing Alan started using the patio for dinner service or we might still be there."

"Leaving him wanting to see you again is never a bad idea. Do you know where he's taking you on Sunday?"

"He asked me to let him know where I'd like to go, but I told him to surprise me. He'll call later in the week so I'll find out what time, but I'll make dinner so all you'll need to do is heat and eat."

Steph waved a hand through the air. "We can keep them overnight here if you want."

"I'll need to get them to camp, so being home would be easier for me Monday morning."

"We're flexible."

Liza looked over her shoulder at Leo in the kitchen and dropped her voice. "No pressure, but did the two of you talk? Are we going to have a family wedding or are you going to elope?"

"We wanted to talk to you together."

As if on cue, Leo came out of the kitchen carrying a plate and a tall glass. He set them on the table next to Liza. "Are you still talking about the big date?"

"We've moved on to another big day." Steph patted the chair next to her. "Have a seat. We've kept your sister in suspense long enough."

Liza looked from her brother to Steph and back again. The boys were hanging on to the side of the pool, talking.

Leo took Steph's hand and kissed it. "What you said to

Steph made a lot of sense. I will marry her wherever and whenever she wants. We would like for you to plan a small family wedding but instead of holding the ceremony at Sand Creek, we want to get married in the church in Black River where Steph was baptized and then have the reception at Creek, if that's okay with Tessa and Max."

Tears misted Liza's eyes. "I'll make it the best wedding I've ever done."

Stephanie dropped her voice. "Tonight, I want to ask the boys if they'd walk me down the aisle."

"I thought you might change your mind and ask Dad to do the honors."

"It would mean a lot to me if they would." She squeezed Leo's hand. "To us."

"Of course." Liza glanced at the boys. They would be thrilled to be a part of the wedding.

"That leads me to another question, sis."

"Anything you need. Just ask."

"Would you stand up for me as my best person?"

She was taken aback. "Don't you want to ask Don or Jack?"

"You're my twin. We've shared our lives right from the very beginning of conception and it only seems right that you're by my side when I marry the love of my life."

"Leo." She placed a hand over her heart and blinked away tears, telling herself not to cry. "I would be honored to stand next to you." She got up and hugged them both. "Have you chosen the date?"

"We have. The third Saturday in November. At two in the afternoon." Steph gave her a smile. "One last thing. Do you think all the Price women would go with me when I shop for my dress?"

"Just try to keep us away." Thrilled didn't begin to capture how Liza felt as she watched her brother and his future wife talk about the start of their married life.

"When are you going to tell the family?"

Leo said, "I called Mom and asked if we could have a family dinner one night this week. She's got the phone tree going to work out the best night for the majority. You know any sort of major announcement is so much easier when we're all together."

"Especially now that we've grown by leaps and bounds. When you tell everyone, I'll act totally surprised." She just had a thought. "You might want to wait until after the get-together to ask the boys. They'll never be able to keep a secret. Remember how Owen blurted out Peyton and Jack's news?"

Leo nodded. "True."

Stephanie's eyes shimmered. "We want the boys to be the first to know. When I saw Leo with them, it melted my heart. They're the reason we fell in love. It won't matter if they blurt it out." She glanced at Leo. "Right?"

"As long as I'm marrying you, that's all I care about. Heck, I'd take out a billboard if you asked."

With a laugh, Liza said, "I've warned you." She was thrilled they wanted to include her boys in their big news. Leo really had found a gem.

She finished eating her dinner while the boys got out of the pool and dried off. Steph went inside to get dessert and when she carried the tray out, Leo got up and took it from her.

He said, "Let's sit at the table."

The boys were ravenous, and both were asking to have the biggest piece of blueberry pie and two scoops of ice cream.

As Stephanie dished up dessert, she said, "I cut them exactly the same so everything is equal."

Johnny eyed each slice as if making sure Steph wasn't trying to pull something over on him. Satisfied, he asked, "Are we having whipped cream too?"

Liza shook her head. "John Bradford, that was not polite."

"Sis, it's okay. What's pie without a squirt of cream?" Leo stepped inside and was back in a flash with the can.

The boys shoveled dessert into their mouths and on the tip of Liza's tongue was a reminder for them to not rush, but Leo would overrule her anyway. Sometimes it was just easier to let go and worry about manners another day.

As their spoons scraped their plates clean, Leo bobbed his head in their direction.

Stephanie said, "Hey, guys, I was wondering if I could ask you to do me a favor?"

George stopped his spoon with the last drip of vanilla ice cream midway to his lips, and Johnny set his down with a clatter against the glass plate, and they both looked at Steph.

"Are we in trouble, Stephie?" George asked and he was totally focused on her.

"Not at all," Steph began. "You know that Uncle Leo and I are going to get married soon."

"Yup, and you get to officially be Aunt Stephie."

She smiled. "I do. But we need to have the ceremony first and I was hoping that you two would agree to give me away?"

"Give you to who?" George asked.

Liza held back a laugh.

"You would walk me down the aisle in the church and once we got to the altar, the pastor would ask who gives this woman, and you would both answer *I do*. Then you'd give Uncle Leo my hand and sit down."

"Oh, like Poppi gave Aunt Anna to Uncle Colin." Johnny beamed.

"That's right. Since my dad passed away, I need someone who I could count on to be there for me on my special day."

It suddenly dawned on the boys what Stephanie was asking them. Their eyes grew wide. Johnny asked, "So we each stand by your side and hold your hand too?"

She gave them a broad smile. "You wouldn't have to hold my hand unless you wanted to, of course."

George piped up. "Do we have to wear a tie?"

"Spoken like a true man." Liza laughed. "You'll wear whatever you're asked to wear. I'm going to guess it will be a tuxedo."

"Is Uncle Leo gonna wear one too?"

"George, all the men in the family will wear one, except for Spencer. He's too young."

They both shrugged. "That sounds cool. We'll give you to Uncle Leo."

Steph pulled them against her body and gave them each a fast hug before they wriggled out of her arms.

"Thank you both. You've just made our special day even more so."

Johnny rubbed his eyes with his fists and wrinkled his brow. "Poppi made a speech after Aunt Anna was married, before dinner."

Liza was surprised he had paid that much attention. "You remember that?" Her son never ceased to amaze her.

"Yeah. Poppi said it was part of his duties as the FOB. So I'll make the speech for both me and George, but we can stand up together."

Steph looked at Leo and then Liza and then at the boys. "FOB?"

"You know, father of the bride, and even though we're not a dad, we can be a NOB instead." He gave a nod to Steph.

"Nephews of the bride," she said. "I get it, and if you want to give a speech, then by all means go for it. All I ask is that you think about what you want to say before you have to do it."

Liza wanted to jump in and say they shouldn't, but the look of pride on their faces stopped her. She would offer to help them write it and maybe they could do a dry run or two. She pointed to the kitchen. "Why don't you put your dishes in the sink and gather up your stuff? It's late and you still need showers and to pack for camp tomorrow."

Johnny rubbed his forehead and winced as they scraped their chairs over the wooden deck.

"Johnny, are you okay?"

He looked at her through squinted eyes. "Ice cream headache." The boys took their plates and spoons into the kitchen.

Liza could hear them talking, but not what they were saying.

"Leo, don't you think it's a little risky agreeing for them to toast you at the wedding?"

With a snort, he said, "Are you kidding? If I know you, you're going to be all over that speech like a bee to flowers on grapevines. I have no doubt they'll do a great job. And if worse comes to worst, you can give a speech when they're done. After all, you're the best person."

"The last of the bachelors is getting married." She grinned.

He leaned back in the chair and trailed his fingertips over Stephanie's arm. "I can't wait."

She gave Leo and then Steph a hug. "We'll talk tomorrow. There are plans to make."

9

onday morning, Liza was in planner mode. She held the phone to her ear while it rang and glanced at the page of notes to discuss with Steph. First, was about *the* dress.

"Hello. This is Stephanie."

With a laugh, Liza responded, "Hello. This is Liza."

"Hey, sorry it took so long for me to answer. I'm up to my elbows in Bondo."

"We can talk later if you want." She doodled flowers on the pad in front of her.

"No, I've left the car in Zira's capable hands. What's the good word?"

"I've made a couple of calls to three different bridal shops and we have tentative appointments based on your schedule. But there is one I really want to take you to. It's called It's Your Day. They're the best." With a flash of sadness, she remembered what it had been like to find her gown there.

"Leo and I still need to talk with the family tonight."

"I know, but we should get a jump on the appoint-

75

ments. Sometimes it's hard to get them for a larger group in a short timeframe. Besides, you can share the dates when you ask everyone to come with us."

"That's a good idea."

She smiled into the phone. "That's why you're paying me the big bucks."

Steph's laughter warmed her heart. "I'm glad you've got the details covered and I'm getting the family discount."

"It's going to cost you in babysitting."

Steph laughed again. "What we do for love, right?"

Liza agreed. Love was essential and even if the family was sometimes a little too nosy, they had come through after Steve died and made sure she and the boys knew they were never alone until they were ready to handle it. "I'll text you the specifics after I confirm the times."

"You said a couple of shops. Are they all good? I want to make Leo's eyes pop out of his head when he sees me."

Liza would make sure Stephanie would be the most beautiful bride that graced the altar at Black River Congregational Church. "Don't you worry. He won't be able to tear his eyes off you."

"I'm going to ask all of the girls to get a special dress and coordinate with the theme."

She was touched by Steph's thoughtfulness. "Who's going to stand up for you?"

"Since we're going nontraditional, I thought I'd ask Gary. He works for me and he and Dad were best friends forever and in a small way, it would make it feel like Dad's with me. Do you think that would be weird?"

That was a sweet idea. "It's your day and you can have anyone you want be a part of it."

"Then that's settled."

"Have you thought about colors or a theme?" She was prepared to write down whatever Steph rattled off. Free thinking usually generated the best ideas.

"Leo said he doesn't care, so I'm leaning toward silver and sage green for the basics."

"Those are beautiful fall colors." She scrawled a note across the pad. "Have you thought about dress styles for the Price women?"

"I would like to give them a palette of colors and let them choose whatever dress they feel comfortable in, and that includes you."

She let out a low whistle. "Whew. I thought Leo was going to ask me to wear a tux."

A hearty laugh came through the phone. "I can tell you Gary will flatly refuse to wear a gown. What do you think about wearing sage? It'll be lovely on you with your coloring."

"Not a problem." Liza wrote that down and thought she might leaf through some bridal magazines to see if she found a style that would work in her dual roles as best person *and* the planner, one that would also be easy to dance in.

"Of course we'll talk to Tessa about the arrangements for the reception at Sand Creek?"

"Have you decided how many guests?"

Steph laughed. "Things have grown a bit. I'm going to guess around a hundred. Do you think Creek can hold that many people? I want to include my team here and I have a couple of friends from Portland that might want to come, and of course the entire extended family. My new family."

Liza could hear the catch in her voice. She wished they were face-to-face so she could give her a hug. "Stephanie, you know that you're loved by all of us. And besides, there is plenty of room at Creek. I've coordinated several large events there and it was perfect."

"I never thought I would find a man who had a big, amazing family. Being an only child was hard and as I got older, it was even harder. I realized what I had been missing after I met Leo."

Liza thought of Drew being the only child too. Did he find it lonely as an adult?

"Liza, did I lose you?"

"No. I'm here. I was thinking about something you said."

"Care to share?"

She thought about asking Steph if she thought kids who grew up without siblings felt isolated and alone as a child and an adult. Maybe that's why Drew opened the camps—to help others find companionship during the summer months like he had, in addition to giving kids a great experience.

"No, but thanks." She tapped the pen on the paper. "I'm going to put together some floral arrangement ideas for you to take a look at."

"Alright. I need to run, but I'll see you at your mom's."

"Have a great rest of the day."

"You too."

She set the phone aside and brought up her email. A message from Drew was waiting. For half a second, she wondered how he had gotten her email address, but it was her work email, which was posted on her website.

She smiled as she read the short note.

I had a great time with you and looking forward to Sunday. He signed it with a capital *D* and a smiley face.

The email was thoughtful and proof he'd thought about her after their date. Should she respond or wait and reply later or tomorrow? But she wasn't into playing games.

She jotted off a quick response. *Thanks for a wonderful afternoon. See you on Sunday!* She hit send and then settled back into work mode.

*L*ater that day, Liza parked the van in front of her parents' garage and turned in the driver's seat. She looked at the boys. "I want you to promise that you won't tell anyone, and I do mean anyone, that Uncle Leo and Stephanie have an announcement tonight. It's their news to share at dinner, not yours."

"Mom." George rolled his eyes. "You don't need to keep telling us. We're not blabbermouths."

She smothered a smile. They'd never ruin a surprise intentionally but… "I just wanted to remind you one more time."

"We've got this." Johnny's voice was mature beyond his years. These little moments gave her glimpses into the man he'd become. Steve would have gotten a charge out of him for sure.

"Can we go inside now?" he asked.

"Will you each take a tote bag with you from the back?"

When the boys tried to get the hatch open, it was stuck. She depressed the release button and it still didn't budge.

"Can you climb over the seat, George?"

He scrambled over and handed the totes to Johnny. Then he made a big show of sliding over the seat again, whacking the glass with his sneaker, and leaving a smear on it. He beamed when he got out of the van.

The boys lugged the overstuffed bags to the house and

Liza grabbed her computer bag. She had printed lists she wanted to give to the happy couple, things they'd need to decide before she could do final bookings. Oh, and they needed to make sure that Sand Creek was available too. Just one more thing to add to her mental list.

She and the boys seemed to be the last to arrive and everyone was in high spirits. As usual, the kids were running around until Mom shooed them out the back door. The three youngest ones were playing in the sandbox with plenty of toys to keep them occupied, and the adults were sitting in various spots around the spacious family room with a clear view of the kids.

Leo winked at her. He pulled Steph up from the sofa. "Can I have everyone's attention for just a minute? Steph and I have an announcement." His deep voice stilled all conversations.

Liza thought she could hear a pin drop.

"We'd like to request that you keep the third Saturday in November open as"—he held up their clasped hands—"we're getting married."

Jack, who was the closest, clapped him on the back and hugged Steph.

Leo grinned. "Hold on for another minute. It's going to be easier for me to just keep talking."

Anna smirked. "That's nothing new."

Laughter rippled across the room.

"It's going to be a small family wedding. We plan on limiting the guest list to less than one hundred people. So, by Price family standards, it'll be tiny." He smiled at his twin. "I've asked Liza to stand up for me, and Steph asked Gary to be her wingman. George and Johnny will walk my bride down the aisle."

Steph hugged his arm close to her body. "I'll take it

from here." She kissed his cheek. "For the rest of our news, I'm going dress shopping." She looked at the women in the room. "If you agree, I'd like for each of you to wear a dress that reflects your style but is still a part of the fall color scheme. This way, you'll be honorary bridesmaids."

Leo looked at Don and Jack and then Max and Colin. "I'm hoping I can count on you to be ushers and basically keep things running smoothly."

Don said to Leo, "You can count on us."

Mom wiped a tear from her cheek. "We'll have a small engagement party the first Sunday in August, after the tasting room closes."

Leo and Steph beamed. "Sounds good, Mom."

Liza could only imagine how Mom was feeling, knowing that her youngest son was going to be married in less than five months.

Dad sat in his leather recliner. Steph crossed the room and perched on the arm of his chair. She bent her head low, and the conversation was between the two of them. He was nodding, and then he beamed. She bent down and kissed his cheek and he slipped his arm around her waist and pulled her close.

When he released her, Dad stood up. "This calls for a toast."

Leo followed Mom and Dad from the room while the ladies clustered around Steph. She pulled a slip of paper from her jeans.

"Here's the scoop. Liza has made a couple of tentative appointments for dress shopping. We could go Friday night at eight, Saturday at eleven, or the following Sunday at three." Her gaze took in the group. "Who can go when?"

Tessa said, "What works best for you?"

"I kind of like the idea of Saturday. I was thinking when we were done, we could go have a bite to eat and celebrate. Make it a girls' day."

Everyone agreed Saturday would work, and the logistics of who was driving was ironed out in a flash. Liza pulled out her phone and confirmed the appointment with the bridal salon and canceled the other two.

"Why don't we gather here at nine thirty? As long as we are out the door within fifteen minutes, we should make it to Rochester in plenty of time."

Steph said, "Would you mind nine? What if we get caught in some traffic on the highway? I don't want to be late."

"You're the bride. Nine it is." Liza trusted that everyone would agree. Being a part of this group of women warmed her heart. And this gave her hope that she'd find her happily ever after, maybe even with someone she already knew.

10

The next night, after Liza had gotten the kids into a shower and then pajamas, her phone rang. It was Stephanie.

"Is it okay if I stop by? I have a couple of things I want to show you."

"Sure, come on over."

She went into the kitchen and put on the teapot. Steph had a passion for all different kinds of tea, and for Christmas she had given Liza fancy loose leaf tea. It was fun to have someone to share it with.

As she was finishing putting cookies on a plate, she heard a car in the driveway, and then the back door burst open.

Steph was grinning and did a little jig. "Can you believe your brother and I are getting married in fifteen weeks?"

"I can, and that time will fly." She poured water over the infuser and the citrus aroma teased her senses.

"You made tea." She sank onto a stool at the breakfast bar.

"I did." Liza gestured to the folder on the counter. "Grab that and we'll take a look."

Steph ignored it. "I didn't come to talk about the wedding. Well, not as the first topic. We haven't had a minute to talk about your date on Sunday, at least not alone. And I couldn't ask you the most important question in front of the boys or your brother." She wiggled her eyebrows. "Did he kiss you?"

"No. It was our first date and my first in a million years." Heat crept up her face and she even felt her ears grow warm. She groaned. "I have no idea how to date in the twenty-first century and I wasn't sure if I should hug him, so I didn't."

With a laugh, Steph said, "Take a breath. We'll drink tea and dissect it."

Liza slid mugs across the countertop, the teapot in one hand and a plate of shortbread cookies in the other. "Let's sit over near the bay window."

After they settled into overstuffed chairs, Liza brought the mug to her lips and sipped. "You had a first date just over a year ago. How did you know Leo was someone special, not just a body to fill up some time?"

"That was easy. I liked talking to him and he's genuine." She nibbled a cookie. "How did you feel when you were with Drew?"

She kept her hands wrapped around her mug. "It was amazing. I was so comfortable with him. Talking to him wasn't awkward and even if I said something that I thought was cringeworthy, he was still interested."

"When did you know you wanted to see him again?" Steph set her tea aside.

"I said I was switching to lemonade because I had to drive the boys later and he switched too. I told him it didn't matter if he had another glass of wine. He seemed to enjoy just being there. And then we sat there for another two hours. It was effortless, not awkward at all."

"He sounds considerate and I'm happy you had fun."

Liza leaned forward. "Do you know that he owns summer camps? He went to sports camp as a child and he wants kids to have a similar experience."

Steph finished her cookie. "I knew he owned car dealerships but didn't know about the camps."

"Mom!" George called from the living room.

"What?" She didn't get up from her chair. This was part of the nightly ritual in the summer.

"Can we watch one more show?"

"No. Brush your teeth and get ready for bed. I'll be up soon."

"P…leeze…"

"Nope."

The television fell silent, and then she whispered, "I may have won that skirmish."

Steph arched an eyebrow. "But who wins the battle?"

With a soft laugh, Liza said, "It's still up for grabs." She held up a finger and tilted her head. Feet pounded on the stairs. "Hopefully they'll brush their teeth."

"So we can get down to a few tougher questions. Have you thought at all about becoming intimate with him?"

Liza's mouth dropped open. She had given it a lot of thought, but each time she circled back. Having a date was one thing, but actually starting a physical relationship was something else entirely. She fidgeted. "I've thought about it, but that's as far as I'm prepared to go at this point."

"I just want you to mull it over. You're a beautiful woman and you deserve to live a full life, which includes being intimate with a man if you choose."

Liza blinked tears from her eyes. She didn't want Steph to see that. "I've had two babies and my body is not what it once was. What if he doesn't find me desirable when I take my clothes off?" She looked at her hands. "He could date women who have plenty of time to spend hours in the gym, who are beautiful and toned. I spend my days taking care of my family and working."

"If that was important to him, Drew wouldn't have asked you to have dinner. He's obviously attracted to you." Steph jumped up. "Come with me."

Liza allowed herself to be guided down the hall to a large wall mirror. Steph stood behind her and looked at Liza's reflection.

"This is the woman Drew sees when he looks at you. Strong, confident, smart, loving, and yes, stunningly beautiful. He's an intelligent man who wants to be with you."

Liza studied her reflection. She appreciated what Steph was saying, but she had her doubts.

⁂

*L*iza woke at the first light of the gray dawn. She crossed the room to the window seat in anticipation of the sun's first streaks of pale orange and pink. The sky grew brighter as the rays crept across the dew-dampened grass. She hadn't slept well. Steve weighed heavy on her mind and she wished they had talked more about the what-ifs of life. But they had been young and thought they'd grow old together. Now she was faced with living a life without him. Was it too soon to be dating, and how would the boys react? It had been over five years, but still…

She liked this time of day, alone with her thoughts. Once she left her sanctuary, life would move at full speed.

The door creaked open. "Mom?" George was in the doorway, wearing Superman pajamas. His blond hair was spiked up every which way.

"Come here, kiddo." He wasn't too old to snuggle with her. She treasured these rare moments. Soon they'd just be a memory.

He padded across the plush beige carpet, sat next to her, and placed his head against her body. She circled her arms around him.

"Did you have a bad dream?"

He nodded. "I couldn't find you."

She smoothed his hair and kissed the top of his head. He shivered and she drew him closer.

"Can we have pancakes for breakfast?"

It would mean shifting her schedule, but her son needed reassurance that she was right where he needed her to be. Her not-so-little boy was the more sensitive of the two. Johnny seemed to take everything in stride. He'd have a quick outburst and then whatever had been troubling him was off his chest and he was fine. George bottled his emotions up.

"Just plain?"

He tilted his head back and his cute face wore a smile. "Do we have any blueberries?"

Tapping the tip of his nose, she smiled. "I think we have some in the refrigerator." He lay his head against her chest. "Do you want to help?" She felt him nod.

They sat there watching the colors on the horizon deepen.

"It's going to be a hot day. We'll have to make sure you don't forget your hat for camp."

"Is Owen coming today?"

"Aunt Peyton said next Monday."

"Good."

"Is everything going okay with your new friends?"

"Yeah. It'll just be more fun when Owen's there. He's gonna like the ropes course. I get to do that with Johnny and it's a blast." He wiggled out of her arms. "Do I have to get dressed before breakfast?"

"It would be a good idea. Why don't you wake up your brother and let him know we're having pancakes today."

"Mom?" He tipped his head and scrunched up his face. "Can I ask you something?"

"Of course."

"Are you gonna get married some day?"

That would have knocked her over if she wasn't sitting down. "Why do you ask?"

"Me and John are the only kids without a dad or stepdad and I kinda want to have one someday."

"No one could replace your father. What would you think if I did want to get married someday?" She could see his wheels turning.

"You'd marry someone who liked kids, right?"

"If he didn't, that would be a deal breaker, as you and Johnny are the most important men in my life and you'll always come first."

His face relaxed. "When we had dinner at Mimi's, I heard Aunt Peyton and Aunt Kate talking about you going on a date. Does that mean you're getting married?"

"Oh, George. First, you shouldn't have been eaves-dropping, but to answer your question, a date is when you're getting to know someone to see if you have interests in common and if you have fun together."

"Oh."

"Is there another question?" With George there always was.

"Will we have to move to a new house? Stephie doesn't live at her house anymore. She lives with Uncle Leo."

She opened her arms. "Come here and let's talk."

He leaped into her arms and she held him tight.

"If, and I do say if, I meet someone who I think will fit into our lives, we'll spend time together to make sure we all get along. Remember we discuss all important decisions as a family."

"Like with a vacation when we talk about it and make plans?"

"Exactly. There are some things that will never change." She gave him a big squeeze and a kiss on the top of his head. "Do you feel better now?"

"Yup." He slipped out of her arms and raced to the door. "I'm gonna wake Johnny up." He shut her bedroom door with a thud.

The sun flooded her bedroom with bright sunshine. She was going to have to speak with the family and ask them to keep talk of her dating to a minimum when the boys were within earshot.

11

*A*fter dropping the boys at camp, Liza headed to the park where the wedding this weekend was to be held on Saturday. It suddenly dawned on her that she couldn't go dress shopping with the girls.

She slammed her hand against the steering wheel and depressed the hands-free button and called Steph as she pulled off the road. Her family would have to go without her. There was no way she was going to even suggest a date change. It worked for everyone else.

When Steph answered, Liza dove in. "Hi. I have some bad news."

"What?" The concern in Steph's voice came through the line loud and clear.

"I won't be able to go dress shopping. In my excitement for you, I completely blanked on my event on Saturday. What kind of professional am I to forget a job?"

"A busy one, and you have a lot on your mind—work, the boys, dating, and now our wedding."

That wasn't an excuse. Liza prided herself on being an organized professional in this competitive business. And as much as she wanted to be there, it just wasn't feasible. She shook her head and kept her tone neutral. "Go without me."

"Well, that's not happening. What were the other times?"

"Friday night at eight. The couple's having an afternoon rehearsal and I'm waiting for her to confirm or Sunday. I'll postpone my date. Drew will understand and if he doesn't, oh well."

"You will not cancel your date."

Liza could hear the clipped sounds of Steph's shoes against the floor loud and clear. She could envision her pacing.

"I want you to call the bridal shop and see if you can still get the eight o'clock appointment on Friday," Steph said, "since that's our best hope for this weekend. If the timing doesn't work out, ask about an appointment for next weekend. Problem solved." She sounded like a woman who knew exactly what she wanted and there was no dissuading her at this point.

"If you're sure, I'll make the calls, but first I'll confirm with my client for Friday."

"Call me when we're penned in."

Relief coursed through Liza. She had wanted to be with everyone when Steph tried on dresses. It would be fun to poke through the racks for something pretty to wear too. "I'll call you in a bit."

"Liza, to be clear, there's no way I'm going to go shopping for my wedding dress without you there. It's important to me that all my sisters are with me."

She loved how Steph emphasized the words *all my sisters*.

The next step was a quick call to her bride, and Liza

was happy to hear she wanted the rehearsal at two, which would mean at the latest, she'd be free by four. This was going to work if the bridal salon hadn't booked that slot yet.

She called Steph and confirmed Friday was a go. "I'll text the family and then get back to planning the wedding for Saturday."

With a short laugh, Stephanie answered, "I'll talk to you later."

And then Liza could focus on her date with Drew.

*L*iza heard a thud under the van as she pulled back onto the road and muttered under her breath about potholes. They had better not damage her new tires. Fifteen minutes later, she slowed when she saw the sign for Fountain Park. This was a beautiful venue for a wedding and reception but a bit difficult, as she had to have the entire experience created from the ground up. She strode across the grass, relieved to see the tent company on-site. The tent was nearing completion for the ceremony location and happily the enormous tent for the reception was complete.

She waved at the foreman, Marcus, an older gentleman who was never in a hurry to get anywhere. They had worked together for several events and she knew he'd do a good job.

"Liza. Good to see you."

"How's everything going?" She looked around at the buzz of activity. "Everything seems to be running on schedule."

"Like clockwork." He smelled of pipe tobacco and Old Spice. "Gonna be a pretty day Saturday."

She glanced around. "We have the tent sides stashed just in case it rains, right?"

"Now, Liza, I've been in this business for a long time with a tad bit of experience."

"I know, but I feel better asking the question. Better to know the answer than freak out later."

"You have one of the coolest heads in this business, but to ease your mind, not only do I have the sides tucked over yonder"—he pointed to the far side of the park—"but I have men on call if we need to have them installed."

"Just what I needed to hear." They walked to the stacks of chairs and tables. "Are the linens here too?"

"Those will be delivered in plastic totes by midday on Friday. That'll keep them protected until Saturday."

"Excellent." She took a few pictures, as the bride wanted to be kept in the loop on every detail. "Thanks, Marcus. You have my cell if you need something. I'm off to meet with the florist."

"I'll be around Friday afternoon too. What time's rehearsal?"

"I expect the bridal party here by two, but I'll be here by eleven if you want to meet me."

He touched his fingers to the brim of his straw fedora. "I'll be here."

She did a full three-sixty and marveled at the beauty of the park. It was a wonderful place to start married life and who knows? Maybe someday it could be where she tied the knot.

*I*t had been hectic for a Thursday. Picking up the boys was something Liza looked forward to, and today was no exception. She parked next to the curb and walked over to a group of kids. Sandy, the counselor in charge of pickup and drop-off, got the boys' attention with a sharp toot of a whistle and pointed to her.

For a change, they walked at a sedate pace, except of course George who was jumping over all the cracks in the sidewalk. Well, they had been going full speed all week.

"Hey guys, how was your day?" She took their backpacks for them.

"It was good," Johnny said. George nodded in agreement. "What's for dinner?"

"Spaghetti and meatballs."

"Yum." George smacked his lips. He stopped short when they got to the van. "Mom?" He pointed to the back tire.

She groaned. "Oh no, not again. A brand-new tire." She bent down to inspect her very flat tire and muttered under her breath, "I don't remember running over anything." Maybe when she hit that hole yesterday, she had picked up a nail or something.

Johnny set a comforting hand on her forearm. "Don't worry, Mom. We can handle this."

"The way the van is parked might make it hard to get the jack in there." She really didn't want to call Leo again, but if she started changing it, the boys would insist on helping. It didn't look safe. As she was trying to figure out the best way to approach it, she was interrupted when she heard, "Hi, Liza."

She was pleasantly surprised to see Drew. He looked at

the van and then at her. With a smile, he said, "I think this is a replay of another time we ran into each other."

"Well, at least this time we didn't crash into you." She smiled at him and then looked at the boys. "You remember Mr. Cameron?"

"Hi," Johnny said. "Mom, if you unlock the hatch, we can get this tire changed."

Drew cocked an eyebrow. "Need some help?"

"I can change it." She smothered a smile as Johnny seemed to size up Drew again, asserting his place.

Over their heads she mouthed thank you. This was important for her boys to try and she wanted him to understand their point of view.

"I'm going to talk to your mom for a minute. Just let me know if you need a hand."

Liza hit the button and the hatch released. George took the backpacks from her and tossed them on the back seat. He strutted around the back of the van.

She hid a smile behind her hand and half turned away from the boys. "This is a nice surprise."

He arched a brow. "The flat or seeing me?"

"Seeing you, of course."

"It's a nice bonus for having to stop by camp today." He reached out and then glanced at the boys and withdrew his hand. "Have you decided what time on Sunday?"

Liza noticed Johnny was watching them closely. It was obvious he was listening to their conversation.

She inclined her head in the boys' direction and changed the subject. "John, how's it going?"

"Okay."

Drew turned his attention to the boys. "Need a hand?"

"Well…"

He pointed to the spare. "Johnny, is it okay if I take this and you carry the jack?"

He nodded. "Yes, sir."

"You can call me Drew."

George shot a quizzical look at Liza.

She nodded. "He gave you permission."

Johnny's face relaxed into a smile. "Drew, I'll put the jack under the van."

The boys knelt beside him, contemplating the flat. He walked them through the steps of changing the tire, basically letting them handle everything except the extra muscle for loosening and then tightening the nuts. It took about twice as long by the time they stored the jack and flat, but it was worth every extra minute to see the boys' beaming smiles. Her little men. With Drew helping, she hadn't worried about the way she had parked the van.

"See, Mom? I told ya we could change it." Johnny slid open the van door and plopped on the seat. George was right behind him.

She turned so they couldn't see or hear her. "Thank you."

"They're great kids." He grazed her cheek with his finger. "I'll call you later and we can make plans for Sunday."

She felt a quiver of anticipation race through her. "If you call after nine, the boys will be in bed. It'll be easier to talk."

A little louder, he said, "You might want to think about having the van checked out before you drive too far. There might be damage from driving on a flat."

"I'll call Leo and see if he can take a look tomorrow." She frowned. "I've been toying with the idea of getting a new SUV. But I won't have time until the fall to even think about looking."

He wiggled his eyebrows. "I can get you a good deal. I have a few connections, you know."

She wasn't going to ask him to help her shop for a new vehicle. "Thank you, but I like to research, test drive, and then haggle. It's all part of the fun."

"What are you thinking about?"

She brushed back her hair and said, "An SUV like Kate has, with the bells and whistles. The boys are getting older and that would give us more room for sports equipment and their friends, and in case you haven't noticed, I tend to hang on to a vehicle a long time, maybe longer than I should, but I like to extract my money's worth."

He gave her a wide smile. "If you change your mind, just let me know. I'm happy to help and there's a friends' discount too."

George called to her. "I'm starving. Mom, can we go now?"

"Coming." She gave Drew a flirty wink. "Talk to you later." She felt his eyes on her as she got in the driver's seat.

He waved to the boys. "See you later, guys."

"Thanks for the help, Drew." Johnny grinned. "You made it fun."

He leaned in through the open passenger window. "Drive careful on the way home."

"Thanks again for everything." She eased away from the curb and in the sideview mirror saw him wave. She was already looking forward to his phone call.

George caught her eye in the rearview mirror. "Hey, Mom, why are you smiling like that?"

"I'm just happy, son."

12

Friday night was warm and the sun was beginning to dip toward the horizon. The Price women were gathered on the front porch at Mom's house. Liza sent the boys inside to watch a movie with Dad.

Kate dangled her keys in the air. "Who's ready to hit the road?"

Steph stepped forward. "I'm with Liza."

Peyton held up her hand. "Me too."

"Sherry," Kate announced, "you, Tessa, and Anna can ride with me."

As they descended the front steps, Liza glanced over her shoulder. "Kate, you have the address, right?"

She held up her phone. "All set."

With a bounce in her step, Steph said, "Meet you there." She slid into the passenger seat and Peyton got into the back.

Liza grinned at Steph. "Are you ready to try on wedding dresses?"

Stephanie looked at Peyton and then Liza. "Yes, but I'm

nervous. What if I don't find a dress? Then we'll have to make another trip to a different shop and we don't have a lot of time."

Peyton piped up. "I know exactly how you feel. When I went shopping for my dress, I was convinced before we got there it was going to be a huge waste of time." She gave Liza a little poke in her shoulder. "Do you remember what you said to me? I'll never forget how sweet you were."

Steph said, "I think I could use some calming words of advice right now to keep me from going off the deep end."

"I promise you, Steph, that we will find the perfect dress for you. If we don't find it in this shop, then we'll go to as many as needed until you say YES to the dress and they ring that bell."

Steph's eyebrow arched. "What bell?"

Liza started the van. "Each time a bride chooses her dress, they ring this bell so everyone in the salon knows the bride made her choice. People clap and it's just a fun thing to do." She glanced at Steph and grinned. "You'll see, and I have a good feeling about tonight."

Steph leaned back in the passenger seat. "Peyton, have you been kept up to speed about our sister-in-law here having another date with the handsome Drew Cameron?"

"What?" She leaned between the seats as far as her seat belt would allow. "That's wonderful. Jack never said a word."

With a dry laugh, Liza said, "I'm shocked Leo didn't take out a billboard with the news." She was pleased that the ladies were supportive of her dating Drew.

Steph shook her head. "I told him if he was a blabber-mouth, we'd have a serious conversation about privacy."

Peyton poked her shoulder. "Spill the details."

Liza adjusted the air conditioner. "Do you think it's warm in here?"

"Nope. It's only because you're on the proverbial hot seat," Peyton said. "So you had a first date and now it's progressed to dinner?"

"Prepare to be shocked. I asked Drew to meet me for a drink at Sawyers last Sunday."

"You? Asked him?" Peyton clapped her hands. "What have you been drinking lately, something with a heady bouquet?"

Liza tipped her chin up; she was proud of herself for asking him out, like starting her business to prove she was a strong woman so was asking out a handsome man. "I'm taking charge of my happiness and I wanted to ask him, so I went for it. If he had said no, well, there would be another guy at some point, right?"

"Good for you," Peyton said. "Now, details. Like, is he as charming and funny as he seems?"

"Yes." She caught Peyton studying her in the mirror. "I was stunned when he said yes."

Steph turned so she could see Peyton. "We kept the boys for what we thought was going to be a couple of hours and it lasted over four."

"You had a four-hour first date." Peyton nodded. "Well done."

"We had a glass of wine and then lemonade and we lost track of time." Liza grinned without looking at the girls. "I never expected the conversation to flow so easily. He's a good listener, asks questions, and, well, before we knew it, they were seating people for dinner. Looking back, I should have talked to him when he was at family events. Maybe we could have gone out sooner." She shrugged and glanced at Steph and then in the mirror at Peyton. "I guess I wasn't ready yet."

"I'm thrilled for you. But is it still a secret or can I tell Jack? He'll be happy to know you're having fun again."

"Sure, you can tell him, but just remind him I am a grown woman and don't need my older brother showing up."

Peyton groaned. "Steph, Don and Jack were seriously overprotective when we were growing up. They were always checking up on us and they'd just show up, hovering close enough to eavesdrop until they were satisfied their sisters were fine."

Steph glanced between the two women. "That had to have been embarrassing."

Liza chuckled. She had forgotten her brothers were always around until Peyton brought it up. "It got worse. If we had a date with a guy, they'd grill us when we got home about exactly what had happened and if they didn't like the guy"—she threw one hand in the air—"well, they'd badger us, hoping we'd agree to break it off."

Steph's mouth gaped open. "Please tell me Leo wasn't like that too?"

Liza gave her a side-eye. "He was overprotective, but in a different way. He usually would show up wherever I was with a date, but he'd be with a girl. It was never overt as to what he was doing. Well, at least not to the guy. But I knew."

"Did they finally outgrow that boorish behavior?"

Peyton snorted. "We can only hope. That's why Liza wants to keep dating Drew on the down low."

Steph nodded. "I can promise you if Leo showed up and embarrassed you, I'd have some pretty strong words."

With a laugh, Liza said, "I appreciate the support."

Peyton asked, "Do you really like him?"

Liza didn't have to think before answering. "I do. A lot."

"I'm guessing the feeling is mutual." Peyton settled back against the seat. "What do the boys think?"

"Nothing about Drew specifically." She looked in the rearview mirror at Peyton. "How did Owen handle it?"

"He was younger, and Jack had been around for a long time before we started dating. The boys have seen Drew at a few parties, but I'm guessing they haven't interacted with him much."

"No. Not really." She grew thoughtful. "It is different from you and Jack, but the boys have seen Drew at camp, and then when I picked up a nail in my tire, he hung around while the boys thought they could change it. Well, he was really sweet, giving them the chance to do it before jumping in. It showed that he respected them, and I liked it and I think they did too."

Stephanie asked, "Do you think they'll know it's a date?"

Peyton said, "Be up front and say you're going to start dating Drew. It'll lead to some questions, but better than letting them think you have something to hide. After all, they're getting to the age where they may want to pull one over on you and if you can point back to this, being honest might go a long way during the dreaded teenage years."

"Peyton's right. My dad didn't date much when I was growing up, but he always was up front about it when he did."

"Okay then. While they're with Mom tomorrow, I'll figure out how to bring up the topic and let them know. Thanks, ladies." She slowed the car.

Steph peered out the windshield. "We're here. I'm so excited."

Liza parked next to Kate and the ladies walked as a group to the large white double doors trimmed in pale yellow. They hadn't changed since Liza came here to buy her wedding dress.

They were greeted by a woman whose skin was flawless. She was dressed in an elegant black sheath, her hair secured into a low bun.

"Welcome. I'm Betty." She scanned the family. "Which one of you is the bride?"

Steph held up her hand. "Me," she squeaked.

"Excellent. And the mother of the bride?"

Mom stepped forward. "I'm the groom's mother and will be standing in for Stephanie's mom."

Liza's heart warmed as she watched as Steph gave Mom a grateful smile. She said, "The rest of us are all related to the groom, and we'd also like to shop for dresses while we're here, if someone is available to help us?"

Lila turned and waved toward another woman who was dressed in a similar style, but she looked older and had salt-and-pepper-colored hair. "Maeve will help you select dresses."

Liza and Mom went with Steph while the other girls headed toward racks of dresses.

Before following, Tessa paused to ask Steph, "Long or short for our dresses?"

Stephanie smiled. "Decide as a group whatever makes you all happy."

Liza scanned racks and racks of bridal gowns, wondering how Leo would react when he saw his bride for the first time and in a blink wondered how Drew looked in a tux. They continued to walk to the back of the shop, where banks of mirrors lined the walls. Several sofas had been arranged so a small platform was the focal point.

Liza touched her shoulder. "Tell me what you like and what you don't. It will help Betty to narrow the scope."

Steph absentmindedly twirled a lock of hair around her finger. "I don't want anything too poufy or frilly. And cream would be good."

"What about sleeve length?"

"Well, it's in November, but we won't be outside all that much, so I guess it doesn't really matter, but nothing strapless. I don't want to have to worry about the front of my dress slipping down and above all, I want to be comfortable." She held up her hand. "That is the most important factor."

Betty listened to the list. "I'm going to grab a few dresses and you can try things on." She glanced at Steph's curves. "Size ten?"

"How did you know?"

She gave her a broad smile. "I've been in the dress business for a long time. If I didn't know, I should hang up my pincushion." She slipped away.

Stephanie snapped her fingers. "Oh, shoot. I should have told her about the pockets. Do you think we'll find a dress tonight?"

Mom placed a hand on her arm. "Don't put any pressure on yourself. Just have fun and enjoy this experience, and we will make sure you have pockets."

"I want the dress to be perfect so when Leo sees me, he thinks, *Wow. She's beautiful.*"

"My dear Stephanie. My son looks like that every time you're in the same room. You don't need a beautiful gown for him to be reminded how stunning you are. He already knows it."

"Sherry, you're sweet." Tears formed in Steph's eyes and she blinked them away. "If Mom couldn't be with me today, I'm glad you're here."

"I'm pretty lucky that Leo had the good sense to propose to you."

Liza handed Stephanie a small packet of tissues. "There are more where those came from."

Steph took one and dabbed her eyes. "You really do think of everything, don't you?"

"Part of my charm. And I'm an up-and-coming event planner, so being on top of all the details goes with the territory."

"I'll return the favor someday when it's your turn to get married."

Liza felt her cheeks getting warm. "Let's concentrate on your big day." Out of the corner of her eye, she could see Betty coming toward them.

"Time to try on dresses. I'll go get the others."

She passed Betty and tipped her head to the side. "Thank you for everything."

"Now comes the exciting part for the bride and her family." She bobbed her head at the hangers in her hands. "Somewhere in this shop is a dress Stephanie will say yes to."

"I don't have a doubt in my mind, Betty. You've always had the knack for finding the perfect dress."

"Just like I did for you. What was that? Fifteen years ago?"

Liza was surprised she remembered and forced herself to keep her smile bright. "It seemed just like yesterday."

13

By the time Drew turned onto Liza's road, he had to admit his nerves were slightly rattled. Sunday evening had finally arrived and he was eager to see her boys again but nervous that this time was as their mother's date. What would they think of their mother having dinner with a man who was not their father? Would they even care? Hell, yeah, they would. If he was their age and his mom was dating someone, he'd care and so would they. What if they gave Liza a hard time? It was natural for them to want to keep things as they were.

Drew was drawn to her like he had never been attracted to another woman, and he had dated plenty. This woman was different. Her strength and grace were just two of the qualities he admired. In addition, having a thriving business within the first couple of years indicated she had a good work ethic—something that was important in Drew's opinion.

He noticed a cream-colored vintage Chevy pickup in the driveway. Relief eased the clenched feeling inside of him. Leo and Steph were already here.

He was walking to the house carrying a bouquet of pink sweetheart roses when Johnny and George appeared around the side of the house.

He gave them a friendly smile. "Hi, boys."

"Hi." Johnny eyed the roses with a furrowed brow. "Mom doesn't like flowers."

George nodded. "She's allergic to bees."

"I didn't know that, but I got these from a florist, so they should be bee free." He was impressed with their protective side.

The front door opened and Liza stepped onto the wide front porch. She was wearing a pretty floral dress and her blond hair was loosely curled. A smile spread over her lips and warmed her eyes. "Hi."

He walked up the steps. "Hi. You look beautiful." He held out the flowers. "These are for you, sans bees."

She glanced at the boys, who stood at the base of the steps, glued with interest to the exchange.

"I'm guessing the boys said something?"

"They did."

She accepted the flowers and inhaled their heady scent. It was one of the prettiest things he had seen in a long time.

"I'm glad they told me."

"Occasionally we have a bee issue around here and I've had to use an EpiPen once when we were alone. It scared them, so now they're extra careful." She stepped to one side. "Come in."

Liza looked at the boys. "Are you guys coming?"

Johnny shrugged. "Yeah."

They trudged up the steps and past Drew. He held back a chuckle.

The center hall of Liza's house was spacious and more

luxurious than he thought it would be; however, it was decorated just as he had imagined. Soft florals mixed with solid durable fabrics on the furniture, suitable for the boys without fear of dirt or tears. It wasn't at all like his parents' house when he was a boy. That was like something out of *Architectural Digest*; this reminded him of an upscale *Better Homes and Gardens*. When he had been here before for a family barbeque, he had only made it as far as the kitchen. A formal dining room to the right of the door had been converted into an office, complete with computer desk, printer, and stacks of manila folders on the table.

Liza noticed him looking in the dining room. "I have an office here and at CLW; this way I can be home when the boys get home from school." She pointed down the short hallway. "Come on into the kitchen. Leo's getting ready to grill."

The boys had gone ahead of them, and he followed Liza down the short hall. The back side of the house was an open kitchen and family area. To the right was a closed door which he knew from his previous visit was a combined laundry room and half bath.

"Drew. Welcome." Leo's smile was friendly and Steph was at the sink, rinsing a bowl.

She called over her shoulder, "Hi."

Leo glanced at Liza. "If you didn't have plans I'd say stay, but Liza looks too pretty to be eating in the backyard."

"Leo." Her voice held a warning tone.

Drew thought the look on Liza's face would cause anyone to wither, but Leo grinned and held up his hands. "Just being a good brother."

Steph playfully snapped him with a towel. "No. You're

just being a pain." She took the flowers from Liza. "I'll put these in water if you two want to take off."

"Thanks, Steph." She picked up a small clutch and added her cell phone to it. "If you need something, my cell will be on."

"Stop worrying and have fun." Stephanie waved her hand at the couple. "We're having dinner and then playing board games and maybe s'mores before bed."

Liza turned to Drew. "I'm ready."

He looked at Steph and Leo with a stab of sadness; he didn't have family like this. "Thank you for watching the boys so I could take your sister out to dinner."

Leo looked him in the eye. "These kids are a lot of fun to hang with. I hope you have as much fun as the four of us are going to have."

Drew looked at Liza and he hoped the night would go off without a hitch.

*B*efore they left, Liza turned to say goodbye one last time to the boys. They were slumped in deck chairs. "Drew, I need a minute. I'll be right back." She stepped onto the deck. "Guys, I'm leaving now."

"You look really pretty, Mom." Johnny poked his brother.

"Yeah, Mom," George said.

She perched on the edge of the chair and faced them. "We talked about my date. Are you guys okay with me going?"

They nodded in unison.

Johnny raised his eyes to meet hers. "It's just weird."

"I know it's different, but Drew's nice and he's a good friend to Uncle Colin."

He didn't avert his eyes. "I know."

She touched the arm of the chair. It was unusual when she couldn't tell what either of her boys were thinking, but hopefully this wasn't a bad sign. "Be good tonight."

"Bye, Mom," Johnny said. "Have a good time."

George slid out of the chair and gave her a hug. "Bye, Mom."

She kissed the top of his head and savored the smell of sun and little boy sweat.

"I'll come see you when I get home."

They got up and raced down the deck steps to the backyard. Minor skirmish averted. At least for now.

Drew eased his car into a parking space at the entrance to Fountain Park. He looked at Liza. "I thought we could have a picnic."

She glanced at her dress and her smile dipped.

"You really do look beautiful."

She said, "I'm not dressed to sit on the ground."

He pulled the keys from the ignition. "I had hoped that would be the case." He gave her a warm smile that she couldn't help but return. "Ready?"

She pulled her cardigan sweater on, anticipating cooler temperatures as the sun set. "I am now." If she had known they were going to be outside, she would have worn slacks.

Drew opened the passenger door and helped her out. She didn't let go of his hand as they strolled down the brick path.

She glanced at the car. "Shouldn't we bring the cooler?"

"Let's pick our spot, and then I'll come back for it. No sense lugging a heavy cooler all over."

She exhaled. It was nice to let go and have someone make plans for her for a change. "I do love this park," she said as they strolled along the path. It was familiar and comfortable, and she was glad Drew had picked this park for their date. "There's a little gazebo near the pond and I've organized three small weddings there so far this year."

He gave her hand a gentle squeeze and Liza realized their hands were still interlaced and she was pleasantly surprised how natural it felt.

"I bet it is a gorgeous setting for a small wedding. When I was a kid, my parents and I would ride the bike trails."

"There are some geocaches hidden around here too. Have you ever done that?"

He slowed his steps and scanned the area. "Geocache? No. Is it fun?"

"I haven't been, but the boys are talking about it. I guess it's all the rage at the moment with their friends."

Drew casually steered her to the middle of the park where the pond was located.

"It sounds like fun. If there comes a time when you want to go, maybe it's something we could do with your boys."

She glanced his way, surprised he wanted to spend time with her boys too. "I'll keep that in mind."

Liza wasn't ready to start making plans for the four of them. She was going to take her time and see how things went between the two of them first before they did family events. It was enough they knew she and Drew were dating.

He let go of her hand and looked deep into her eyes. "You set the pace on when we do anything with the boys. I'm enjoying our time getting to know each other."

The path was lined with a mix of wildflowers and ferns. The late-day sun dappled through the maple and oak trees overhead, creating a patchwork of light as they strolled closer to the pond.

"There are picnic tables if we take a right at the corner." She pointed to a curve in the path up ahead.

"Let's look at the water first. I'll bet the view is stunning tonight."

She was content to walk close to him. His spicy cologne was tantalizing and she wanted to hold him close and savor it. It was surprising to feel this way for someone who wasn't Steve but she liked it and Drew.

They strolled to the left and she could see the roofline of the gazebo up ahead. Her steps slowed. "We should go the other way. It looks like there is some kind of event going on based on the glow of lights."

His voice held a light tone. "Just a peek, and then we'll slip away before we're even noticed."

She dropped her voice and gave a soft laugh, giving in to the mischievous twinkle in his eyes. "Then we'll need to be very quiet." She really wasn't sure they could slip in undetected, but it was a public park. When she had done a wedding at the gazebo, there had been a few onlookers at a respectful distance. It wasn't like they would crash the party.

They walked quietly down the path and as they grew closer, her breath caught in her throat. She had never seen the gazebo more beautiful as the sun bathed it in a golden glow. Twinkle lights were wrapped around each column and in the middle, a table was set for two. Vases of pink roses were placed on the steps leading up to the center.

Her heart skipped. How utterly romantic. Whoever did this went to a lot of effort to make it look like something out of a magazine, right down to soft piano music drifting from hidden speakers. No one had arrived yet.

Drew said, "Let's take a closer look." His eyes twinkled.

"We can't." The words died on her lips as his smile grew and her heart skipped. Was it possible he did this for her?

"But we can. This is where we're having dinner tonight."

Her eyes grew wide and her lips parted. "You," she stuttered. "You did all of this for me?"

"Do you like it?" He gazed into her eyes.

"It's unbelievable and so"—should she say romantic? Why couldn't she?—"Drew, it is very romantic." It wasn't about the place, dinner in a gazebo, like she knew Leo had done for Stephanie, but it was the effort he had made to sweep her off her feet and it was working.

He tucked a lock of hair behind her ear and a pleasant shiver slid down her back.

His voice was soft. "I wanted tonight to be very special and something you'll always remember."

"It is and I will."

He took her hand as they ascended the stone steps. Chilling in a wine bucket was a bottle of Chardonnay that bore the Sand Creek Winery label.

It was the attention to detail that astonished her. "How did you know about the wine?"

"I noticed at the picnic you hosted for Anna and Colin

it was the only thing you drank. And also, Tessa had mentioned Max put a case in the pantry for you."

"That was months ago." She couldn't believe he remembered such a minor detail, but she knew the shirt he was wearing tonight was the same one he had worn at the Memorial Day picnic so maybe they both paid attention to the little things.

He gave a one-shoulder shrug and pulled out her chair. "Details are important to me."

She looked around and it was then she noticed chafing dishes on a table at the back of the gazebo. She caught a whiff of something spicy that made her mouth water.

"Did you cook too?"

He chuckled. "Not tonight, but if you'd like, I will cook for you sometime. I can burn a steak on the grill with the best of them."

Somehow, she doubted he'd burn anything but just in case, she said, "So, I should plan on being the grill master?"

He laughed. "Yes, please, or maybe you can teach me. I know today's men should be able to grill but the technique escapes me. Thankfully, I can do this instead." He raised a hand, gesturing around the gazebo. He looked over her shoulder and gave a slight nod. A young woman appeared on Liza's left and she poured and handed them each a glass of wine before stepping back.

He tapped his glass to hers. "To a very special evening."

Her eyes met his over the rim. This was going to be a night to remember.

14

When they had finished dinner and dessert, Drew walked around the table and pulled Liza into his arms. She longed to be kissed under the stars. He gazed into her eyes, leaned in, and kissed her cheek. The brush of his lips sent a shiver racing down her arms. She turned her head, offering her lips to his while his hands slid down her arms to take her hands.

"I've loved every minute tonight." Disappointed he didn't kiss her, she murmured, "It's been an enchanting evening."

"Does this mean you'd go out with me again?"

"Yes." Her voice was soft but it seemed to carry across the silence. She shivered. As she anticipated, the night air held a chill.

"We should go."

"Don't we need to clean up?"

"No, it will be taken care of." The way he spoke was confident that whoever was waiting to dismantle the scene would be there the moment they were gone.

It was funny how they had such different ideas about

money. She liked her bank balance to grow, and he seemed to have no problem spending freely. But she had to remind herself, it was his money to do as he wished and there was no harm enjoying being pampered a bit too.

"Wait." She pulled her cell phone from her clutch. "I want to get a couple of pictures."

"That's a great idea. I can have Celia come back and take them."

His finger trailed down her cheek and she tilted her head to the side. "Sure." Her voice was shaky and she could feel heat rise in her cheeks.

Celia came in and Drew asked if she'd mind taking a few pictures. She took both their cell phones and asked, "Where would you like to pose?"

Liza moved toward the steps. "Can you get the moonlight on the pond and the twinkle lights in the picture?"

With a small laugh, Celia said, "And the two of you?"

With a sheepish grin, she laughed as Drew pulled her close. She molded to his side and his arm relaxed around her, as if they had been posing for pictures for years, and it felt good and something she had thought about occasionally since the first time they met. She never would have dreamed, as a widow with two kids, she would be crushing on a handsome man, posing for pictures under the moonlight.

Celia said, "Smile." She clicked away as she moved from side to side. Then she handed the phones back to Drew. "There should be a couple of keepers."

"Thank you. You did a wonderful job tonight."

"My pleasure." She slipped out of sight.

Drew scrolled to the right with Liza looking over his arm. "There isn't a bad picture in the group. Let's look at the ones on your phone."

They were pretty much identical and something Liza would enjoy looking at tonight after she went to bed. The evening had been magical, better than she had hoped.

"Are you ready to leave?"

"I am." He wrapped his arm around her as they strolled through the park to the car. He opened the door for her and she settled in the passenger seat.

"I'm curious. Are s'mores a favorite with the kids?"

Liza laughed softly. "That's an understatement. We have a special box that holds all of the fixings for s'mores and from spring through fall, it is ready for an evening fire."

By the light on the dashboard she could see the grin on his face. He said, "I've never heard there was a special kit, but I like that idea."

"Mom gave it to them for Christmas a couple of years ago and I swear it's their favorite gift of all time."

She leaned her head back on the seat. "It was nice the town gave you permission to be in the park after dark. The view of the pond from the gazebo was breathtaking and it was wonderful to witness the day come to a gracious close."

"Renting the gazebo was straightforward and I had to sign a document that it would be left in the same condition it was in before our night." He took her hand and gave it a squeeze. "You have a way with words."

She gave a small laugh. "I'm always encouraging my boys to use different words to describe something. At times, I do it without even realizing it."

"Please don't censor yourself around me. Just be yourself; it's charming." His eyes twinkled in the dashboard light.

She could feel the blush wash over her cheeks, glad she could hide under the cover of darkness.

"If you're up for it, we could go for a drive."

She looked at the time on the dashboard and sat up straight in the seat, shocked at the late hour.

He noticed. "What's wrong?"

"Would you mind if I took a rain check? It's getting late, and I have to work tomorrow. I'm preparing for a wedding on Saturday, the day before July Fourth, so it's added some layers of complexity."

"Of course. I should have been more aware of the time. We'll go straight to your place."

"Thank you for understanding. Weddings are exhausting and yesterday I was running from the moment I arrived at the ceremony site. It's like that for every event."

"You seem to love what you do."

"To be part of a couple's special day is wonderful."

Drew pulled into her driveway and doused the headlights. He turned off the car and turned to her. "Liza, I had the best time tonight."

"It was amazing."

He lifted her chin so they were looking at each other. She barely dared to breathe and all but melted when he grazed his lips across hers. That now familiar thrill raced through her. He seemed to wait, silently asking her if she was comfortable with more.

Her hand slipped around the back of his neck. His skin was warm under her touch. She breathed, "Kiss me again." This was what she wanted. It had been a long time since she had wanted to be kissed, and with this new foray into dating, she was going to ask for what she wanted.

Without hesitation, his mouth seared hers. She was

drowning in the thrilling pressure of his lips and the taste of him. The kiss deepened.

The floodlights came on, illuminating the interior of the car. With a low chuckle, he said, "Déjà vu."

She brushed a finger over her tingling lips. "My dad was famous for flicking lights on when me or my sisters came home from a date."

"So now is Leo in charge of lights?"

With a slow shake of her head, she pointed to the house. "See two short shadows in the front window?"

"Are you going to have some explaining to do at this hour?"

She gazed into his eyes. "There will be a conversation, but it will be about respecting their mother's privacy."

"Can I call you tomorrow?"

"I'm working, but I'll be home by six."

He pecked her lips. "Then I'll call after nine." He opened the car door and said, "Wait right there."

She held back a grin as he came around the front of the car. He took her hand and pulled her to his chest. He lightly kissed her lips one last time before taking her hand and they strolled slowly to the steps, making the moment last.

*

*L*iza sailed through her week. She was still riding high from her dinner with Drew and they talked every night since Sunday. On Monday she had sat the boys down for a talk. She smiled at the memory of their questions and what-ifs. After reassuring them that Drew was a nice man and it was okay to ask questions, she reminded them that she was the parent and they needed to trust her judgment. The most important takeaway for her was the boys seemed glad they knew Drew was their uncle's very good friend. That gave him extra credibility.

That was still on her mind as she had checked in with the caterer before heading home. The luncheon was over and so was her day when she noticed the bride alone and off to one side.

She hurried over. "Kathy, is everything alright?"

"It is. I'm just taking a moment to soak it all in." Her arm swept the dance floor. "Look at those happy faces. Everyone's having a great time."

"They're here to celebrate your special day. Where's your new husband?"

"One of his buddies had to borrow him for a minute so I slipped away to take a breath too."

"Want me to keep you company, or would you prefer to be alone?"

Kathy looked at her. "If you don't mind, I'd like to continue to be a wallflower, but I want you to know that today was absolutely perfect, right down to the last detail. I'm so glad you were our event planner."

"I'm thrilled to hear you say that. You and Jag deserve to have a happy, stress-free day and it's my job to do just that."

"There's a couple of recent engagements in our group and I'm going to twist a few arms to make sure they call you first." She laughed. "Not that I'll need to twist hard after today." Kathy threw her arms around Liza. "Thank you again."

"It was my pleasure. Enjoy your honeymoon."

"Thank you. We will."

Liza walked through the grass to the prep tent where she had stashed her tote bag. Her keys were in her jacket pocket and her cell was in her dress; it was all about the pockets on event day. With a final look over her shoulder, she knew that someday she wanted to have someone look at her on their wedding day as Jag looked at Kathy. Marriage wasn't easy and as much as she loved Steve and the life they had built, she was ready to find her future and it started by enjoying what was left of the holiday with her family.

She popped the hatch on her van and stowed her bag before she called Mom.

"Hi, Liza. We were just talking about you."

"Hey. I'm leaving the reception now and I'll swing by to get the boys."

"It's nice you're getting out early, but I have a better idea. Head home, get a shower, and change. Dad and I will pick up pizza and bring the boys to you."

"Wouldn't you rather enjoy a relaxing dinner? I'm sure they kept you on your toes today."

"Actually, we spent the afternoon at Leo's. They swam while I got to talk wedding plans with Steph, and we barbequed with the rest of the family. It broke up early, with all the kids being exhausted from too much fun in the sun."

She had a twinge of regret that she had missed it, but she had to work. "That sounds like fun." She watched a couple stroll arm in arm down the path. "If you're sure you don't mind, a nice cool shower sounds like heaven right now." She glanced at her slim silver watch. "Can you give me about an hour?"

"We'll see you soon."

•   •   •

*O*n the drive home, Liza concluded there was more to the impromptu pizza dinner. She could read between the lines. Mom was dying to know firsthand how her date went, and Liza had been too busy this week to stop in. All Mom wanted was for her kids to be happy, and Liza got it. She'd want the same for her boys if they were in a similar situation.

She adjusted the air conditioner vent in an attempt to get more cool air flowing in her direction, but all she got was hot, heavy air. She smacked the dash, wishing that would be all it took to get the AC working, and pushed the button to have the two front windows go down. The van was approaching twelve years old and well over ten times that in mileage. She might just have to bite the bullet and trade it in before she got stranded. It always started with the little things such as tires, air conditioners, windows not functioning properly, and then the bigger systems, like brakes and the transmission. The list was endless. She'd meant to talk to Kate about her SUV to see what she liked and didn't like about it and made a mental note to do that soon. Whatever she bought would need to last her another ten years.

When she parked in front of the garage, she was surprised how quickly the drive passed. She grabbed her tote bag from the back. A spot of color resting on the front step caught her attention. She was delighted to discover a small basket filled with fixings for s'mores inside. There was a note.

Thought you could share these with the boys some night soon.

In a large scrawl there was a capital *D*. She clutched the

paper to her chest for a fraction of a second. Her silly story was something that stuck with him. Tonight it would be fun to have a fire in the backyard. George loved to help build the fire and Johnny always burned the marshmallows. Maybe Mom and Dad could stay too. It was something they hadn't done since last summer.

She smiled and tucked the note in her bag. Drew Cameron was certainly full of surprises. She scooped up the basket and ran up the stairs to get ready for a fun evening with her parents and children.

15

*L*iza was in the kitchen when she heard the doors on her dad's truck slam.

"Mom!"

Footsteps thumped on the back steps and the door burst open. Johnny and George tumbled inside and grinned. "You're never gonna guess what we did today!"

She had opened her mouth to speak when George continued. "We went fishing and caught a huge fish from the dock near Uncle Jack's boat." He held up his hands as wide as he could. "And then we went swimming at Uncle Leo's."

She held back a laugh. "Are you sure it was that big? Seems it might be a bit of a fish tale."

Mom walked in and a set a large pizza box and a container, which Liza guessed was salad, on the counter. Dad came in behind her and closed the screen door. "Before the story gets too out of hand, they each caught a nice rainbow trout almost a foot long."

Her mouth formed into a large O. "My mistake. That sounds like dinner to me."

Johnny waved his hand in the air, his excitement bubbling over. "We did catch and release today. But Uncle Don was at the big house and everyone's going on the boats tomorrow afternoon and invited us to come with them. Can we go, Mom? Uncle Jack said we could go fishing off the back of the boats too."

"Did you want to go to the fireworks tonight?" She ruffled George's hair.

He looked at his brother and Johnny said, "Nah. Can we go fishing with everybody tomorrow instead?"

"That sounds reasonable. We can." She glanced at Mom. "Don was at your house today to make plans? Is the whole family taking tomorrow off since the winery is closed?"

"From what Don said, Jack was the one who got the ball rolling and Leo jumped in too. I've called Anna and Tessa and so with the three boats, we can anchor in the middle of the lake. It'll be fun."

"I had yardwork and laundry planned." She looked at the boys.

"Please, Mom, can't we miss one day?" Johnny tugged at her hand. "Uncle Don said it's a do-over get-together since you had to work today. We'll help with laundry before we go. I'll fold. And we'll help you in the gardens too, Mom." He frowned. "Even though weeding is the worst job ever."

The way he groaned made Liza laugh out loud. "Stop being so dramatic. How do you think we get fresh veggies on the table if it weren't for the garden?"

"You could be like other moms and just buy them at the store." His face brightened. "Or we could go to Blake's Farm Stand. Aunt Kate gets a bunch of stuff from there for her restaurant. I heard her and Aunt Peyton talking about it before."

She crossed her arms over her midsection and leaned against the counter. "Buying it isn't nearly as rewarding as growing it ourselves and besides, it's more cost-effective this way too."

"You're always trying to save money, just like Mimi." Johnny rolled his eyes. "She won't buy any of the good cereals unless she has a coupon."

Mom said, "Then I taught her well."

Dad said, "Money doesn't grow on trees, boys. It takes hard work, whether it's in the garden or taking care of you boys, and your mom works hard." He pointed to the bathroom door. "Go wash your hands."

Once the boys disappeared from view, Liza said, "Thanks, Dad, for having my back. It's hard to teach these two about money when so many of their friends at school get everything the moment they ask for it."

"You're doing a fine job. Stop worrying."

Mom opened up the cabinet door and withdrew a stack of plates and then, from the drawer, silverware. "Are we eating outside or in?"

"Let's sit outside."

Dad opened the slider door for Mom. He took the pizza box and salad container. Liza carried the plastic cups and a pitcher of lemonade with her. The boys reappeared, shaking water droplets from their hands.

She frowned. "We do have towels you can use."

"We're starving." Johnny wiped his hands on the back of his shorts while George wiped his on the front of his shirt. With a mischievous grin, he said, "And besides, we're saving on laundry."

"You keep up trying to be funny and there will be no

roasting marshmallows tonight."

"Did you get stuff so we can have s'mores?" Johnny asked.

"Actually, when I got home, I discovered a package on the step. Drew dropped off the fixings for us."

George looked around the room. "Cool. Is he coming over too?"

"No, it's just the five of us." She looked at her parents as they came back inside. "It would be nice if you'd stay for the fire."

Mom patted George's shoulder. "We will if the boys promise to toast a marshmallow for me. The last time they did, it was delicious."

"Sure, Mimi." His face lit up. "I can make two if you want."

With a laugh, she said, "One will be plenty."

Liza was lucky to have great kids and parents. She was looking forward to tomorrow with the family, but nights like this were rare. It was good for her and the boys to have some time with her parents. It reminded her after Steve died and they would stop over and lend a hand with an evening meal or help the boys work on a school project. It had taken her a while to get acclimated to being a single parent, but with the unwavering support of her parents, she had learned how to be independent. But she also understood when to ask for help when she needed it.

The boys took two slices of pizza and started eating before they even sat down.

"Boys, slow down and chew your pizza. There is plenty of time to get the fire going."

With his mouth full of meat, cheese, and crust, Johnny muttered, "You won't change your mind?"

"Are you kidding? I'm counting on one of you to make me a s'more too."

With cheeks that looked like a chipmunk, George held up his half-eaten slice. "Dibs."

She ruffled his hair. "Chew."

The next day, sitting in the middle of the lake with her boys and the family turned out to be just what Liza needed to unwind. She reclined on a bench seat with a book in one hand and a bottle of water in the other. Leo's boat was anchored at one end of the trio. Jack's was in the middle with her boys, Owen, and Ben jumping off the swim platform with their uncles. Peyton and Kate were getting the younger trio ready to swim from Don's new pontoon boat. Anna and Tessa were taking a dip, and Mom was taking it all in. Everyone was accounted for except Dad.

She sat up and looked around, pleased to discover him on the front of Jack's boat with a line dangling in the water. If she had to guess, there was no bait on the hook and there might not even be a hook. He liked to create the illusion he was fishing when he was really just being in the moment. Dad's open-heart surgery had done wonders to get him to slow down and savor life. Thankfully he had gotten the message before it had been too late.

He looked over his shoulder as if he could feel he was being watched. He patted the spot next to him. She set her book aside and secured her hat before making her way across adjoining swim platforms.

"Hi, Iz."

She smiled at the childhood nickname. Dad didn't use

it often, usually when it was just the two of them. She sat down and shoulder bumped him.

"Dad? Are the fish biting?"

He flashed her a telling grin. "Been a little slow today. I think when the boys decide to fish, it'll be better."

"Hook optional?"

He held his finger to his lips. "Shh. Don't tell anyone."

"Your secret is safe with me."

They watched the water as they sat quietly. The sun glinted off the surface and the warm, gentle breeze wafted over her skin.

Dad put his fishing pole aside. "You didn't say anything last night, but your date with Drew was good?"

She had a wide smile on her face. "There are no secrets in this family, are there?"

"Did it not go well?" The tone of concern was hard for Dad to hide.

"Sorry, Dad. That was snarky. It was really nice." Should she share all the little details or would Dad find it too much information or, worse, stupid?

As if he read her mind, he patted her hand. "I want to hear everything."

"Are you sure?"

He gazed across the water. "I remember the first time you came home and told me about a boy you liked in your class. His name was Billy." He looked at her. "Do you remember?"

She nodded, surprised he did. "I liked him but he pushed me down on the playground and I cried."

"He did. But you poured your heart out to me. I think it was because your mom wasn't around, but secretly I was glad you told me what happened. I was ticked that someone would bruise your heart and I certainly wasn't happy he pushed you down."

She felt a tug at her heart. They didn't have this kind of heart-to-heart conversation. "I vaguely remember you wanted to call his father."

"Probably. He wasn't the first or the last boy whose parents I wanted to call when it came to my little girl."

"Dad, you never got involved. It was always Mom who would talk to us and soothe the heartaches."

He nodded. "And then at night, after you girls were asleep, Mom would fill me in. You may have thought I was clueless, but I always knew."

He fell silent again. Liza knew this was how he worked. Talk and then wait for her to open up. He was a master at it.

"The date was amazing. He got permission to have dinner at the gazebo in Fountain Park, and it was draped in white lights and the food was delicious. He got my favorite wine and pulled out all the stops." She let out a breath.

"And?"

She twisted her hands in her lap. "Dad, is it too soon for me to date? I worry about the boys. They flicked on the porch light when we pulled in the driveway, then snuck into the front hall and waited in the window."

He chuckled. "Those knuckleheads. Have you talked to them about this new chapter in your life?"

"A couple of times. I told them that I loved their father very much but I would like to be able to go out to dinner and do things with a nice man. At first, I thought they got it but after that stunt, I'm not sure. And you heard how they reacted at first to Drew's s'mores box. The first question was if he was coming over too."

"But it didn't sound like they were opposed to the idea, just curious. Be patient; it might take them some time. The most important thing is for you to have fun, and when you're ready, let the boys hang out with him too."

"That's my plan, and I do like him. Dad, you're one in a million and I love you."

"Iz, you deserve all the happiness in the world and I'm here if you need to talk."

*L*ater that night Liza was reading a novel when her phone rang. She said hello and a slow smile spread over her face. "Drew, it's nice to hear from you."

"I hope it's not too late to call. I know the last few days have been pretty busy for you."

His deep voice caused her cheeks to grow warm and she was glad he couldn't see her face. She sat up in her bed. "No, I was just reading, you know unwinding. What did you do today?"

"I caught up on some paperwork for a board meeting I have coming up and puttered around the house getting a few chores done."

"Don't you have people for that?" She held back a laugh and hoped he didn't take offense to her teasing him.

"You're too funny, but I happen to like to do things around my house."

Now that was something they had in common. "What's your favorite home project?"

"I love to do yardwork, like mow the lawn, and I've been planning how to update the flower beds in front of my house. It might be hard to believe but I like getting my hands dirty."

She leaned back on her pillows and put her book on the nightstand before settling in for an unexpected and hopefully interesting conversation. "I love to garden. Tell me what you have in mind."

"How much time do you have?"

With a smile on her face and in her voice, she said, "All night."

16

The house was quiet and Liza lay in the dark of the night after a long conversation with Drew. If she were being honest, she longed to be held at night. To have someone to whisper good night in her ear as she drifted off to sleep. It was the little things that smoothed out the rough edges after a long day. The last thing she thought before she closed her eyes and gave in to sleep was she wanted to find love again.

"Mom. Mom. Wake up."

Her eyes fluttered and George was mere inches from her face. Instantly alert, she bolted straight up. "What's wrong?"

"I heard Johnny calling to you and it woke me up. Now he's making funny sounds."

She leaped out of bed and raced down the hall. The cool bare wood floors barely registered as she burst through Johnny's bedroom door. The room was filled with the glow of predawn. She eased onto the edge of the bed and placed a hand on his forehead. His skin was cold and clammy and his breathing shallow.

"Johnny, what's going on, buddy?"

"My head hurts really bad and I'm very thirsty." He blinked hard. "Things look fuzzy."

"George, get my cell phone for me." She kept her voice controlled but inside, a shiver of fear raced over her. Johnny was never sick.

George raced from the room and was back in a flash. "Here." He thrust her phone toward her. His voice quivered. "Is he going to be okay?"

"Of course." She held George's hand and dialed Anna.

She did her best to keep her face neutral despite her blood roaring in her ears.

The phone rang three times before Anna answered. "Liza, what's wrong?"

"Can I talk to Colin?"

"Hold on."

"Liza?" Just hearing his deep voice gave her comfort. He'd know what to do.

"It's John. He has a headache, his vision is fuzzy, his palms and skin are cold to the touch, and he's thirsty. I've never seen him like this. Can I give him something to drink? Should I take him to the ER?"

"Have you called his pediatrician?"

She shook her head.

"Liza?"

She blinked tears away; she didn't need to upset the boys any further. "I called you first."

"Can you get him to the car?"

"I don't know if I can carry him." She moved the phone away from her mouth. "Kiddo, can you walk down the stairs?"

He nodded but kept his eyes closed.

"He said he can walk."

The phone line was muffled as if the receiver had been dropped. "Colin, I'll take him to the emergency room."

Anna's voice came on the line. "It's me. Colin said he'll be there in less than ten minutes. Wait for him."

"Okay." She put the phone on the nightstand and rubbed Johnny's hands, trying to take the chill from them.

Without looking at George, she said, "Honey, can you get dressed and wait for Uncle Colin in the kitchen? The door is locked."

He hesitated. "But Mom."

"It's okay. I won't leave your brother." She hoped her voice sounded comforting because she certainly didn't feel that way on the inside.

"Mom, can I have some water?"

"We should wait until your uncle gets here. Does your tummy hurt?"

"No."

So maybe it wasn't appendicitis, and she was pretty sure he'd also have a fever if it was. The minutes dragged. She kept checking the time on her phone. She'd get dressed once Colin arrived.

She checked the phone again. It had been nine minutes, not that she expected Colin to get there in ten, but it gave her something to focus on as Johnny lay in the bed.

The sound of voices drifted her way. She breathed a sigh of relief. Colin had arrived and he'd know what to do.

He rushed through the bedroom door with Anna right behind him. George trailed after them. Colin gave her a reassuring smile as he dropped on his knee next to the bed.

"Hi, Johnny. Mom said you're not feeling so hot."

His eyes fluttered open. "No." His voice was weak.

Liza was quiet as Colin checked Johnny's pulse. He leaned in and hovered over Johnny's face and then turned his ear and listened to the boy's breathing.

"Have you been thirsty a lot?"

"Uh-huh."

"Mom said you're having trouble with blurriness?"

"Uncle Colin, am I dying?"

He patted Johnny's arm. "No, but we do need to get you to the hospital so they can check you. Do you think you can walk down the stairs if I'm right there with you?"

"Can I go pee first?"

Colin flicked back the covers. "Sure." Over his head, he said to Anna, "Can you keep an eye on him while he gets to the bathroom? He might be a little dizzy. I want to talk to Liza."

Her brow arched and Liza knew that look. Anna had questions.

"Let's go down the hall." Colin walked out of the room and, over her shoulder, looked at George.

"Kiddo, wait for us in the kitchen." She walked into the bedroom but stopped and faced Colin.

"What's wrong with him?"

"I suspect he may be diabetic. His breath has a sweet, fruity smell. Combined with the other symptoms, it's an educated guess. At the hospital, they'll run some blood work, primarily a glucose test and if it is, they'll give him medicine to get it under control, but this will be a lifelong change, Liza."

Tears slipped down her face. "Oh, no."

He put his arms around her and hugged her tight. "It'll be okay. Put some clothes on and I'll help John. Do you want Anna to stay here with George?"

With a firm shake of her head, she stepped away from him. "I want him to come with us. Do you think we should test him too?"

"That's a question for his pediatrician, but nothing you have to worry about today." He closed the door behind him as he left the room.

She stepped out of her pajamas and pulled on shorts and a t-shirt and slid her feet into sandals. As an afterthought, she ran a comb through her hair.

Once she got in the kitchen, George was holding the door open for Johnny and Colin. The sun was coming up and it promised to be a beautiful day. Except for the dark cloud hovering over her son.

She grabbed her bag and ran down the steps to her van. Johnny was making his way under his own steam, with Colin and Anna at the ready. The hospital was a short drive and soon she'd have the answers she desperately needed and then, if Colin was right and John had diabetes, it was time to begin life, again, with a new normal. Whatever that meant.

⁂

The emergency room doctor held a tablet and walked around the gurney. Colin was next to the head of the bed and acknowledged the physician. "Liza, this is Dr. Ny. We've worked together before, and this is my sister-in-law and nephew."

"Mrs. Bradford, the tests confirmed our suspicion. All indications are that Johnny is a type one diabetic."

The words hung in the air like an ominous death threat hanging over her precious boy. "How could this have happened? We don't eat a lot of junk food; he's very

137

active. He's always been very healthy; he barely ever gets a cold."

Johnny looked at Colin. Liza could see his eyes wide with fear, not understanding what was being said. "Did I do something wrong?"

Dr. Ny said, "No. You have an organ in your body called the pancreas and although we don't understand why, sometimes it stops working correctly. When it does, your body works very hard to keep your blood sugar levels stable and when it can't, it starts sending us clues, like getting very thirsty and headaches."

"Like today?"

"Exactly. So through education and medicine, you'll learn how to regulate your blood sugar. With your mom's help and the right combination of foods, you should start to feel better soon."

"Does this mean I can't play soccer anymore?" He averted his eyes to the floor.

"Not at all. In fact, exercise is part of the treatment. But you will need to check your blood sugar levels often and make sure your coach knows about your condition. The added bonus is that you'll get to eat an extra snack before you hit the field."

Dr. Ny looked at Liza. "I'll refer you to an endocrinologist for follow-up."

Colin cleared his throat. "Liza, I can help Johnny learn how to test his levels and how you and he can manage the shots."

Johnny went visibly pale. "Shots?" The quiver in his voice was unmistakable. "I don't want to have to get stuck. Can I just swallow a pill instead?"

"Unfortunately, no. With your type of diabetes, shots are the only solution." Dr. Ny's voice was very kind as he spoke with Johnny, and Liza appreciated that he didn't talk to just the adults. Johnny needed to be included in all difficult conversations; he would be living with this for the rest of his life.

Dr. Ny said, "Here's what we're going to do. A nurse will come in and show you how to check your blood sugar. He'll give you a chart to check your numbers against. Once we have that baseline, he's going to give you a shot of insulin."

John vigorously shook his head from side to side. "Nope, not happening."

Liza placed her hand on his leg. "John, please listen to what Dr. Ny is telling you."

He crossed his arms over his chest. His lower lip quivered. He blinked away the tears building in his eyes.

Colin sat down on the edge of the bed. "Buddy, I know this sucks, but you have to learn how to take care of your health. I promise I'll help you every step of the way, just like your mom will. What do you say? Are you ready for the nurse to come in and get things rolling?"

He didn't look up but picked at the white sheet under him. "I guess so."

Somehow, he seemed small lying in the hospital bed and Liza wished this was just a bad dream and they would wake up. She forced a small smile to her face.

"Maybe we can think of this like a science experiment. You know how much you love to see how things work."

"I'm not a test tube, Mom."

"I know but—" She faltered, at a loss how to comfort him.

Dr. Ny looked at Liza. "Why don't we go out in the hallway and talk for a moment."

Colin gave her a reassuring smile. "Go ahead."

She followed the doctor into the hallway. "Is there something more about his condition you didn't want to say in front of him?"

"Not at all. I know this can be a lot to take in. The specialist you'll see is experienced with kids, so it should go smoothly. I would suggest you have Colin help him learn how to inject himself. It might be easier, given that his body will begin to change and it might be less embarrassing for a boy to talk to his uncle."

"I never thought of that." She crossed her arms over her stomach and then dropped them to her sides. "How long before we see an improvement in his levels?"

"He'll feel better after the first dose of insulin and from there, monitoring him throughout the next few days is critical, and don't forget the nights too. I'm going to ask for the first available appointment with the specialist."

"Thank you, Dr. Ny."

"Good luck." He moved down the hall and disappeared into another examination room. Liza's emotions ran the gamut: happy it wasn't worse but heartsick that Johnny had to grow up that much quicker once again. It wasn't fair. Bits of his childhood were being stolen from him.

She rolled her shoulders a few times and forced a relaxed smile to her face before she walked to the waiting room where George waited with Anna.

17

The phone didn't stop ringing over the next few days as word spread throughout the family. Liza was slumped in the kitchen chair while the boys watched television in the other room. She was glad she didn't have to call everyone, but they all needed to know since the boys stayed with various family members when she had to work. She dropped her head in her hands. How could she leave Johnny with anyone? She didn't even know how to manage his condition; how could she explain it to anyone else? It reminded her of when she brought him home from the hospital as a newborn. She felt as helpless today as she did eleven years ago.

"Mom?"

She lifted her head and opened her arms. Johnny sat down on her lap. His long, gangly limbs seemed to be everywhere. They hadn't been like this the last time he had wanted to sit in her lap. She wrapped her arms around him, holding him tight.

"I'm sorry I got diabetes."

"Oh, kiddo, remember what the doctor said? You didn't do anything to make this happen."

His voice broke. "Am I going to die?"

Her heart sank as that almost did her in. "No. We just have to understand what to do to keep your blood sugar stable." She smoothed a hand over his head and kissed his cheek. "What do you say we check your blood sugar? Uncle Colin said we should test before meals and before bed."

"Is he coming back to help me with my shot?"

"He is, and he said to call with your numbers after we test and he'll be over in a few minutes."

He got up from her lap and crossed to the island, where the small black bag rested on the counter. He brought it back to her and sat down in the chair next to her. He laid everything out on the table: a meter, test strip, and the lancet to prick his finger.

"Don't forget to wash your hands first."

Without speaking, he did as she asked.

Her heart constricted. She wished it was her issue and not his. She sat quietly while he seemed to steel himself for the jab.

A floorboard creaked. George crept up to her and she slid her arm around him.

"Johnny, can I watch?"

"Whatever." He picked up the small strip and the monitor. Moving with care, he stuck the testing paper in and watched the screen. "Did I do that right?"

"So far so good."

He inspected his index finger. "It looks purple. Do I have to use the same one?"

"Not at all. Try the middle finger. Just hold the edge of the lancet firmly against your skin and hit the trigger.

Remember, after you feel the prick, squeeze until a little blood appears and hold it to the strip."

"I'm gonna use my thumb." He chewed on his lower lip and held the flat part of the lancet against the skin. He squeezed his eyes shut as he depressed the button. With a little cry, his eyes flared open. "Ouch!"

"Squeeze."

He followed through with the instructions and then stuck his finger in his mouth. Liza looked at the monitor. The reading was one-twenty. She made a note on the tracking app on her phone that Colin had her download and remembered it was within an acceptable range.

"Do you want to call your uncle and see what he says?"

He held out his hand and took her cell.

"George, how would you like to help me make dinner and give your brother some privacy?" She really wanted Johnny to be actively engaged in managing his diabetes and having him call Colin was a good step.

They walked to the counter and she laid out salad fixings.

George began to tear the lettuce while she chopped a cucumber.

"Mom? Am I gonna get it too?"

She stopped what she was doing and placed a comforting hand on his shoulder. "Well, I don't have a crystal ball, but I'm going to make an appointment for you to see the doctor and get you checked out too."

He grew quiet. "I hope not."

She didn't know if she should agree or just let it go for now.

Johnny handed her the cell. "You got a text message."

Setting the phone aside, she said, "What did Uncle Colin say?"

"Are you gonna look at your message? It's not from Colin; it's from Drew."

"I will later but right now, I want to know about you."

He brightened for the first time all day. "He said that was super good for my first few days and I told him we were gonna have dinner soon. He'll be over in a couple of hours to check for my shot."

She breathed a sigh of relief. The cavalry would be over later.

With a twinkle in his eye, he popped a cherry tomato in his mouth. "What's for dinner? I'm starved."

*A*fter the meal and while she dried her hands, Liza thought about Drew. She checked his message. He had texted her a hello with a smiley face. *Hope things are good there.* She replied asking if they could talk later.

The response came back quickly with a *yes*. She was already looking forward to talking with Drew later. It would be nice to just be a person and put all of this on the back burner for a bit. Now it was time to see if she could distract her boys with something besides video games while they waited for Anna and Colin.

*T*he house was quiet like a church as Liza silently crossed the thick carpet of her bedroom. She felt compelled to check on the boys one more time before she settled in for the night. She placed her cell phone on the bedside table and put lotion on her hands. It pinged with an incoming text.

Expecting to see it was from one of her family, she was surprised it was from Drew, and then she remembered she hadn't called him back.

Want to talk?

YES!

She smiled in spite of the long day, and she settled in bed and dialed his number. He answered on the first ring.

"Hello." His deep, rich voice was a balm to her weary soul.

"Hi. Sorry I didn't call you back before. Things went wonky this week and this is the first moment I've had to myself."

"If you want, we can talk tomorrow."

She smiled at his kindness. "No. I could use some easy adult conversation."

"Do you want to talk about it?"

She hesitated, wondering if she should really dump her day onto him. But he had always been sweet and easy to talk to.

"You sound tired. I was hoping we could have lunch tomorrow."

"That sounds nice but another time perhaps. A lot has happened since we talked on Monday night."

"Anything I can help with?"

The concern in his voice was genuine, and she paused. "Tuesday, Johnny woke not feeling well. Colin and Anna rushed over and we ended up taking him to the emergency room, only to discover he has type one diabetes."

"Liza, I am so sorry. How did he take the news?"

His reaction soothed her soul. She got up and crossed to a comfy chair where she had a view of the backyard.

"Like you'd expect. I think we're all a little shell-shocked and I'm over here like a helicopter, constantly checking on him, watching him. I'm sure he's starting to wonder if this will be his new normal, living with a crazy, overprotective mom."

"Give yourself a break; it's only been a few days. Do you have a plan on how to educate him so he understands the signs his body is going to give him?"

"We have an appointment with the specialist on Monday and until then, Colin is going to be coming over twice a day, in the morning and before bed. We're testing four times a day, so if something gets really out of whack, I have someone to call."

"He's the man to have on speed dial for all things medical. He doesn't fluster easily."

She stretched out her legs. "We saw that when Dad was in the hospital. I'm sure that's one of the reasons Anna was attracted to him—well, that and she thought he was the most handsome man she had ever met."

He chuckled. "I hope she didn't tell him that. It'd go straight to his head."

"They make a good couple. He's levelheaded but has a strong sense of fun. I've played golf with them a couple of times and he's funny on and off the course."

"I didn't know you played."

She perked up at the distinct interest in his voice.

"Would you like to play a round as a foursome with them?"

"I would but"—she glanced toward the hallway—"I won't be going anywhere until we get Johnny's condition under control."

"Understood."

Did she hear disappointment in his voice? "For the time being, I want to stick close to home."

"Are the boys in camp?"

"I didn't send them this week, trying to get a handle on things. All I want to do is keep them next to me, wrapped up in a blanket, safe inside the house."

"A Liza cocoon?"

"Something like that." She brushed her hair from her face and let her shoulders slump. "I think I'm going to say good night. It's been a very long day."

"Can we talk tomorrow?"

"Would you mind if it was around this time tomorrow night? I have to work, and then I thought I'd take the kids to Leo's so they could go swimming."

"Of course, and you should think about sending them back to camp. Call the office and coordinate a conversation between the medical staff, you, and Johnny. They're amazing and prepared to deal with all kinds of health concerns. They'll be able to handle checking his sugar levels and be on hand if he needs to have a dose of insulin. I have heard that in the beginning, it's hard to get someone regulated."

"You seem to know an awful lot about diabetes."

"My mom has it."

He said the statement in a matter-of-fact way, like it was no big deal when it was. "I had no idea."

"That's why it was just me. Being pregnant was hard on her body and the doctor told her it was a one and done situation."

"So, you do understand how hard this is." She sat up in the chair.

"Some. Mom was pretty regulated unless she ate off schedule or overindulged in the wrong kinds of food."

"You really think he'll adjust?" For the first time in a few days, she had a glimmer of hope.

"He doesn't have much of a choice, but yeah, I do."

"That makes me feel a little better." She muffled a yawn. "I want to thank you again for Sunday night and the basket of s'mores fixings. It was very thoughtful of you to drop it off."

"It was not that big of a deal. I was at the market and saw a display and thought of you and your boys. It was something I would have liked to have enjoyed with my parents when I was their age."

"Sometime you'll have to join us."

"Does this mean we'll be seeing each other again?"

She wished she could brush her lips against his, just once. Who was she kidding? Once was not going to be enough. She really liked kissing him.

"Liza, are you still there?"

"I'm here. Sorry. I was just thinking about something." She felt her cheeks get warm. "Yes, I want to see you again."

She heard him exhale and she smiled. It was good to know she wasn't the only one interested.

"I'll leave it up to you to make the next move. But until you're ready, can we go old-school and use our phones and talk?"

"I'd be disappointed if we didn't." She traced the outline of her lips with her finger, remembering what it had felt like just a few nights ago. "Thanks for under-standing."

"I get it. You're a mom first and I admire that."

"I appreciate it."

"Sleep well, Liza."

Softly, she said, "Good night, Drew."

18

The following Tuesday morning the boys came thumping down the stairs with their backpacks and upon entering the kitchen immediately asked what was for breakfast.

"Well, good morning to you too." She grinned, happy to see them full of smiles and energy.

"Morning, Mom." Johnny plunked down at the table and drank his milk. "I gotta test, okay?"

He should have tested before he drank any milk, but it shouldn't change the number too much. "Sure. I'm fixing scrambled eggs with cheese, English muffins with almond butter, and there are strawberries too."

George gave his belly an exaggerated rub and smacked his lips. "I'm starving."

"You're a goofball this morning." Liza kept one eye on Johnny while scooping the eggs onto three plates. She inwardly flinched as the lancet popped against his skin.

He looked up. "Eighty."

"Okay. Log it and then come have breakfast." She knew

this was okay since his numbers had been good at bed and she reminded herself this is just another data point.

He jotted down the number on the pad stuck to the refrigerator and added the time and date. He was doing a great job taking control of this aspect and he was much better at giving himself the shots. He slid into his chair and popped a berry in his mouth. While he chewed, he asked, "Why were you laughing last night after we went to bed?"

"We don't talk with our mouths full, and I was on the phone." She thought about the call with Drew and how he made her laugh.

She put ketchup on her eggs and passed George the bottle.

He said, "We hear you talking at night and you laugh a lot more now."

"I'm having fun." This wasn't a conversation she wanted to have but felt she needed to have.

Johnny added berries to the top of the almond butter. "Mom, is Drew your friend?"

There wasn't anything that escaped her sons and she wanted to be open and honest with them to a degree.

George handed his brother the ketchup. "We saw them kissing, so he's her boyfriend." He scrunched up his face when he said the word *kissing*.

She held her face neutral, unsure where this was going. "We're friends. Does that bother you?"

"Nah, me and George talked and if you wanted to ask him to come with us tomorrow night to the food truck festival, you can." He began to shovel eggs into his mouth.

"What made you think to suggest this?"

They both shrugged. "No reason."

Then George said, "We see him sometimes at camp and

he's really nice to us." He scooped up a forkful of eggs covered with a liberal dose of ketchup.

"Well, I'll give it some thought." She sipped her coffee. It would be fun to see him, but would Drew even want to go to the festival with them?

"You could ask him this morning when you drop us off at camp." Johnny didn't lift his eyes from his plate.

"We don't usually see him during drop-off."

They didn't say anything.

"Boys, is there something I should know?" Now her curiosity was piqued.

"Well, ya never know when he's gonna pop up." George drained the last of his milk. "Just one favor, Mom."

"What's that?"

"If he says yes, no kissing. You can hold his hand but nothing smoochy."

She swallowed her laugh. "What makes you say that?"

Johnny groaned. "It's embarrassing. That's all."

"Let me get this straight." She set her fork aside and suppressed a smirk. Her boys thought she needed their encouragement to go out with Drew again. "Are you giving me permission to ask Drew to go on a family date?"

"We were talking to Uncle Leo last weekend—ya know, man to man. He said it's a good thing when your mom laughs and is all smiley."

It felt as if her heart sighed in her chest. All they wanted was for her to be happy.

"He's around camp sometimes and he's okay, so yeah, if you wanna date him, it's okay with us too." George grinned.

"That's a lot of okays." She smiled. "I'll think about it. Finish up and put your plates in the dishwasher. We don't want to be late for camp."

She continued to sit at the table, contemplating what her sons had just said. She was glad the boys felt they could go to Leo when something was on their minds.

Once she pulled the van out of the drive, Johnny asked, "So are you gonna ask Drew if he wants to come with us tomorrow night?"

She glanced in the rearview mirror and George poked his brother in the shoulder. They were up to something.

She got in the drop-off line and as they approached their turn, she was surprised to see Drew on the sidewalk just beyond the crush of kids.

"How did you know?" Those little monkeys had something to do with Drew being there, of that she was sure. Her voice faded as Johnny slid open the back door.

"Come on, Mom. Don't you want to talk to Drew?"

She got out of line and pulled the van into a parking space, curious to see what those boys were up to. He walked in their direction.

"Hey, guys." He looked at Liza and gave her a blood-humming smile.

"Well, good morning."

"Hey, Drew. Mom has something she wants to ask you." Johnny beamed.

This was not how she thought she'd ask Drew to join her and the boys at the festival.

George said, "Mom…" Both kids were looking at her and bobbing their heads in his direction.

She took a breath to steady her nerves. "Would you like to grab a coffee?"

"Mom!" John sputtered. "That's not—"

She looked at him and narrowed her eyes with a slight shake of her head. Coffee first and she'd feel him out about the festival.

"Sounds great, should I meet you somewhere?"

Liza could see out of the corner of her eye the boys looked pleased with themselves. Before she could firm up plans with Drew, George said, "Gotta go, Mom. See ya later."

"Have fun George, and John, remember to…"

Johnny held up his wrist. He wore a brand-new watch with timers. "I know. Check my levels at ten and let the counselor know if I start to feel weird."

She longed to pull him into her arms but resisted the temptation. They had agreed no hugs or kissing in public.

"I'll see you at four." She watched as her young men blended into the group of kids heading through the gates.

Drew touched her arm and pulled her attention away from the boys. "About coffee?"

"We could go to Daisy's on Oak Street. They serve the best coffee in town other than the roasting company and I need a large cup to jump-start my day."

He gave her another heart-melting smile. "I'll meet you there."

She got in the van and gave him a final wave before she pulled out of the parking space. Maybe going to Daisy's wasn't the best idea. Should she have asked him to have lunch instead? She was an adult who had the right to have coffee with a very handsome man and who knows? Maybe she'd ask him to lunch too.

*D*rew watched Liza pull away. So that's why the boys had asked him to be here this morning. They were trying to play matchmaker and he was pleased that, for whatever reason, they had decided it was okay for him to date Liza.

He strode to his SUV. Having a relationship with Liza would mean developing one with her sons. They were good kids, full of energy, smart, and kind. He had observed them in their groups and both Johnny and George would find a way to pull the quieter kids into all activities. They had an innate ability to make everyone around them feel included.

Once he parked next to her minivan at Daisy's, he went inside and found her sitting at a table for two off to the side, away from the path of customers. He smiled at the countergirl and held up two fingers and pointed to the table. With that taken care of, he sat down.

"I didn't expect to be having coffee with a beautiful woman this morning."

He liked how her cheeks flushed pink when he gave her a subtle compliment. He leaned over the table and pecked her cheek.

The countergirl came over and set two mugs on the table and poured coffee. "Can I get you something from the case?"

"I'd love an apple muffin with maple glaze if you have any this morning." Liza smiled at Drew. "They're delicious."

"Make it two, please." He couldn't take his eyes off her. Only talking on the phone this last week had been torture. Yes, he had gotten to know her, but this is what he longed to do—just be with her.

She stirred some cream into her coffee and handed him the pitcher as if she knew how he took his even though this was the first time they'd had coffee together.

"Thank you." He added a generous splash. "So, tell me, how's Johnny doing?"

Her smiled dimmed as her eyes met his. "He's on top

of the testing and still hesitant about doing the shots, but he's doing almost all of them now."

"And George? This has to be hard for him too."

She held the mug to her lips and blew on the hot coffee. "We went to see his pediatrician as a precaution and the doctor was great with him. He explained that because Johnny has diabetes doesn't mean he'll get it. And like always, George does what his brother does, so eating according to the food plan has been easy. Well, so far."

"That does make life a little simpler." He wanted to take her hand to let her know he was here for her and the boys. But he was letting her set the pace of their relationship.

The apple muffins were delivered. Liza cut hers in half. "How did you happen to be waiting for us this morning?"

"Funny you should ask. I ran into the boys yesterday right after lunch. Johnny asked why I was never a greeter in the morning and George said I should try it today."

"Really?"

"I didn't think much of it to be honest until he piped up this morning and said you had a question to ask me. Then I got the feeling we had been set up." One of these days, he'd have to thank the boys.

"Oh yeah, they're playing matchmaker." She smiled. "Would you like to go with us to the Food Truck Festival tomorrow night?"

"Are you kidding? The chance to spend time with you and your boys. I'm definitely in, but what exactly does one do at a food truck festival?"

She laughed out loud. "We eat."

"Is that all?"

"There's music and more food. It's fun; you'll see."

He took her hand and caressed it. "What about Johnny's diabetes? Do you think he's ready for the challenge?"

Her face fell. "I hadn't even thought of that. But I said we could go and I hate to go back on my word."

"I can help steer him to the best choices, if that would help."

Her eyes grew bright. "That's right. I knew you worked with a juvenile diabetes foundation."

"There is that and with my mom's diabetes, I grew up being sensitive to her testing and how she needs to eat to control it."

She leaned back in her seat, her eyes wide. It was as if a heavy weight had been lifted from her shoulders. "Thank you. I would like it if you'd just keep a casual eye on Johnny tomorrow night and if you see him choosing not such great food items, let me know and I'll rein him in."

"You got it." He leaned in close and said, "I can't wait for tomorrow night."

Her eyes twinkled and she laughed softly. "Oh, but be warned, the boys have made one little request."

"What's that?" He wanted to keep that smile on her beautiful face.

"No kissing, but we have permission to hold hands."

He gave her hand a squeeze and laughed, remembering what it was like to be their age when his parents kissed in public; it was mortifying. "What if they're not looking?"

She gave him a flirty wink. "We might sneak in a goodnight kiss if we're careful."

He brought her hand to his lips. "I'm highly motivated to find a way."

$\mathcal{L}$iza descended the stairs after double-checking her hair and makeup. She had taken extra care to dress casually but knew the lilac-colored top complimented her eyes and she even added the hoop earrings the boys gave her for Mother's Day. They looked up when she walked into the family room.

Johnny's face scrunched up. "Hey, Mom, how am I gonna check my diabetes since we're not gonna be home? At camp I go to the nurse's office."

Anxiety was written on his face, but she wasn't about to let on that she was worried.

"Actually, I thought about that. We'll put your test kit in my backpack, and I picked up a small insulated bag that can hold your insulin and a needle. But you'll need to choose your dinner carefully; we don't want to overdue on the carbs if you want to have a scoop of ice cream later."

"Do you think I could test while we're still in the car and not where everyone can see me?"

"That's a really good idea." She gave him her best reassuring smile.

"Will Drew be okay with it?"

She crouched near the edge of the couch. "Why don't you ask him when he gets here?" She was determined to empower Johnny to take control as much as possible. It wasn't her place to tell him about Drew's mother, but she was sure that given the chance, he would share.

A knock on the back door caught George's attention. "I'll get it."

Johnny stood up and she touched his arm. "If you start to feel like you need to come home, just let me know and we'll leave."

"Mom," he groaned. "I'm not a baby and besides, you can't worry about me all the time."

Once again, she saw that he was aware of the seriousness and was able to handle it. "It's hard. I've been doing this for a lot of years. You could say it's an ingrained habit."

He flung his arms around her neck. "I know; it's a mom thing."

She held him tight and swallowed the lump in her throat. "Yeah, buddy. It is." She kissed his cheek and then ruffled his blond hair. "Let's see what George's telling Drew."

When Liza and Johnny entered the kitchen, George was saying, "And we have a fort outside. Wanna see it?"

Drew looked at Liza out of the corner of his eye. Her youngest was talking as fast as his jaws could move. He wasn't this talkative at camp, but maybe it was because there, he let Johnny take the lead during the camp-wide group activities. It had to be easier to let your older brother blaze the trail.

"Hey, Drew."

"Hello, Johnny." He glanced at Liza and the way her eyes lit up said she was happy he joined them. "You look nice." He flashed her a smile. "Purple is your color and nice earrings."

She touched one of the hoops. "Thank you. They were a gift from the boys." Her cheeks flushed a sweet shade of pink and she focused on the kids.

He took the hint and directed his attention back on the boys. "Who's ready to go eat?"

George piped up, "Me."

"Drew?" Johnny looked at his mom, who gave him an encouraging nod. "Would it be alright with you if I tested my blood sugar before we start walking around, like sitting in your car? I won't make a mess or anything."

"Not a problem. I'm not sure if your mom shared with you"—she shook her head—"but my mother has diabetes too and I understand about managing it."

"She does?" His eyes grew a little wider. "I don't know anyone else who has it."

"She's had it her entire life."

"That's a long time."

Drew couldn't help but chuckle. "She's your grand-mother's age."

Liza picked up her bag. "What do you boys say we stop talking about how old people are and get to the festival before all the good food is sold out?"

"Oh, Mom. That'll never happen." Johnny let out a groan. "If they do, we'll just eat when we get home."

"A backup plan, I like it." Drew grinned. "And spoken like a man after my own heart."

George nodded. "We think alike." A look of acceptance flashed across his face.

"Johnny, why don't you get your medicine and a small ice pack from the freezer and put everything in this bag." Liza held out the insulated pouch. "And then put it in my backpack." She looked at Drew. "Would you like me to drive?"

"No. I'll do the honors."

Johnny slipped the zippered case in Liza's bag. "It's a good thing. Poppi says Mom's van is on its last legs."

"George, it is not." She popped her hands on her hips. "The van is just fine and has plenty of life left in it." Her cheeks went crimson.

Maybe she wasn't sure about picking out a new vehicle and being independent, she might not want to ask Leo for advice. Before he could think about how to respond, he said, "If you need to buy a new vehicle, I can get you one at cost at one of my dealerships. Just say the word."

Her mouth went into a thin line. "Thanks, but we're fine."

"Mom, can we get a new car? Something that isn't a van?"

"John Bradford, we will when the time is right!"

Drew regretted ever saying a word, but if she really did need something to drive, he'd find a way to help.

"*A*re we ready to go?" Liza did a quick shoulder roll to release the tension that had flared up and then forced a smile at the boys. She wasn't about to spill that she didn't have time or that she liked to pinch pennies until they squealed.

She checked the lock on the doors as the boys raced to

Drew's luxury SUV. They wouldn't be eating ice cream in his SUV on the way home.

"I'm sorry if I upset you about the van." He grazed her hand with his.

"It's not a big deal. I like my van. It may have a few miles on it, but it's comfortable and I have plenty of room if I need to carry stuff around for work."

"It is practical." He opened her door and without looking at the boys, she got in. To their credit, they didn't make a peep or other noise of disapproval.

She pulled her seat belt across her chest. "Exactly."

He got in the driver's seat and looked over his shoulder. "Everyone buckled in? Next stop, food truck festival."

When they parked, Drew and George got out while Liza stood in the open door next to John and waited for him to do his test. He gave her the reading, which she added to the ever-growing list of numbers, and then put everything back in her bag.

"Now, remember. If you start to feel overly hungry or anything at all, you have to tell me right away."

"I know. It's not like this is the first day being a diabetic."

He was talking like it had been years instead of less than two weeks. She wanted to pull him into a hug, but she knew he'd be less than thrilled with that public display of affection. Instead, she brushed the hair from his forehead.

He glanced around. "Can we go now?"

She nodded and swallowed the lump in her throat. It was a comfort that Drew understood the condition.

With the SUV locked, they set off in the direction of the

growing crowd. The boys were ahead of Liza and Drew as they made their way to the main entrance. People were sitting on blankets, enjoying dinner, and there was a smattering of picnic tables outside the gates.

While they were walking she noticed Drew scanned the area. "Should we have brought a blanket? It doesn't look like we'll get a table."

She looped her arm through the crook of his. "That's part of the fun. Keeping an eagle eye open. When one does, you swoop in and grab it ahead of someone else."

"Sounds like a lot of aggressiveness goes into this event."

With a laugh, she said, "Come on or we'll lose sight of the boys."

At each truck, they stopped to look at the posted menus. George and Johnny wanted something from every truck they'd passed so far, but she reminded Johnny to try and avoid a lot of the options with bread and maybe go for barbeque chicken instead.

Drew leaned into her. "Is this typical for them?"

"To be indecisive? Yes. Their eyes are much bigger than their stomachs. Fair warning. This will take a while. But if you see something you want, order it and it might hurry them along."

"I'll wait for the boys to decide."

Grinning, she said, "I hope you had a big lunch." She slipped her hand in Drew's and gave it a gentle squeeze. She was having a good time despite the lingering concern about her son.

After one full circuit was completed, the boys were still talking about what they should order.

George asked, "Johnny, what do you think about barbeque? They even had corn on the cob at one truck."

He looked at her. "Mom, do you think it's okay if I eat it?"

"I do, and remember if your body reacts to the carbs, we can make sure you have some extra protein when we get home to balance it out." She smoothed his hair back.

He pulled back. "Mom," he hissed, "someone might see us."

"Sorry. I lost my head for a minute." She suppressed a smile.

George shook his head. "I'm with Johnny. No Mom stuff here." He glanced around the crowd and his head bobbed. "We have reputations to protect."

This time, she had to laugh, and Drew turned away from the boys as he struggled to contain his laughter.

"I didn't know you were concerned with your reputation and that you even cared what other people thought."

"I'm going into sixth grade, and Johnny told me it was important to not act like a little kid." He took a step closer and whispered, "You can still hug me at home."

Even though her heart was light, she nodded solemnly. "Good to know." She wanted to ruffle his hair but clasped her hands together and watched their grins emerge again. Since when had they gotten so preteen-ish? But there were physical signs right in front of her. Johnny was shooting up. Within a few months, he'd be taller than she was, and George's round, chubby face was becoming lean and he too was starting to grow. She missed having a little one around.

Drew gave her hand a tug and Johnny was watching them but didn't say a word. Instead, he smiled, probably relieved she had something else to do with her hand.

"Guys, since this is my first time, maybe you could suggest what's good. I'd hate to blow it."

She felt light pressure on her fingers and smiled. "I'm getting hungry too. We should decide. Maybe if we're lucky, we can get a table near the bandstand so we can listen to the music while we eat."

"I'm having barbeque," Johnny said with finality.

George grinned. "Me too."

Drew looked at her. "What do you want?"

"A burrito." She pointed over her shoulder. "Would you mind going with the boys and I'll get my dinner and meet you back here?" She dug in her handbag and handed Drew cash. "For their dinner."

He gently pushed it back to her. "I'll take care of this."

She shook her head and handed it back to him. "I asked you. Therefore, I'm buying dinner."

He relented. "I'll get ice cream later. Agreed?"

She tipped her head and grinned. "We'll talk about it."

His finger grazed her arm as he took the bills from her. Her skin tingled where he had touched her. She didn't dare look to see if the boys were watching them or not. Technically, it wasn't anything more than the touch of a hand. It was a good thing the boys didn't understand the sensations a simple gesture could elicit.

"Come on, Drew." George cut short her train of thought. "The line's getting longer."

Drew followed the boys with a smoldering glance over his shoulder that made her knees knock. It had been a very long time since anyone had looked at her like that, and she liked how it felt.

rew walked Liza and the boys into the house. The festival had been fun and the boys could eat like men. They had to be going through a serious growth spurt. He had been around enough preteens at camp to see Liza had installed good manners while letting them be kids.

"Mom, we should have a fire tonight." George held open the door for her.

"Drew, would you like to join us?"

He looked at Liza. "I'd love to if you aren't ready to send me home."

She began to smile and Johnny said, "Come on!"

The boys dashed into the house, and over his shoulder, John shouted, "We'll get it set up."

"They love showing off their skills. Dad taught them how to build a fire with an upside-down *V* technique and it works like a charm every time."

He cupped her cheek and brushed her lips with his. "They're good kids, Liza. You've done a great job with them."

She looked out the back door. George was adding crumpled paper to the center of the pit and Johnny was carefully setting up the small sticks around it.

"Thanks."

"How long has your husband been gone?" He knew part of the story and maybe he shouldn't be asking, not now when they were having a great evening, but was she ready for a serious relationship? It was something he wanted to have with her.

"Five years."

It was stated simply, without tears, just resignation in her voice.

Liza said, "We need to join the boys, but first let me put Johnny's insulin in the fridge."

"What can I do to help?" His question was loaded with much more than this moment. He wanted to offer her everything to make her life easy and fun.

"If you open the drawer at the end of the island, the s'mores kit's in there."

He slid open the drawer and found a box that had a picture of a marshmallow on it. "Ah-ha, I've found your special s'mores kit, but I didn't expect it to look like a plastic tackle box. I was thinking just a cardboard version."

She flashed him a heartwarming grin. "Everyone should have one, don't you think?"

He placed a hand on his chest in mock horror. "I don't."

"Not to worry. You can borrow ours if you ever find yourself in need of one." She grinned and pointed to the box. "Besides, that holds more than the essential ingredients for a classic summertime treat."

"Such as?" He leaned into her and slid his arm around her waist. He could feel the quickening beat of her heart and the warmth of her breath on his face. He lightly pressed his lips to hers. Before he could deepen the kiss, one of the boys called out, "Mom, we're ready to light it."

She placed her free hand on his chest and eased herself back. He was reluctant to let her go.

"Can we pick this up later?" His voice was husky.

"Maybe." She cocked her head toward the back deck. "Coming, boys."

With a small groan, he stepped back so she could pass him. He took pleasure in knowing she wanted to kiss him as much as he wanted to kiss her.

She paused at the door. "Are you coming with?"

He liked how she dropped the word *me*; it was cute and just a bit flirtatious. "Right behind you."

The fire crackled as the boys burned marshmallows for the construction of s'mores.

"Why don't you guys tell me what you like about camp and what you think could be improved." Drew licked a glob of melted chocolate from his thumb.

The boys looked at Liza and didn't answer him.

"Did I say something wrong?" He looked at her and the boys. "Or should we talk about something else?"

George didn't look at him. "It's fun."

Johnny nodded in agreement, but he wouldn't look at Drew either.

"Well, now you've really made me curious." He looked to Liza for guidance.

"Boys, we always speak the truth when asked a question. If there is something you don't like or have seen, try to explain what you mean, constructively."

"Like when we show you our report card and we got a C. You say what could we change to get a *B*, right?"

"Basically."

Johnny put his stick aside and leaned forward in his seat to poke at the fire. "Ya know how we have a bunch of activities every day?"

"I think you have what, five different things that you do, plus lunch and breaks."

"Well, we just start having fun at something and it's time to change. Like, we never get to finish a soccer game or a canoe race. It's like bam, bam, bam. Move to the next activity."

"Yeah," George chimed in. "I don't have enough time to eat my lunch either."

"Why not?" This concerned him. If other kids felt the same way…

"The bathroom is a long way away from the lunch tables and you know, I have to go, and then I have to wash my hands." He looked at his mom before he finished his explanation. "Mom is physic, and if I didn't before I ate lunch, she'd know."

"Physic?"

She smiled. "He means psychic."

With a knowing smile, he nodded. "Bottom line is you don't have enough time during the day to finish a game or eat lunch and use the restroom." He would have to look at the schedule tomorrow to see what could be changed. Not for this year, but next season. Also, maybe change where they gather for lunch too.

"But the best part is when we get to have the Friday night sleepout," George announced.

Johnny said, "Yup, that's the best. It's too bad it isn't every Friday night."

Liza chimed in, "If it was every Friday, you might not have as much fun since it wouldn't be as special."

The fire shifted and Johnny picked up the poker and moved the wood around. "Maybe."

He started to toss another log on the fire when Liza said, "Hold on there. It's getting late and you need to start getting ready for bed."

"Already? I'm not tired yet."

George was quick to chime in. "Me either." He picked up another log and looked between Drew and his mom. "You guys could sit out here."

Drew held back a laugh. George was acting like he was giving Liza permission to stay by the fire with a boy— well, in this case, a man.

She grinned at her kids and pointed to the house. "Son, I don't think we need your permission to stay up late."

Johnny stood and slipped around the back side of his mom's chair.

"John, call me when you're ready to check your insulin levels."

The screen door banged after them and she got up to fix the fire. "I'm sorry about that. He sees himself as the man of the house since Steve died." With a snort, she said, "I am so looking forward to when he starts dating and I get to turn the tables on him."

Drew extended his hand to her. "Does this mean we are officially dating?"

The firelight danced in the reflection of her eyes. He couldn't tell if the glow was from within her or from the heat of the fire.

"I guess we are, if you like how that sounds."

She took his hand and he scooted their chairs closer together.

"Could we go a step further and say we're going steady?"

"Drew." With a nervous laugh, she said, "Isn't that a bit like high school?"

"Okay then, how about we say we're exclusively dating each other?" He kissed her cheek and looked into her gorgeous hazel eyes and moved his mouth to hers. "I really like you, Liza Bradford, and I want to see where our relationship might lead."

She licked her lips. "Drew." She breathed his name. "I…" She stopped and looked away. Then she got up and stood in front of the crackling flames. "You're the first man I've dated since my husband died. I have no idea how to do"—she waved her hands between them—"any of this. Dating. Dating with kids in tow. My life is crazy and busy, and my big, nosy family is in and out all the time. Are you sure you want to be with a woman with so much baggage?"

In one short step, he was standing in front of her. The fire warmed his leg. "We all carry different kinds of baggage into any relationship. I happen to be very fond of your two carry-ons."

"I'm assuming you mean my sons." She tilted her head to one side and looked into his eyes. It felt as if she was probing his heart and soul.

"Yes. I had fun with them tonight and I look forward to the four of us spending more time together. I get that your boys are number one on your priority list, which means for you and me to have any kind of a relationship, it will include them too."

"Are you sure?"

He could see the cloud of doubt in her eyes. "All I ask is that we have time, just the two of us too. I want to take you dancing, to concerts, and plays. Things that wouldn't be fun for them. But in return, we can go hiking and biking and do things they'd enjoy."

She glanced to the second floor of the house. It was lit up like Christmas. The sounds of running water drifted out the window.

"We can be a lot to handle."

"Are you trying to scare me off? Because it won't work."

"How about we table this conversation. I'd like to ask you to come with us to an engagement party for Steph and Leo. The entire extended family will be there, and after you've been submerged in that as part of me and the boys, you can decide if you want to stick around."

"You make it sound so appealing to attend a party with you and your sons." He pulled her close. "Challenge accepted." He dropped his head and waited for her to kiss him. She tipped her head to the side and claimed his mouth. He loved a woman who knew what she wanted and took it.

21

The next morning Liza called her mom and had to leave a voicemail. "Hey, Mom? It's Liza. I'm going to bring Drew with us on Sunday for the engagement party. I know food isn't an issue, but I didn't want to catch you off guard that I'm bringing a date. Yes, you heard that correctly. It's a date. Call me back."

She set the phone aside and wondered how fast that news would hit the family grapevine. No pun intended, but she did love that phrase since the family was all about grapes. The boys had been nonchalant this morning when she mentioned Drew was going, and she was taking that as a positive sign. Maybe it was because they'd had fun with him last night at the festival.

Less than ten minutes later, her phone was buzzing and she didn't need to check caller ID to know it was Mom.

"Liza, I got your message and I'm thrilled Drew is coming. Would you like us to keep the boys overnight after the party?"

"Mother!" She tried to add an extra zing of shock to the word. "We are not ready for spending the night with each other."

"Why on earth not? That man is handsome as sin. Long legs, toned body, those green eyes, and that little scar give him a distinct sex appeal factor of ten on a scale of ten."

With a laugh, Liza said, "Mom, I can't believe you're encouraging me to have sex."

"Just because I color my gray doesn't mean I don't know what it is to enjoy a healthy sex life."

"Mother. Stop. I do not want to hear about your and Dad's intimate affairs."

"We've had six children. How do you think you all got here? It's not like we found you hanging from a vine, ready to be plucked."

She could hear the smile and laughter in her mom's voice. "Even still, I don't need to think about it."

"Well, if I was young and was dating Drew, I'd want to have at least one sleepover just to see if the chemistry was there."

"Okay. Change of subject." She wasn't about to confess there was more than enough chemistry between them.

"If you insist. But do yourself a favor and get a sexy nightgown, something silky with lace. Just in case."

"Mom, if I'm going to do what you suggest, why on earth would I need a new nightgown?"

"It creates a more interesting evening if he has to work a little bit for it."

Liza was grateful no one was around to see her flaming-red cheeks. Talking about sex with Mom was not something she had on her to-do list today—or ever. She wasn't a prude, but really. "I'll think about it."

"Good. Now does your date know this is his first Price event where he won't be allowed to fade into the background and just be Colin's good friend? There are high expectations for the men us Price women include in our lives."

Now she groaned at Mom's emphasis on *your date*. "That's another reason why I'm calling. When this hits the family announcements, I would like to make sure you tell *everyone* there will be zero questions about what anyone's intentions are. We're enjoying each other's company and having fun."

"Honey, the man has been around our family before and you're making us sound like we're a bunch of busybodies."

Liza swore she heard her mom sniff. She wanted to say *if the cork fit* but instead said, "No. That's not what I'm saying. Our family is close-knit, which he is very well aware of, having attended events as a friend of the family. It is entirely different when someone dates a Price."

"I understand we can be a bit much to take. But if he can't stand the heat, then he should stay home in the air conditioning."

"Mom." The warning tone was light but intended. "Now, what would you like me to bring?" It was time to change the direction of the conversation. Hopefully she'd take the hint and move on.

"Finger-size desserts would be good. Maybe some of those small cheesecakes you make and whoopie pies?"

"Can do. Let me know if you need something else."

"Who's taking the boys on Friday?"

"They're going to Jack's after camp and then for dinner. I'll pick them up on the way home."

"It's too bad they can't spend the night. It would be good for you to have a break."

"Neither Johnny nor I are ready for that yet. He still needs to be able to give himself shots consistently. He's gotten the testing down, but we have a ways to go on the next and final step."

"Why don't you see if they can go to Anna's? You know they are happy to help."

She bristled. "Because we have to be independent, Mom. The only way I can show Johnny is by example. We can't have Colin give him shots for the rest of his life. Each time, I use it as a learning opportunity."

"I do understand. I just wish…"

"There are a lot of things I wish, Mom, but we don't always get what we want, do we?" The moment the words left her lips, she was sorry she had just snapped at her mother. She didn't deserve it.

"I'm sorry, honey. I didn't mean to upset you."

"No, I'm sorry. Johnny's diagnosis has been harder than I imagined. This changed his life permanently. I know he can live a very long and healthy life, but sometimes I just want to scream at the top of my lungs about how life isn't fair. To have another tough blow after losing his father… Well, I don't want him to give up."

"You're kidding, aren't you? He has an excellent role model who never gives up on anything. If there is a road-block and you can't climb over, you either go around or tunnel under. I'm so proud of you, Liza. The boys couldn't ask for a better role model."

"I learned from the best."

Mom was quiet for a few long moments.

Liza dropped her voice. "Are you still there?"

"I am, and thank you. That is one of the nicest things you've ever said to me."

"I love you, Mom. I need to run and double-check my arrangements for Friday."

"What is this event? I forgot."

"It's a christening."

"On a Friday night? That's an odd time."

Liza smiled since that was exactly what she had thought before she learned the baby was a boat. "Don't laugh, but it's a boat christening. The owners bought a new yacht and it's on Lake Erie. I need to be there by late morning to check on the caterers and the band, and then I can head back. The event starts at two."

"Don't you need to be there to oversee everything?"

"Normally I would, but when I spoke with the clients and explained what was going on with John, they understood. As long as I take care of everything up front, they were fine."

"It's time for you to seriously consider hiring an assistant. Having someone you trust that works exclusively for you would be the best and you could do more than one event on any given day."

"I know, but it takes more time than I have right now to advertise and interview."

"What about talking with Peyton? She's excellent at hiring people. You know she takes care of all the special event staff for CLW. And you could talk to Barb Peters, see if she could help out for the event. Remember, she started in the tasting room before taking over marketing and she's excellent with people. Might be worth a shot. And I'm sure Don would be fine with her helping out for the day."

"Good idea but I'm still going to ask Don first. I'll give her a call and see what I can work out."

"If she can't, let me know and I might be able to come up with another name or two. In fact, there is one person who might be perfect; her name is Dawn and she's from my book club."

"Thanks. I appreciate your support." She jotted down a few other names that popped into her brain while talking. She'd also have to talk to the accountant and see what she needed to do to hire someone and maybe for now, someone could work for her on a per diem basis.

"Let me know what Barb says."

"I will."

Liza got up for another cup of coffee and changed her mind and poured a cold glass of water instead. Mom was right; it was time to expand her business, as there were times where she could have easily been in two places at once. She called Barb to see if she'd want to help out on such short notice for Friday.

*After Liza had cleaned up her lunch dishes, a sharp knock on the kitchen door caught her attention. She wasn't expecting anyone.

A tall, slender woman about her age was standing on the back step, looking through the screen door. She wore her dark-red hair with light-purple highlights in a pixie cut. Her eyes were pale blue; her complexion was dusted with light freckles, and she was dressed in a cotton floral skirt, matching blouse, and flat sandals.

"Hello. Can I help you?"

"Hi, I'm Dawn Moritz and your mother said she was going to give you a call and gave me your address and suggested I stop by to see you."

"She did?" Her cell phone rang. "Can you wait just a minute, please?"

"Sure."

"Hey, Mom." She glanced at Dawn, who was still standing on the step. "Did you forget to tell me something perhaps?" Frustration bubbled but Mom was notorious for butting into all her kids' lives.

With a small laugh, Mom said, "I'm guessing Dawn is already there."

"Um, yes."

"Remember I mentioned the woman from my book club and that she's fairly new in town? Just this morning, she said she's been looking for a job. She's starting over after a divorce and moved here from Ohio. Anyway, she has experience in event management from some big hotel chain and I thought she might be a good fit for you to hire, at least for Friday."

Liza turned her back on the door. At least Dawn wasn't some whack job just showing up. "Did you tell her I'd give her a job?"

"Heavens, no. I'm not sure if you checked with Barb yet, but Don mentioned she was going out of town this weekend. I know I'm overstepping a lot, but I thought this was a good solution for both you and Dawn. Give her some local experience and you some support and I can vouch for her; she's a good person but she just needs a break."

"I hadn't heard back yet from Barb. I'll talk to Dawn, but no promises." She turned to smile at her visitor. "And since this is all spur-of-the-moment, could you pick up the boys and bring them home?"

"I would love to. See you later."

Before Liza could respond, her mom had disconnected.

She held the screen door open wide. "Dawn, please come in."

Dawn stepped inside and looked around the spacious kitchen. "Your home is lovely. Have you lived here long?"

"Thank you. Almost fourteen years." She gestured to the table and chairs. "Please have a seat. Can I get you something to drink?"

"Water would be nice, thank you." Dawn pulled out a chair opposite where Liza had been working and settled in.

"I guess I should have waited for Sherry to call you before I rushed over. But when she told me you were looking for part-time help for your event business, well"— she held up her upturned palm toward the ceiling—"it seemed like it was an answer to my prayers."

Liza placed a glass of ice water in front of her and then sat down.

"How so?"

"I'm unemployed and when I left the hotel business, I found the one thing I really missed was the one-on-one contact with people. Making an ordinary day extraordinary for someone else."

"Did Mom tell you I've only been in business a few years and currently I'm looking for someone to work part-time, and it would be per diem. This way, if either of us finds we don't work well together, we can walk away."

"She did, and that's what I love about this. It allows us to work without company manners clouding our judgment."

Liza instantly liked this woman and believed her mom was right. Making a snap decision, she stuck out her hand. "What are you doing tomorrow? Want to go to Buffalo for the day? I have an event Friday, but tomorrow is the walk-through."

Dawn grinned and shook Liza's hand. "What time do we leave?"

"I'll pick you up at eight." She held up her coffee mug. Sometimes her mom was right, and a thought began to form. If this worked out, she'd have more free time to spend with a very handsome man. "Cheers."

22

Sunday dawned and it was going to be a beautiful day for Leo and Steph's engagement party. Liza was behind the wheel with Drew riding shotgun and the boys were in the back. She really hoped her family would behave themselves and go easy on Drew as her official date. Was she making too big a deal out of this whole thing? It wasn't like she had never dated before; hell, she'd been married and had two kids and she wasn't a babe in the woods.

Drew half turned in his seat. "Guys, tell me. Is there anything I should know before we get to your grandparents' house?"

"No. Just make sure you tell Mimi her cooking is the bomb." Johnny grinned.

"How about I just stick with tried-and-true compliments?"

George half shrugged in the rearview mirror. "Suit yourself."

"Hey, Drew, did you know that George and I are giving

Aunt Steph away at her wedding? The only part that stinks is we have to wear bow ties."

He looked at them with a broad smile. "I'll bet you'll do a great job."

"Are you gonna come to the wedding too?" George asked.

He glanced at Liza. "I have to get an invitation first."

Johnny reached out, patted his shoulder, and tried to wink, which Liza found comical. "I'm sure you'll get one, especially after today."

She felt her cheeks go scarlet. "Boys!"

"It's okay, Mom. We like Drew."

She silently laughed, her shoulders shaking the only indication she found this entire conversation somewhat funny. She firmly believed in being open with the kids, to a point of course, and having this type of conversation had never been off-limits.

"Guys, you know what we talk about as a family is private."

"We know," they chirped in unison.

Johnny continued. "Aunt Kate says—" He finally looked at her giving him the mom look in the mirror. "Oh, look at the balloons and streamers Poppi put up." As further explanation, he said, "Poppi won't let Mimi on a ladder. Ever."

"Good to know." Drew flashed her a grin and wiggled his eyebrows. He must be enjoying all these insider tidbits.

Before the van was parked, the boys were out the back door and, as usual, running to the house. Johnny then reversed direction and came back to the van.

"I forgot my bag." He slid open the door and plucked the small black insulated bag from the seat. "I'll give it to

Mimi." This time, he walked at a slower pace, as if he bore a heavier weight on his slim shoulders.

Her grip tightened on the steering wheel. "Please tell me it will get easier for him."

Drew gave her hand a supportive squeeze. "I hope you don't mind, but I called my mom to see what it was like when she was diagnosed. She remembered those early months clear as a bell. It was difficult for her to control it in the beginning, so Johnny has it a little easier than she did. Also, she wanted me to tell you to check into different devices that can be used for both monitoring and giving the insulin when he needs it."

She loosened her hands and looked at him as she exhaled and released some of the tension in her shoulders. "I really appreciate you getting a firsthand perspective. I mentioned the monitor to his doctor, but he prefers Johnny learn how to manage his condition using the basic tools. It will help him be aware of how he feels, since what he does and eats will potentially affect his numbers. Especially as he goes into the teenage years, when hormones will really wreak havoc on them."

"Makes sense. Chin up. Mom said it gets easier."

"Good to know."

He grazed his lips over her knuckles. "When they come for a visit in a few weeks, I'm sure Mom would talk to him about how she handles it, if you'd like. She's very active—not like Johnny, of course. But she golfs, swims, plays tennis, and hikes."

"I'll think about it. Thanks." She was distracted by Peyton waving to them from the front porch. "Our quiet time is over." With a grin, she asked, "Are you sure you're up for this?"

"I like your family. Everyone has been friendly and

welcoming. You need to relax and just go with the flow. I've got this." He wrapped his fingers around the door handle. "You're more nervous about today than I am." He flashed her that heart-melting smile. "It'll be fun."

She got out of the car and popped the hatch on the van. "No drinks today. Just dessert."

"Good call. But your expression was awfully cute when you dropped the jug of tea."

"It took a lot of scrubbing to get the tea out of my brand-new capris."

"I know it was distressing but the look on your face was something I'll never forget; you were so cute." He picked up the two trays. "These look delicious."

"Mini cheesecakes with fruit topping and whoopie pies."

"And the lady bakes. Is there an end to your talents?"

With a throaty laugh, she said, "You've seen just about all my party tricks."

"Oh, I certainly hope you have a few others up your sleeve."

The intensity of his gaze made her heart dance and the blood hum in her veins. It was a good thing Drew didn't know it didn't take much to get her motor running.

"Time will tell." A band of fresh nerves tickled her stomach.

"Relax," he breathed in her ear. "We have all the time in the world for everything." He pecked her cheek and glanced toward the house. In a playful voice, he asked, "Do you think the boys saw that?"

"Maybe, but they didn't mention seeing us after the festival, so I think we're in the clear."

"In that case…" He set the trays down in the back of the van and slipped his arms around her waist. "I've been wanting to do this since the moment I saw you today." He lowered his lips to hers and kissed her breathless.

*I*f anyone in the family noticed Liza's lips were well kissed, no one said a word. Drew was introduced to a few people who worked at Steph's garage. He offered to help her mom whenever he could, carrying coolers or trays. Liza caught his eye from across the yard and smiled. She was glad he didn't feel the need to be glued to her side.

*D*on walked over to where Drew was standing and handed him a beer. "How's it going?"

He accepted the bottle and twisted the top off. "Good. Nice party." He took a pull, surprised at the pleasant taste. He looked at the label. It was from a microbrewery that just opened up. "The Price family knows how to do it up pretty good."

Don drank some of his own beer. "Mom's a pro. Been like this for as long as I can remember."

Drew nodded, not sure where this conversation was going but he noticed Jack was headed their way. So now Liza's two oldest brothers were flanking him.

"I hear you, Liza, and the boys went to the food truck festival. Must have been pretty good; the boys are still talking about it."

"It was fun." He drank some more of his beer. He had never been at a loss for words, but he discovered there was a first time for everything.

Jack was smiling without looking at him. "We've been

told we can't ask you certain questions when it comes to Liza."

"Oh." *Here it comes. The inquisition.*

"Don and I worry about her, especially now that Leo is getting married and we all have families. You understand we're just looking out for our youngest sister."

Drew could appreciate their point of view. "I would never do anything to hurt her."

Don pulled the corner of the label from the dark-brown bottle. "I'm going to sound like a jerk, but it seems like you have a lot of free time. Being that we're both working our family business, we're just not sure how that happens. You don't seem to spend much time at your businesses."

So that is where this line of conversation was going. He hoped he could reassure them he wasn't just a *trust fund, figure head for charity* kind of guy. "Gentlemen, let me reassure you the reason why my time is so flexible is my parents set up two companies with an amazing staff, so they practically run themselves. I've built a great team to run the camps which allows me some flexibility to expand, but my real focus is my charity work. I believe in giving back, not just money but my time too." He thought they knew about his dealerships. But maybe Colin hadn't ever talked about it.

Jack turned so his back was to Liza, who was now looking their way but couldn't see his face. "All legitimate businesses?"

Drew wanted to chuckle, but if he had a sister, he'd probably be a little overprotective too. "Of course. I'm expanding my summer camps and chain of sporting goods stores to add a few on the West Coast and I own a dozen car dealerships." He pointed to the bottle they had in their hands. "I'm also thinking of dipping my toe in the beer business too."

Jack broke out into a grin. "Now we're talking. A good beer is critical to life. Well, of course, along with wine."

Don clapped Drew on the back. "Good. And now I can tell Kate there is nothing to worry about." With a laugh, he moved away and then looked over his shoulder. "And for the record, I never asked what your intentions were." With a grin, he walked in the direction of his wife.

Jack stood next to him as Liza came closer. She cocked her head and her eyes narrowed. "Jack, what were you guys talking about?"

He grinned. "Drew's got his hands full with work." He dropped a kiss on her cheek and whispered in her ear, "For the record, we like him." Louder, he said, "I'm going to get something to eat and then talk to the happy couple." He clapped Drew on the shoulder. "And if you need any help checking out breweries, just let me know. Always happy to put my taste buds to good use."

Drew gave a sharp nod. "I'll keep that in mind."

Jack left them alone and Liza said, "I saw they cornered you. Please tell me they kept their word."

He crossed his heart and smiled. "They did not ask what I was planning for our future."

"Well, that's a switch. They never listen." She glanced at her brothers as they joined their wives, who were chatting with Leo and Steph.

There was no way he was going to tell her they wanted to know if his businesses were legal, and besides, with their line of questions, it felt for the first time like he wasn't a guest but he had the potential to be much more.

"Come on, let's get something to eat." She took his hand and led him toward the patio.

"Your family puts on quite a spread. What are Thanksgiving and Christmas like?"

With a laugh, she said, "Huge in food volume, not people. Each smaller family does something at their own homes, and then we gather here for a big holiday dinner. We all bring different things. Like at Thanksgiving, Peyton does pies; Kate does whatever anyone else doesn't want to; Dad fries turkey in the backyard, which all the kids love to watch, and Anna and Tessa make side dishes. Then, of course, the extended family come too, like Peyton's parents, Max's sister Stella, and now Colin's family. It just continues to grow. I suspect at some point, we'll be holding holiday meals at one of the wineries, both of which can accommodate a lot more people."

"It must be nice to be a part of a close-knit family."

"There are moments when I wish I could stay home and hang out in pj's on Christmas Day. We try to get to Mom's by two, eat around three, and the kids play. My parents always have a few board games or a movie for them while the adults relax."

Sam wandered their way and gave Drew a welcoming smile. "Having a good time?"

"Yes, sir, I am."

"The name is Sam." He pointed to his wife, who smiled and waved from the other side of the deck. "Sherry."

"Got it."

Sam gave Liza a wink. "Liza, you're looking pretty today."

"She certainly is, sir. I mean Sam."

"You two have fun and make sure you get more to eat." He pointed to the platter of cut fruit with a chocolate dip. "Make sure you have some of that. It's Sherry's specialty. I don't know what she puts into it but every time she makes it, I sneak some into a container before the party so I can have leftovers."

Drew slipped his arm around Liza's waist. "Thanks for the tip."

Sam descended the stairs and beckoned his grandchildren to come over and Drew watched him. "He's like the Pied Piper."

"You have no idea."

He kissed her temple. "I really like your family. Their warm welcome made me feel less like a guest and more that I belong."

She tilted her head back and looked up. "Yeah, you kind of fit right in."

23

The following Sunday, Liza invited Drew over. While they were relaxing with the boys on the deck after lunch, Johnny sat up in his chair.

"Can we go geocaching this afternoon?"

She gave him a slight frown. "We invited Drew over."

His smile widened to include Drew. "He can come with us; it'll be fun." Johnny focused his attention back on Liza. "Come on, Mom. Some of the kids at camp were talking about it and there's an app you can put on your phone and we can find treasure."

George wiped up some ketchup on his plate with his finger and licked it off. "Come on, Mom. Summer's almost over and you know once school starts, there's games and practices all the time and there won't be any Sundays to go."

Drew glanced at the boys and then said, "It does sound like fun, and I'll drive."

"See, Mom? Drew's in."

Outnumbered, she easily relented. "Everyone needs to pitch in and clean up the kitchen, and we need to pack supplies." She didn't want to remind anyone about Johnny's specific issue, but this was another first for them, post-diagnosis. They wouldn't be able to quickly jump in the car and run to the hospital if something went sideways. With Drew along, she didn't have to worry so much about every little thing that might go wrong.

The boys jumped up and hastily cleared the table of all dishes.

"I should get into the kitchen before they try to load the dishwasher; I kind of like my plates. I'll need to pack drinks, a few candy bars or fruit, and some crackers and nuts."

Drew touched her arm. "Yes, snacks and drinks make perfect sense and we'll be gone just a couple of hours, good for a first geocache adventure."

Johnny popped in from the kitchen. "When Mom goes hiking, she has to pack like we're going to get lost in the woods for days," and then he disappeared just as fast.

A tingle of fear raced down her spine as she looked at all the items going into her pack. She dropped her voice. "Could this be dangerous with Johnny's diabetes? Maybe we should do something else, like a movie."

"Liza, you can't put him in a bubble. I understand how you must feel. I always worry about Mom, but she didn't stop living. In fact, I think it made her even more aware that she needed to be in tune with her body."

She took a deep breath and exhaled. "No, you're right. The helicopter in me is preparing to take flight."

"I see it a lot with parents at camp." He gave her a bear hug. "I love that you want to protect your son, but also there's wisdom to know when to let go a bit."

She breathed in his musky cologne. It eased her

nagging fear. "How did you get so wise without having kids?"

"Observation of what's worked at Cam's."

"And I'm not really letting go. That's giving me way too much credit." She flashed him a smile. "My gut is screaming to wrap him in cotton."

With a soft chuckle, he murmured, "Thank heavens you're a logical woman."

He had to lean in to kiss her lips when she heard, "That's gross."

With a laugh, she bussed his mouth and gave a side-long glance at George, who was standing in the doorway, holding his backpack in one hand and his sneakers in the other.

Drew let go and gave him a wink before saying, "One of these days when you meet a girl, you won't think so."

"I'm never gonna wanna kiss one."

With a short snort, Liza said, "Put your shoes on. Don't forget a hat and bug spray. We'll go as soon as Johnny comes down."

She called up the stairs to him before stowing the items she had pulled from the cabinet. Huh, still no Johnny. That was odd.

"John, are you coming?"

A muffled response reached her ears. "Be right there."

She went back to the kitchen. Drew was coming through the back door. He held up lightweight shorts and a light-colored t-shirt.

"Okay if I change before we go? Jeans and a polo will be a bit hot for hiking."

"Make yourself at home. You're like a Boy Scout, always prepared." She glanced at her outfit and said, "I'm going to change too. I'll be right down."

She climbed the stairs and looked into Johnny's room. He was putting his testing kit away which she thought was in the kitchen. She paused in the doorway. "Everything okay?"

"Yeah. Just checking my numbers."

"They might not be accurate since your lunch hasn't digested yet."

He blinked hard and looked at her. "Just a data point, as Uncle Colin says."

"Do you have something in your eye?"

"Nope." He didn't seem to be upset so she brushed it off.

"I'll meet you downstairs. I'm going to change."

Within a few minutes, she joined Drew and the boys. They were talking about the treasure they might find.

"Oh, I need the app thingy." She grabbed her phone and started to hit the search function.

Drew held his up. "I got it. Let me see your phone and I'll make sure it gets loaded."

"Thanks, and then we're off. Next stop, the hiking trail near Crescent Lake."

*D*rew adjusted the straps on Liza's backpack and pulled it on and then his faded Baltimore Orioles hat. Liza had a breathable fedora style hat, and the boys also sported ballcaps from their favorite sports teams.

He pulled up the app and waited for it to point them in a direction.

George peered over his arm. "Which way?"

"According to this, we hike about a half mile west and we should find our first treasure."

"How'll we know when we find it?" Johnny asked. Liza handed him her phone so he could check it out too.

"I'm not sure, but hopefully we'll figure it out when we see it."

The boys started down the path first. The hike at this point was more of an easy walk, the path flat and wide. The sun dappled through the leaves and despite the heat and humidity, which were both running high, it was a nice day to be outdoors.

Liza reached for Drew's hand. They strolled as the boys pointed out a frog here or a bird there. They were playing a game of I Spy when Drew called out, "We should be getting close. Keep your eyes peeled."

Johnny scanned in one direction and George looked the opposite way. Drew consulted his phone and said, "We're almost on top of it."

Liza pulled her hand away and walked to where Johnny was looking. "What's that under the brush over there?"

He scrambled down a soft embankment and dropped to one knee. "It's a box." His eyes were bright. "George, come 'ere quick."

George raced over, slightly out of breath. Beads of sweat were on his upper lip. "Let me see." He wiped the back of his hand across his forehead. "I think this is it." He smacked his brother on the back. "Good job!"

"Can we open it?"

Liza laughed. "I think we're supposed to, and then sign the log inside."

George slipped the latch and flipped back the top to reveal the contents. Inside was a smooth polished rock, a bandana, a small brown notebook, and a stubby pencil.

Johnny withdrew the pad and pencil. He gave them to his brother.

"You sign first."

Johnny blinked and gave a very small, almost imperceptible shake of his head. Drew wouldn't have seen it if he hadn't been watching him at the moment. George scrawled his name and then handed it back to Johnny. He stood up and looked unsteady before walking over to Drew. Liza peered over George's shoulder as they examined the contents in the box.

"You feeling okay?" he asked John.

"Yeah, just a little thirsty. Can you grab my extra water bottle from my backpack?" He turned for Drew to unzip it and once it was out, he took a long drink and replaced the cap. "Thanks." He pointed to Drew's cell. "Where to next?"

"Your choice. Looks like we have two in opposite directions. There is one on the easy trail to the right, which heads back to the lake, or we can take the intermediate trail and give ourselves a bit of a challenge."

"I vote for challenge. Mom, George, whaddya think?"

Liza looked at Johnny, who was wiping the sweat from his brow. "Challenge."

Drew slipped his phone back in his shorts pocket. "It's about a mile and a half. We need to stick to the blue trail."

They set off again. The pace was a little slower, with the incline growing and less shade from the midafternoon sun, but the boys seemed to be having fun exploring the trail.

Johnny stopped and took another long drink of his water. "George, you should drink some too."

Liza stopped under a spot of shade and waited while Drew slid the pack from his back.

She said, "We all should take a drink before we keep going."

Drew was looking at his phone. "We should have seen something by now." He looked around. "We've gone past the mark. I'm going to walk back down and see if I can find anything."

George asked, "Can I go too?"

Liza nodded with one eye on Johnny. "Don't wander away from Drew."

"Mom, I'm not a baby."

"You're my baby. Now, stay with Drew, please."

He kicked a stone on the dirt path. "I will."

Drew and George hiked down the trail a short distance and scanned the area but didn't see anything that might be a marker for a geocache. "We should head back and go on to look for the next one."

George shrugged. "Okay."

Just as they turned, a bloodcurdling scream reached Drew. That was Liza. He glanced at George. "Come on."

They took off at a dead run. Rounding the last bend in the trail, he could see Johnny was slumped over and Liza was next to him, rubbing his hand and talking to him, her tone urgent as she tried to get him to respond.

Drew crouched next to her in the dirt. "Let me try."

He touched the boy's cheeks and noticed his skin was cold, clammy, and pale, his breathing uneven. "John, look at me."

His voice was almost inaudible. "My head hurts and everything's blurry."

Keeping his eyes trained on John, he said, "George, get the black bag for me."

"What's wrong with him?" The fear in Liza's voice snaked around his heart. If he had to, he would run back to the car with Johnny as soon as he knew the EMTs were on their way. But he hoped he could change that outcome.

"I think he has low blood sugar." He nodded toward the pack. "Test his blood." He looked into her eyes. "Trust me."

Liza dumped the contents of the pack on the ground and withdrew the testing kit. She held the lancet to his finger. An uncleaned pinprick wouldn't be lethal, would it?

George thrust the alcohol swab at her. "Mom, remember it's the right way to do it."

She kept her voice calm. "Right."

Johnny didn't flinch as she pushed on his finger to get blood on the test strip. Within seconds, she said, "It's sixty, how did it get so low?"

"George, stick the straw in the juice box and grab a few peanut butter crackers." He did as Drew asked and held the box out for Drew to take.

"Sip." John did as he was told.

"Again," Drew urged. "And try to finish it."

He took another drink. George passed the crackers to his mom. Liza held out one to Johnny. "Try to eat some of this."

Drew hated the panic in her eyes. George was preoccupied with his brother and Johnny was sitting with his eyes closed; Drew guessed probably due to the blurry vision.

"Why is it taking so long?" Liza shook her head. "I always thought something like this would happen when we were home, in a controlled environment."

He made sure he presented a calm front. "A hypoglycemic incident with a T1 diabetic and especially in a child can be dangerous."

She pulled Johnny down next to her and he finished the last of the juice. He ate another cracker. Time seemed to have stopped.

Finally, after about ten minutes, Johnny opened his tear-filled eyes. "I'm sorry, Mom."

She pulled him close. "Stop. You didn't do anything wrong."

Drew wanted to wrap the three of them in his arms and protect them. But he waited. There would be time for that later.

24

$\mathcal{I}$n the week that followed Johnny's low blood sugar incident, Liza had several long talks with him regarding the importance of being honest about how he was feeling. And if she had known his reading was low, all they would have done was give him an extra snack to raise his numbers before the hike. She hoped it was a good learning experience and was relieved Drew had been with them. His cool head had been a lifesaver, maybe literally.

"Hey, Mom." The back door banged and George came in, followed by his brother. "Can we have a snack?"

She looked up from her computer and rubbed her eyes before she looked at the wall clock. "Dinner's in an hour. Can you wait?" She specifically looked at Johnny.

"I'm gonna check." He flicked on the water and scrubbed his hands with a generous pump of liquid hand soap. "What are we having tonight?"

"Burgers and corn on the grill, along with a salad. Aunt Anna and Uncle Colin are joining us for dinner. They'll be here in about thirty minutes."

"They haven't been over in forever." Johnny wiped his

hands on his shorts to dry them. He eyed her suspiciously. "Wait, are they coming to check up on me?"

With a laugh, she said, "Not everything in life revolves around you."

George muttered, "Yeah, it does."

That was like a hot poker to her heart. Did he feel slighted? "George, what's going on?"

He looked at the floor and scuffed the toe of his sneaker over the tile. "Nothing."

"Doesn't sound like it. Come here." She turned a chair around and patted the seat. "Let's talk."

Johnny crossed to the kitchen counter and pulled out his kit. It was where he had started doing his testing and when he was finished, he went into the bathroom.

George dropped to the chair and continued to keep his eyes glued to the floor. "Am I in trouble?"

"Not at all, but it sounds like I might be."

He slowly raised his eyes and stared at her chin. "No."

"George, what is the one rule I insist on?"

"I dunno."

She tipped his face up so he was looking at her. His big brown eyes were troubled. "In this family, we talk to each other and always tell the truth, even when it's hard."

His lower lip trembled ever so slightly. "Okay, but ever since John had to go to the hospital, everyone talks to him, makes sure he's doing okay, comes over to check on him, and nobody asks me anything."

"Oh, George." She realized how it would look to him, and he was right. She had been preoccupied with his brother. "Do you feel like you've been forgotten?"

He nodded. "I don't want anything bad to happen to him like on Sunday but…" The rest of the sentence was left unspoken.

She brushed a fat tear from his cheek. He might be ten, but feeling overlooked or left out had hurt.

"I am so sorry. Johnny being diagnosed with diabetes has caught the entire family off guard and like you, we're learning to adjust. But through all of this, you have been a rock for your brother and me. Like on Sunday, when you handed me the wipe for his finger, that was the best thing you could have done. You had a cool head when everything was happening. He's lucky to have you looking out for him." She pulled him to her chest and held him tight. Then she kissed the top of his head. "And I'm lucky you're my son. I love you with my whole heart."

"Don't you mean half a heart?"

Confused, she looked at his face with the smattering of freckles. "No."

"But if you love me with all of your heart, how can you love Johnny too?"

She kissed his head again. "That's the wonderful thing about love. The more you love, the more you have to give."

"You said you love me and John best cuz you know the beat of our hearts."

"You do listen to me." She gave him a smile.

"Yeah, but you can't say that around anyone else. That's just for us."

Sometimes he acted like a ten-year-old going on thirty, but there were still times he was her sweet little boy.

"Why don't you wash up and you can help me husk the corn."

"What's for dessert tonight?"

"That is your aunt's responsibility." She released him and pointed to the bathroom door. "Now go."

He knocked on the door and yelled to Johnny he was

coming in and then turned, giving her a wide smile. "Mom, I love you best cuz I know the beat of your heart too."

He closed the door and she slumped against the back of the chair. A lump filled her throat. He was a good kid.

She shot off a text to Anna. *No talk of John's diabetes tonight. George needs some attention. Explain later.*

She received a text back less than a minute later. *Okay.*

Then another text came in. *Room for one more at the table? Drew stopped in.*

She didn't hesitate and typed *Sure* and hit send.

The boys would be thrilled to know Drew was coming too.

They came out of the bathroom and ran up the stairs. "We'll be right back."

A short while later, she called up the stairwell. "Boys, I need your help, please."

George came thumping down the stairs with Johnny on his heels.

She pointed to the pile of unhusked corn and said, "Drew is coming over too. He was at Aunt Anna's house and they invited him to come along for dinner."

Before she could continue, they both said, "Cool."

Johnny asked, "Think he'll wanna play catch before dinner, and is Uncle Colin bringing his glove?"

"He usually does," she said.

"You can play too, Mom, if you want."

"Thanks." She grinned. Tonight was feeling easy, like it used to before Johnny's diagnosis. Well, with one exception. There would be an extra place at the table. She gave each of the boys a few ears of corn to husk; they might as well help with dinner prep.

After a few minutes, a toot caught the boys' attention and they dashed out the back door. Liza stepped onto the front porch as her sister and brother-in-law got out of their car. Drew parked his Chevelle next to them. He smiled at the boys and then locked eyes with her. His smile caused a pleasant zing to course through her body. She held up her hand in greeting, her feet momentarily frozen as he broke their connection and gave the boys a grin.

As much as she liked being eye-locked, it gave her a bigger thrill to watch him with her kids. He always gave them his undivided attention, and in her mind, that was sexy. She was surprised that thought flitted across her brain.

"Hey." Anna handed her a bottle of wine along with a dome-covered plate. "I made a cheesecake with berries. I thought it was a better choice than chocolate."

She tucked the bottle under her arm and took the plate and bowl of berries. "I'll put these in the fridge." She lingered and watched Drew with her sons.

Anna followed her gaze, her hand resting on her slightly protruding baby bump. "He's really good with them."

Liza sighed and eased open the door with her foot. Anna followed her inside.

"That's the problem," Liza said. "I don't want a hookup. I really like him, and the boys are getting attached. Maybe I should cool things down." She stashed the cheesecake and wine in the fridge.

"Why? It's obvious you guys like each other and the boys like him too." Anna sat down at the table. "I know you've kissed, but when are you going to take it to the next level?" She held up a hand before Liza could protest. "Wait. I get it. First guy after Steve and then John's issue, but now shouldn't it be time for you?"

Liza glanced at the door to make sure they were still alone. "Are you talking about sleeping with him?"

With a smirk, Anna said, "You can sleep if you want."

With a wave down the length of her body, Liza said, "This isn't exactly twenty anymore. I've got stretch marks, and things aren't as perky as they once were."

Anna waved that comment off. "First, you're beautiful. Second, he knows you've got kids and you're both roughly the same age, so that excuse doesn't cut it."

"It's not an excuse. The last time a man saw me naked for the first time, I was almost fifteen years younger."

Anna snorted. "Okay, I know Steve was not the first guy you had sex with, but even if he was, what difference would it make?" She pointed out toward the guys who were playing ball. "He's interested in you. I can tell."

"I do like him." Liza glanced over her shoulder. Just thinking about being with him in a very intimate way caused her heartbeat to quicken.

"Then make a move. At least toss him the ball so he can get in the game."

"Har har." She pushed open the kitchen door. "Let's see if the men would like us to play."

Anna grabbed Liza's arm and spun her around with a laugh. "My dear baby sister, that tall handsome hunk playing catch with your sons definitely wants to play ball with you, and maybe even hit a home run."

She pushed the fridge door to make sure it was shut. "You know, ever since you got married, you've been incorrigible."

Anna twirled around, laughing. "But you love me." They went back outside.

George caught the ball and gave them a sharp look. "Are you arguing?"

"No." Liza couldn't imagine why he would think she was upset.

"Your face looks bright pink, like it does sometimes when you get mad."

"Oh, your aunt and I were laughing at something funny."

Drew cocked a brow and gave her a questioning look.

Maybe Anna was right. After all, she had made the first move by asking him out for a drink. Maybe he was waiting for her to make the first move with their physical relationship.

Without considering if it was a good idea or not, she walked over to him, stood on her tiptoes, and lightly kissed his mouth. "I'm glad you came over tonight."

If he was surprised, he didn't miss a beat. "Thanks for the invite. Now, if you'll excuse me, you have interrupted a very important game of catch between the old dudes against the young dudes." He winked for her eyes only and kissed her cheek.

She felt a grin spread over her face and was pleased the boys were waiting patiently to get back to the fun at hand.

"I'll start the burgers then." Liza took a step back. At least, from her point of view, there was definitely a smoldering flame between her and Drew. All she needed to do was fan the embers and see if something between them would ignite. "Dinner's in about twenty minutes."

Anna caught up to her as she strolled toward the house. Liza's heart was beating fast just from the way he had looked at her.

"I guess that answered the burning question."

Liza gave her a smile. "If smoke leads to fire?"

"He's smoking and you have definitely lit his fire."

Liza's pulse hammered and she felt flushed. George was right about her pink cheeks. "I hope I don't become a wet blanket."

Anna laughed out loud. "Not likely."

"For the record, I am not giving you all the details. What happens between me and Drew is private."

"You won't need to say a word." Anna gave her a one-armed hug. "It'll be written all over your face. So make plans and we'll take the boys overnight."

"I'll talk to Drew." Liza flashed her a grin. "And I'd better practice my poker face."

25

The upstairs bedrooms were dark and all was quiet except for the crackling fire. Liza and Drew were sitting on the swing, sheltered from the cool evening breeze by the house. Hands clasped, they were thigh to thigh. He slid his arm around her and she looked up. His lips tempted her.

"I'm glad you came over tonight."

He pulled her closer. "I'm glad you weren't upset Anna called and twisted your arm."

"All she did was mention it and I was thrilled to say yes." She stared into the fire. "The boys were excited to see you tonight."

With a quiet laugh, he said, "I think they actually like me."

"You give them attention. It's not just about me and you understand the boys and I are a package deal."

"I'd like them even if they weren't your kids." His lips brushed her temple.

"Thanks." She pulled away from the warmth of his

body and turned slightly to look at him. "Can we talk about our relationship?"

His eyes widened briefly. "What should we talk about?"

She took a deep, calming breath. "I know we have been taking things slow in our physical relationship, and you've been patient."

He lightly touched her cheek. "We have all the time in the world. There's no need to rush into something we might not be ready for. Sex isn't casual for me; it's not just an itch to scratch. When we take that step, we will be making love."

That was sweet, but a niggle of doubt reared its head. "I'm not fishing for a compliment, but do you find me attractive?"

He pulled his arm from the back of the swing and turned so he was looking squarely into her eyes. "You are the most gorgeous woman I know, and not just on the outside. Your heart is just as beautiful." He leaned in and kissed her lips. Lingering there, he said, "You're sexy as hell."

She sucked in a shaky breath. "My knees turn to jelly every time you look at me like you are now."

"I'll remember that too." He kissed her again. This time, his lips traveled to the curve of her neck, taking her breath away. Her body tingled in all the interesting places.

"You're in control of how fast or slow we take this."

Did he mean this exact moment? She didn't want to question anything. Right now, she was where she wanted to be. She slid her arms around his back and neck, pulling him close. He responded with an intensity she hadn't felt before. Kissing Drew like this ignited long-smoldering embers.

He ran his hands over the thin layer of cotton sweater covering her arms. He slipped his hands down her back and under her top, and his fingertips teased her heated skin. Inwardly, she groaned.

He moved slowly. When she moved to mirror his actions, he helped her by pulling his shirt from his jeans. His skin warmed under her touch. She longed to see what he looked like without his shirt, to kiss his toned body.

A light appeared in the upstairs hall window. She froze. Someone was up.

Drew pulled his hand from her shirt and smoothed it back into place. She stood up and took a step back from the swing, waiting to see if one of the boys called to her. She felt like a teenager getting caught making out with her date.

After several long minutes, the window went dark again. She let her breath out. Then the humor of the situation took over. She sat down next to Drew, her shoulders shaking as she laughed softly. "That was, um, unexpected."

He cupped her face. "The next time, I hope we don't have to stop. I want to kiss you, touch you, and spend time with you, alone. Any chance we could manage date night?"

Her heart skipped in her chest. "Yes."

"Good. Now, I was thinking, would you like to bring the boys out to my house tomorrow for dinner? They can swim and we'll barbeque."

"That would be nice. What can I bring?"

"Nothing, except you and the boys. Come over around three? Give us time to swim, and then we can have a beverage while dinner cooks and they can continue to use the pool. In a couple of weeks, I'll close it for the season."

"That sounds nice."

He pulled her up from the swing and took her in his arms. "Walk me to the car?"

She glanced at the last few glowing coals, making sure they were safe to leave. She took his hand. "If you change your mind and want me to pick up anything for dinner, just call."

They crossed the deck.

"I won't. But thank you."

When they reached his car, Drew pulled her into his arms for a long, scorching goodnight kiss, one that left her wanting more.

"Until tomorrow," she said.

"I'm looking forward to it."

He waited until she was at the door before he pulled out of the driveway. She hugged her arms around her body and shivered with anticipation. Tomorrow she'd ask Anna if she'd keep the boys overnight, and soon. She was definitely ready to turn up the heat, and it had nothing to do with the change of season.

George had the van door open as soon as she put it in park in front of Drew's house the next day. He gave a low whistle.

Her head snapped around and asked, "Where on earth did you learn how to do that?"

"Uncle Leo, and he explained what kind of whistle to use when."

She shook her head. "I don't even want to know what that means."

George said, "Drew's house is huge. Does he live here by himself?"

She had to admit the house was impressive, sitting on the knoll in front of them. The blacktop driveway was long, with gentle sweeping curves flanked by perfectly manicured grass. The front of the house had large windows, and flower beds with a riot of colors beckoned to her. She'd love to dig in those, but they were a little too formal and didn't really suit the sprawling country façade. A more casual garden would suit his home. A thick tree line spread from either side of the house, blocking the view to the backyard.

The boys grabbed their backpacks, which held swim trunks and towels. George picked up her bag too. It was funny that they were hanging back, waiting for her. The front door opened and Drew stepped out, flashing a welcoming grin. "Right on time."

"Hey, Drew," Johnny and George said as he came down to meet them and they high-fived him.

"Hey, guys. Do you want to go in the pool or should we go for a spin on the boat first and you can swim later?" He took Liza's bag from George. He kissed her lightly as he slipped his arm around her waist. "Hey, beautiful."

"Hi. Boat?"

"Yeah, it's at the dock." As they got closer to the house, he pointed through the open front door. She could see right through to the backyard.

She stammered, "There's a lake out there."

"Why, yes, there is." He tipped his head and grinned. "You didn't realize that?"

"I mean, I knew there was a lake out here, but I guess I just didn't realize you were lakefront."

"It was my parents' house. When they moved out west, I took it over, gutted it, and put my own mark on it."

She glanced at the flowers. That might explain why they really didn't match.

As if reading her mind, he said, "I think I mentioned I like gardening. I haven't gotten to the front yet. The flowers are left over from Mom's green thumb. The landscaping will be completed next year."

"It's nice." The home was huge but had a cottage flair as if trying to look understated and she liked it.

He laughed. "I guess you don't care for the design." He kissed the top of her head. "You can tell me all about what you would suggest when we get on the water."

He pointed to the stairs. "Guys, there's a bedroom upstairs to the right and a bathroom you can use to change. Make sure you bring a sweatshirt; it's cool on the water today."

They took the stairs at a slower-than-normal pace, but they still hurried.

"Be careful not to make a mess," she called after them, planning to check out the room before they went home.

"They're fine; there's not a thing they can hurt." He set her bag on a chair and said, "Let me give you the nickel tour."

He took her hand as they walked into a spacious living room. A large fieldstone fireplace dominated the far wall. The room flowed into the casual dining space that overlooked the deck and an in-ground pool, and the lake beyond was a showstopper.

"Drew, I've never seen a view like this before. It's incredible."

"This view is the reason I wanted the house. It's impossible to replicate."

She would never get tired of looking at it if she lived here.

"This way is the kitchen."

She gasped. It rivaled the kitchen at Kate and Don's place. The stove was a six-burner with double ovens. There was an additional double wall oven too. The island's prep sink caught her eye, as did a couple of stools at the far end, marking it as a spot for casual eating. There was a large, curved window over the sink with the same lake view and enough light-maple cabinets to hold her kitchen cabinets two times over. From there, the room flowed to a casual seating area, and the exterior wall was four sets of glass doors leading to the immense deck. This house was something from the pages of a magazine.

"You have your own boat dock on your property. Don't let Don see this or he'll want to be your neighbor."

With a twinkle in his eye, he said, "There's a house for sale just down the road with lake frontage."

She gave him a stern look. "Seriously, don't tell him. Kate will kill us both."

His laugh was low and sexy. "Might give you more reason to come to this side of the lake." He kissed her cheek. "Want to see the rest of the house?"

She nodded.

He pointed down a hallway. "There is a full bath at the end of the hall, and that leads to the garage with access to the in-law apartment. It's for my parents when they come for a visit. This is so they can stay with me but still have privacy."

He steered her back to the front of the house. "On this other side, I have my office and a library."

The boys were coming down the stairs. George said,

"Mom, you should see the room we put our stuff in. It's huge."

She glanced at the stairs. "Guys, did you go into Drew's room?"

Johnny shook his head. "We used the one on the right."

"No," Drew said, "The master is to the left of the stairs. It's over the living and dining rooms."

With all these spacious but empty rooms, did he ever get lonely? Her house wasn't as large or grand, but she knew when the boys weren't home, it felt empty, devoid of life.

He rubbed his hands together and looked at the boys. "Who's ready to take the boat out?"

Liza was pretty sure his nonchalance masked the underlying truth; money didn't buy happiness.

26

Monday morning, Liza rapped on Anna's office door before she poked her head in. "Anybody home?" she called out as she eased it open.

"Come on in." Anna looked up from her computer. "Hey, sis. This is a surprise. Everything okay?"

"Why is it when I stop at the winery, that is always the first question I get asked?"

Anna shrugged. "Maybe because since you started working from home, you only come to the winery for board meetings, if you have an event coming up, or you have something on your mind. Since our next meeting is five weeks away and you don't have an event here at the winery for a couple of weeks, that leaves one option."

"Moving my office made things more convenient and I like my house." Liza pulled the empty chair across the lab closer to the desk. "But am I that predictable?"

"Nope. I have been around you a few years." Anna tented her fingers and leaned forward. "Has a certain handsome man got you tied up in knots?"

"Maybe?" Liza twisted her hair into a knot at the nape of her neck.

"I heard through the grapevine you and the boys had dinner at his place last night, did the boat thing, and, by the look on your face, I'm guessing it went well."

"How did you hear?"

"Drew told Colin you were coming over and filled him in on his plans."

She nodded. "It was a lot of fun and the boys like him a lot."

Anna gave her a quizzical look. "That's good, right?"

"Yeah, I'm happy they all seem to like each other, and it makes it easy for us to hang out."

Anna pushed back in her chair and perched on the corner of her desk. "You've got something on your mind. Spill it."

She didn't want to sound paranoid, but Anna would understand where she was coming from. "If he's such a great guy, why hasn't he been snatched up before now? I mean, he's nice, handsome, successful, and overall just a good guy. I don't get it. He has to have a fatal flaw lurking somewhere."

"When you started to show an interest in him, I asked Colin the same thing. You know they've been friends since college. Drew is an old-fashioned kind of a guy. He wanted to meet someone who was real, like you, not someone who pretends to like him because he's uber rich. And since you aren't shallow and can financially take care of yourself, his money is irrelevant."

"You can't get more real than my life. Working mother of two energetic boys, a mortgage, the falling apart mommy van that I don't have time or bandwidth to replace, not to mention I'm always running in multiple directions at the same time with a to-do list a mile long."

"Like I said, you're authentic." Anna got up. "Let's go for a walk. I need to check some vines anyway and the baby could use the exercise." She glanced at Liza's sandals. "Do you have sneakers in the car?"

"Always." The sisters walked down the brightly lit hallway, past a couple of empty offices.

"Where is everyone today?"

"I'm not sure. Peyton should be in the tasting room and Kate's in the kitchen, if you want to swing through on our way out."

"That's okay. I'll say hello before I leave."

They ducked out the back entrance and stopped by Liza's van. She changed into bright-orange sneakers and looked down. "They work with my outfit, don't you think?"

"Hot-pink skirt and sweater set? Not likely, but who cares? You're not walking a runway, just through a vineyard."

Jack waved to them from a distance as he drove in the direction of a warehouse.

"The crush is coming up. Are you ready?" Liza asked.

Anna gave her a grin. "That's why we're checking the grapes. Don needs an estimate on when we'll start the harvest so he can hire temporary workers. You and Peyton are working on the crush party and she's roped Stella in for the weekend too. We all think it's time Stella gets out of her office and meets more people. Ever since she moved here, all she's done is work or hang with us."

"Do you think she's still worried her cancer might return? Maybe holding back on making friends is a mode of self-protection?"

"Maybe, but we need to expand her horizons. She is an amazing person and she needs to live."

"Something I can relate to. Not the life-threatening illness, but getting stuck in a rut."

"Exactly." Anna rubbed her growing tummy. "But back to business. We'll start to harvest in about a month but if the temperatures fall faster than we expect, and the weather forecast says they might, we might have to ramp up sooner. This year's looking to be a bumper crop, and I don't want to lose any of it; I have big plans!"

Liza looked at Anna. "You really do love this place."

"After living in France and working for Henri, I've come to appreciate what we have here. Dad giving me wings to fly only made my roots run even deeper in this valley."

"He's a pretty smart man."

Anna turned down one never-ending row of grapevines. "It wasn't easy growing up as his kid; he was hard on all of us. At times, I wondered why he and Mom didn't stop at two. They had kids to take over the business if that's what they wanted."

"I always thought Mom and Dad wanted to make sure they were surrounded by family. Growing up as only kids, they must have had a quiet childhood. Having a bunch made sure their house was filled with laughter and craziness at all times." She thought of Drew and how his childhood must have been lonely too.

Anna stopped walking. "I never thought of it that way." She looked off at the rolling hills of row after row of grapevines. "Maybe that's why it was important to Dad that we are involved in the business."

Liza thought of her boys and how they loved being at CLW. Did they have juice in their veins too? "I know my boys love listening to his stories about different harvests. I'm going to guess at least one of them will become involved."

Anna began to walk again and she fell in step with her. Blunt as always, Anna said, "Have you decided if you're going to take your relationship to the next step?"

Liza gave her a sidelong look. "Well, that kind of depends on you."

Anna gave her a sharp look and laughed. "You've had kids. I don't need to explain to you how things work."

Liza felt the blush creep up her neck to her face. "I've got that part covered, thank you very much." With a light heart, she gave Anna a playful poke. "I do need a favor."

"The answer is yes."

"I haven't asked yet."

"You need me and Colin to keep the boys overnight so you can get lucky."

She groaned. "Stop." But that was the truth. "Will you take them?"

"Colin's on days right now so just tell me the night and we've got you covered."

"I have an event Saturday afternoon. If you could take the boys during the day and then they could sleep over, that would be perfect."

"Are you going to your place or his?"

"You know, I hadn't thought of that." She couldn't very well invite herself to his house for the night.

"Go to his place, just in case the boys need something and we have to run by your house. I wouldn't want to interrupt anything."

Now she could feel heat flood her cheeks as her sister dragged out the word *anything*. "That's not something I would want to explain to the boys."

"Give your man a call and see if he's free."

"Right now?" Those darn butterflies in her stomach were whipped into a frenzy.

"Yeah." Anna pulled Liza's phone from her skirt pocket for her. "Call him." She wandered down the row to give Liza some privacy.

Ready to leave a message for Drew to call her back, she was caught off guard when he answered. "Well, this is a nice surprise," he said when she said hello. His voice soothed the bouncing butterflies.

"Do you have plans Saturday night?"

"What did you have in mind?"

She could hear the interest in his voice. "I have an event in the afternoon, but I was thinking a late dinner if you're free."

"Do you want me to come to your house and we can go out someplace and then pick the boys up after?"

"They're going to stay with Anna and Colin for the night." She pressed a hand over her midsection in the hopes of settling renewed quaking.

"Well, now. That sounds like fun for everyone, especially us. Why don't you plan on coming to my place? I'll have a cold supper ready and if you want, I can whip up breakfast in the morning. But no pressure at all."

A slow smile spread across her face. He was definitely interested. "I'll be there between five and six."

"I'll be waiting."

She threw her head back and screamed. "I have a hot date for Saturday night!"

*D*rew opened the door before Liza could knock. She had been waiting for Saturday since they made plans. His smile warmed his eyes and he pulled her close to his chest and gave her a searing kiss, kicking the door closed with his foot. He took her bag and dropped it to the floor as he cupped her cheeks with his hands and looked deep into her eyes. "Hi."

Her breathing was rapid and her knees weak. "Hi, yourself."

"How was your event today?"

She placed her hand on his chest. "Good."

He kissed her again. "I'm glad you're here. It's been a long week, waiting for tonight."

That was music to her ears, but now she hoped he wouldn't be disappointed the moment he saw her wearing nothing but a nervous smile. She was proud her body carried the badges of honor of bringing life into the world, but his was perfect—well, from what she had seen so far.

"I've been thinking about kissing you all day."

His admission was sweet and, based on the intensity in his kiss, honest.

"Come in," he said, "We'll have supper and you can unwind after a busy day. I'd like to hear about your event if you want to tell me."

She took his outstretched hand and they walked down the center hallway. When they crossed the threshold of the kitchen, she stopped in her tracks.

Vases of flowers were scattered throughout the expanse of three adjoining rooms. The dining table was set for two. Fat pale-yellow candles burned brightly in the center of the table. More candles were on the kitchen island and in the family room. Soft music came through hidden speakers.

"I planned for us to eat outside, but it's gotten cool. I set everything up in here. I hope that's okay."

"Drew, this is utterly romantic."

He took her hand and molded his body to hers as they swayed to the strains of a popular love song. She felt as if she were in an alternate universe where she was a woman being romanced, not an exhausted event planner.

When the song ended, he gestured to the table. "Wine?"

"Yes, please." She was bowled over by him.

He led her to the table and held out a chair. "I picked up some Fuse from Tessa today. She said to tell you hello." A smile tipped his lips.

"You do know there is nothing secret in my family. If one sibling knows, the rest will know unless you swear them to secrecy."

"I have nothing to hide." He kissed the nape of her exposed neck. "I love it when you wear your hair up."

Unsure how to respond, she smiled. "Is there anything I can do to help you?"

"You've been taking care of people all day. It's time someone waited on you."

"If you keep saying things like that, well, I'm not sure what I will do." This was unfamiliar territory for her, but she liked it.

He poured the deep-red wine into the cut crystal glasses on the table and set the bottle on the polished walnut table. He picked up a small plate from the counter and set it between them.

She was happy they weren't rushing right off to his

bedroom. But she hadn't expected all of this, the slow romantic seduction.

"Tell me about the event. It went well?"

She found herself telling him little anecdotal stories. It had been a twenty-fifth wedding anniversary and the couple had been thrilled with how smoothly everything went.

While she was unwinding, they had dinner and now they were lingering over strawberries and cream with chocolate biscuits. It reminded her of something Kate would have made.

She had completely relaxed and she placed a loving hand on his arm. "You're a very smart man."

He leaned forward and gave her a crooked smile. "Why?"

"You've put me completely at ease."

"I'm glad."

His fingers trailed down her arm, eliciting shivers that raced directly to her heart, which sped up. Now what were they going to do?

"Should we sit by the fire outside, or would you rather sit on the sofa in front of the fireplace?"

"Outside, but I'd like to change first."

"I'll show you to my bedroom." His eyes glowed with desire. "And after you change, we'll enjoy the fire."

$\mathcal{L}$iza's steps were silent on the thick plush carpet as she ascended the curved staircase and they turned left at the top. Drew pushed open the double doors and her breath caught. Now, this room was straight out of a magazine. It spanned the entire width of the house. A small sitting area overlooked the front yard; a king-sized bed dominated the middle, and two over-stuffed chairs were placed to enjoy the view of the lake with French doors leading to an upper deck.

"The bathroom is to the right." He kissed her lightly on her lips. "I'll wait for you downstairs."

If she wanted to heat things up, now was the time to do it. She exhaled her nerves and as he reached the door, she said, "Drew?" She held her hand out to him. "Wait."

"I'm going down to start the fire."

The smoldering heat in his eyes warmed her blood. "I'm warm enough already."

In a few long strides, he was in front of her. She took the final step into his arms and, in one smooth motion, she pulled his shirt over his head and tossed it aside. "You're not going to need that."

He pulled the clip from her hair and ran his hands through the waves, massaging her scalp, sending tingles racing from head to toe.

Anticipation quickened her heart. She let her hands roam freely, without hesitation, over his chest, arms, back, and then across his toned abs. She wasn't quite ready to relieve him of the rest of his clothes, and she tipped her head to the side to deepen the kiss. She moaned softly.

"Liza," he groaned.

Her pulse raced. She wanted to feel his skin on hers. She took a step back. "I'm overdressed."

He carefully unbuttoned the trail of small pink buttons on her blouse and the fabric slipped off her shoulders as his lips caressed her skin. He slipped her bra off and it followed the blouse.

She walked him back to the bed. As much as a part of her wanted to go slow, the other part of her, the more insistent part, wanted him now. His hand hesitated at the zipper on her skirt. She pushed his hand aside and slid the zipper down. The fabric pooled at her feet.

"It seems I'm overdressed now."

She nodded. Her mouth went dry as he took off his jeans and kicked them aside. Every part of him was perfect. He eased her back onto the down comforter. His hands skimmed over her skin, his touch bringing her back to life.

"You are so beautiful."

He spoke the words with intense tenderness. In this moment, she felt beautiful and treasured. One tear slipped from the corner of her eye. For her body to feel alive again after so many years was mind-bending. He stopped kissing her and dried the tears.

"We can stop."

"No." Her voice was hoarse. "Happy tears."

She claimed his mouth while he claimed her heart.

*D*rew was a goner. He lay awake with Liza sleeping in his arms. He looked at the gentle curve of her face, her long, dark lashes gracing her cheeks. She was his angel. The woman who had brought him to life with a simple hello the first time they met at Colin's picnic and the last straw was when she walked into his house a week ago; the house finally felt like a home. It felt different with her in it; it vibrated with life. He felt different when she was by his side, and now she was sleeping in his bed. Liza Price Bradford was the woman he had waited for his entire life.

Could his reality get any better than this moment?

She stirred and he kissed her brow and murmured soothing sounds. It didn't matter how slow they would move because of the boys. He knew she had fallen for him too. He could see it in her eyes and feel it in her kiss.

As he drifted off to sleep, his last thought was of waking up next to the woman he was going to someday marry. He finally knew what love really was, and it had only taken him all of thirty-eight years to figure it out.

*T*he sun streamed through the French doors and Liza stretched her arms out in front of her. She looked around to discover she was alone. At the end of the bed was a folded t-shirt and on it was a note.

When you're ready, slip this on. I'll be in the kitchen, waiting.

She slipped the soft cotton tee over her head. It graced her mid-thigh. She looked in the mirror and noticed a well-faded Orioles logo on the front. She smiled; the boys would try and convert him to be a Mets fan. She made a quick stop in the bathroom, where she finger-combed her hair and brushed her teeth with a new toothbrush Drew had placed on the vanity.

She padded down the stairs. The smell of fresh brewed coffee and bacon made her stomach growl. She took in the vibrant landscape painting in the hallway, signed by B. Ricci. She had never heard of him. But he was definitely very talented.

Drew met her in the hallway. "Good morning." He gave her a tender kiss. "Sleep well?"

She slipped an arm around his waist and leaned in for another kiss. "I did. What time is it?"

"Nearly nine."

"I never sleep this late."

"I'm glad you slept in; you had a busy day yesterday." He turned her toward the kitchen. "Breakfast is almost ready."

"When did you get up?" Her eyes widened. There was a small table outside in a screened-in section of the deck that was set with a small vase of flowers, glasses, and plates.

"About a half hour ago. I wanted to make you breakfast."

"You should have woken me; I would have helped."

He brushed the hair back from her eyes. "When was the last time someone cooked you breakfast?"

She knew exactly the last time. It was a week before

Steve went on his last business trip. Once a month, he had cooked a big Sunday breakfast. It had been their tradition.

She looked away and blinked back the tears that threatened to gather in her eyes.

"Steve?" As if he could sense her sadness, he asked, "Whenever you're ready to talk, I'm ready to listen. Your memories of him are an important part of your past and of who we are as a couple."

She looked into his eyes. Softly, she said, "A long time. Steve used to make breakfast one Sunday a month. He'd go all out. Waffles, eggs Benedict, it was always a surprise." She took a step toward him. "Much like this." She brushed her lips over his and asked, "How are you cooking the eggs?"

"It depends. How do you like them?"

"Scrambled, over easy, omelet, or fried. Your choice."

He pointed to the coffee pot. "You pour. I'll surprise you."

They moved around the kitchen as if they had done this for years instead of for the first time. She made toast and Drew fixed cheese and veggie omelets. Soon they were sitting at the table overlooking the water while they sipped coffee.

She said, "The screened-in part of the deck is a good idea."

"When I was a kid, the bugs were insane and we never ate outside. But Mom would have a picnic on the floor in the dining room so we could watch the water sans bugs."

"Why didn't your parents screen it in?"

"Mom said it would spoil the view." He crunched on the toast. "How did you know I like it dark, almost burnt?"

"I didn't. The toaster took the guesswork out of it." She grinned. "You have it set on dark."

"Do you want to do something today?"

She pushed her empty plate away. "I need to pick up the boys and we have yardwork to do, and I need to get to the market."

"How about dinner?"

"I get the feeling you don't want me to leave quite yet."

He took her hand and kissed the soft part of the underside of her wrist. "I'm happiest when you're around."

She smiled softly as her heart danced. She knew exactly what he meant.

Giving her hand a squeeze, he said, "And that includes Johnny and George. They're great kids and I like spending time with them too."

She didn't acknowledge what he said about the boys. She needed for him to understand how she felt about him. "I *really* like you."

His eyes grew wide as she put extra emphasis on the word really. "The feeling is mutual."

Was she feeling a strong case of like and lust, or had her feelings deepened—and would he reciprocate? She eased her hand away. But this wasn't the time to start panicking about that now. She forced a smile but didn't look at his face.

"Hey, what's going on behind those pretty hazel eyes of yours?"

"Nothing."

"Liza." His voice was deep, almost melodic. "Be honest with me. Do you regret what happened last night?"

She looked directly in his eyes so he wouldn't make a mistake about anything. "Not at all. It was wonderful and this morning"—she waved her hand across the breakfast table—"this was so sweet. Since the moment I arrived last night, I've felt special. I'm not even sure if that's the best way to describe it."

"I hear a but in there someplace." He moved his chair closer to her so their knees were touching. "Talk to me."

"Maybe we shouldn't spend so much time together with the boys."

She watched as his face fell.

"Why? I thought we had a lot of fun together."

"They have had fun with you. It's just, and I don't want this to come out wrong or have you think that I expect something since we, well, you know, last night and all."

"Sweetheart, take a breath and slow down."

She exhaled. "They lost their dad, and it was agony for them. They were much younger and didn't really understand, but the pain wasn't any less real. Now they're older and if they get attached to you and we don't work out, they'll suffer again. Only this time, it will be my fault since I've encouraged the relationship."

"Hey, slow down. You're already thinking we're going to implode or something."

His easy laughter caused her back to stiffen. "Protecting my children is not funny."

"I didn't mean anything by it. Trust me; I've thought about all of this even before we went geocaching. I don't want to hurt them either. Which is why I know what I'd like for our future."

"Our future." Her voice cracked.

He smiled, put his hand under her chin, and looked into her eyes. "I'm not rushing anything between us, so you can breathe, but for the record, I'm not going anywhere. We can take whatever is happening between us at your pace. When the boys are comfortable with more, we'll go to the next logical step. For now, I love being with the three of you, and there are times when I'd like to repeat last night."

She could feel herself relax. This wasn't a fling for him either. "I'm not going anywhere either."

His eyes twinkled. "Now that we have that settled and we both know the other's intentions are honorable, back to my original question; what do you want to do today?"

"Play hooky and toss responsibility to the wind."

"Then do it." His eyes danced with mischief.

"Have you met me? I'm the practical one in the family. Work first and then play." She began to stack their breakfast dishes.

"Then let me help you with the work around your house. Despite what you might think, I can mow lawns and I know how to use a Weedwacker too."

She gave him a long, assessing look. "When was the last time you did?"

"That's not the point, is it?" He cocked his head to one side. "If you're willing to accept my offer to help at your place, we can get the work done in record time, and then the rest of the day is for fun."

She gave him a wide grin. "You've convinced me to say yes." She leaned in and kissed him and then placed the stack of dirty dishes in his hands. "Work first, and then if we hurry, we can have a little more one-on-one time before I need to pick up the boys."

"I like how you think." He set the dirty plates aside and kissed her again.

28

The kids had been back in school a couple of weeks and Liza was in the van, waiting for the boys. They were going to Drew's for a swim and an early dinner and then back home for homework and showers.

Johnny got off the bus after George and Liza's heart dropped. He looked drawn and pale. His shoulders were drooping and he was moving at a snail's pace. George slid open the door and Johnny got in.

George closed the door. "Hey, Mom, where are we going?"

"No place except the house." She put the van in reverse and backed down the drive. "John, what's going on?"

"I dunno. I'm just tired."

"Did you check your blood sugar after lunch?"

"No, I skipped it."

"Why?" She glanced in the mirror. "Skipped testing or lunch?" She threw the van in park. "We need to check your blood sugar and have a snack."

The boys got out and George opened the kitchen door, dropped his bag on the floor, and was already pouring a glass of orange juice when John sagged in a chair at the table.

She handed him the test kit and thanked George for the juice. "Please get my phone so I can call Drew and let him know we're staying home."

Obvious disappointment flashed across his face, but he took her cell phone out of her bag.

Johnny held out the meter, showing he was not in the danger zone but his blood sugar was on the low side. She handed him the juice. "Drink up."

"Mom." George handed her the phone.

When Drew answered, she explained they were going to hang out at the house.

"What's going on over there?"

Tension eased in her chest and she exhaled the breath she had been holding. "For some reason, Johnny's blood sugar is down. I think we'd better just lay low this afternoon. You're welcome to come for dinner here if you like."

"I could come over there. I might be able to help and I picked up the new *Star Wars* movie. That might be a good distraction."

She looked at the boys' long faces. "Sounds good. I'll make the popcorn. See you soon."

"Bye, hon."

The term of endearment lightened her heart and it was always nice to hear.

"Good news. Drew is bringing over a movie and you can do your homework after dinner. So we'll still have a fun afternoon but modified." She looked from Johnny to George. "Sound like a good plan?"

"I'm sorry I ruined your plans, Mom." Johnny hung his head.

"I appreciate the apology, but I'd like to know what happened."

He averted his eyes. "Can I have a snack?"

Since he wasn't about to tell her what had happened now, she'd bide her time. It would come out eventually. This is where the boys being in two different buildings stunk. George would have told her; he was terrible at keeping secrets.

"Some chocolate oat balls and milk for two. Coming right up." These were the best snack she had on hand, filled with peanut butter, oats, and dark cocoa, and thankfully the boys inhaled them like candy. She got the glasses from the cupboard and did a double take; George was almost as tall as his brother and he too was a bottomless pit.

After inhaling the snack, the boys put their dishes in the dishwasher. Johnny was cracking jokes and his color was back to normal, a good sign he was feeling better. She heard tires crunch in the gravel driveway. "Sounds like we have company."

"Mom, Drew's not company. He's your boyfriend." With a slight crack in his voice, Johnny shook his head. "Come on, George. Let's go so they can play kissy-face."

With a sharp knock on the door, Drew walked in. He filled the door with his height. It was the first time she had really noticed how tall he was, almost gracing the ceiling in her nineteenth century farmhouse. His eyes were bright and his smile warmed his eyes.

"Hi." He looked around the room. "Where are the boys?"

"They're in the family room." She chuckled. "And I think I just heard John's voice break."

"A sign of puberty." He scooped her into his arms and smothered her laugh with his lips. When he pulled away, he said, "What's so funny?"

She said, "The boys left the room so you could kiss me."

"Smart young men." He pecked her lips again and looked over her shoulder.

He guided her to the table and pulled a chair out for her. "So, tell me what happened today."

They sat down and she wiped a few crumbs into a napkin. It was interesting to share this with Drew; she hadn't had this kind of conversation with her partner in a long time. "I picked the boys up from the bus so we could head to your place. The minute they got off, I could see Johnny was dragging. He looked drained."

"But it was more than that." His voice was gentle.

"I'm guessing he skipped lunch but won't say why."

He wiped his hand over his jeans-covered leg. "I don't like the sound of that. He knows how important it is to eat on schedule."

She chewed on her bottom lip. "Maybe he got caught up at the library or needed to stay after class and talk to a teacher."

"He's in a new school, with more kids from other towns, right? Maybe it was about a girl he likes."

"I guess, but still." This was something new to worry about. Before his diagnosis, he could have handled anything, but the diabetes had taken the edge off his preteen swagger.

Taking her hand, he gave it a reassuring caress.

"How can I get him to tell me what happened? I can't fix anything if I don't know the details." A wave of helplessness washed over her, almost like when she was a new mother.

"Maybe he can talk to Leo."

"Yeah, but he's been busy with the wedding and hasn't had much time with the boys in a couple of weeks."

"If you want I could try talking to him. Who knows? He might be more willing to open up since I'm not his mother."

She shook her head. "I don't want to put that on you."

"You didn't ask and I want to help." He held up the DVD. "I'm going to get this set up and if you will pop the corn, we can start the movie." He handed her a box of microwave popcorn. "Before I leave tonight, you'll know exactly what happened and we'll figure out the solution."

Liza said, "Then I accept your offer to help."

He kissed her one more time. "I do appreciate the guys giving us some private time."

With a laugh, she said, "They still think kissing is gross."

"Wait until they discover the wonder of it. They'll change their minds. I did by the time I was fourteen. But I might have been a late bloomer."

She sank against the back of the chair. Girls? Johnny couldn't be seriously interested in girls already. If he didn't open up to Drew, she'd ask Leo to pick the boys up from school tomorrow; they always told him everything. Satisfied she had a plan, she noticed the front of the popcorn box. "Extra butter. He does know what I like."

The boys had textbooks spread out across the kitchen table and were working quietly when Johnny slammed his book shut. Drew was working on a supplier contract for camp next year. He gave his head a little shake toward Liza and asked, "What's going on?"

Without looking up from his book, Johnny said, "Math." He propped his head up with his hand. "I don't get word problems."

"Can I help?"

Johnny eyed Drew suspiciously. "Do you know how to do new math? Ya know it's different since you were in school."

Drew's lips tipped up and chuckled. "It doesn't matter. Word problems are the same with new or old math."

Johnny flipped open the pages and slid his book across the table. "See. I have to do problems one through ten."

Drew scanned the text; it looked like something he could handle. "I can help if you want."

"Well," he drawled.

Liza said, "John, the worst thing that'll happen is you get it wrong. Give Drew a shot. Who knows? He might be better at explaining things than Mrs. Rice."

He slid his chair close to Drew's and they spent the next half hour working through his math homework. George finished the book he was reading, made some notes in his journal, and went to take a shower. Liza couldn't help but notice while she worked on the plans for the crush party that Johnny looked more relaxed than he had earlier.

She hadn't had the chance to talk to Drew but if she were to hazard a guess, it was that they'd talked about what happened when she had gone back into the kitchen for more melted butter. She hoped she was one step closer to solving the problem.

Johnny slid his textbook and notebook into his backpack. "Thanks, Drew, for helping me with my homework and if I get it wrong, I'm gonna tell Mrs. Rice that you helped me."

"And if you get it right?"

He laughed. "Then it's our secret, right?"

He ruffled the boy's hair. "Give me all the blame and you take all the credit. Somehow, I got the short end of the stick."

"Well, maybe I'll tell her I had help."

Liza pointed to the stairs. "Shower and then read in bed for half an hour."

"Okay." He got up from the chair. "The movie was good today. Thanks for bringing it over."

"You're welcome, John."

Once she heard the upstairs bathroom door close, she turned to study Drew. "Did he tell you what happened at lunch?"

He dropped his voice. "He can't hear us?"

Liza watched as he frowned. She was not going to like what he was about to tell her. The pipe banged, signaling the shower was running. "Not with the water running."

"Apparently he doesn't want anyone to treat him differently and there was a girl who asked him to go to the library with her and skip lunch period, so he did."

She began to tremble now that it wasn't anything more sinister. He pulled her into his lap and wrapped his arms around her. "It's okay."

She took a deep breath. "I'm going to check on them as soon as Johnny is out of the bathroom. I'd like it if you stayed a while."

"Absolutely." He held her close until the water stopped running.

She lightly kissed his mouth and eased off his lap. "I'll be back in a bit."

"Take your time."

ohnny walked in the kitchen. "Hey, Drew, I just wanted to say thanks for talking to me."

In a rare moment of expressiveness, Johnny put his arms around Drew and hugged his neck. It was over as fast as it began.

"Good night."

"Good night, John." He leaned against the counter and waited for Liza to join him. She walked in and gave him a tentative smile.

"I'm not sure what you did, but Johnny told me he really likes you." She picked up a few loose pieces of paper on the kitchen table and began to tidy the room.

He guessed this was part of the way she calmed herself. Cleaning. He could think of a better way to let go of the worry.

"Come with me." He held his hand out to her. She took it and they crossed to the small reading nook at the other end of the room.

He sat down in an oversized chair in front of the

window and pulled her into his lap. She rested her head against his shoulder.

"What happens the next time a pretty girl catches his eye and he forgets to take care of his health?"

"He won't. Johnny is growing up and this is part of the process, not just his diabetes but girls too."

She kissed his cheek and then his lips, placing her hands on either side of his face, gently at first, but with an intensity and passion that burned him. He didn't want to leave her tonight, but they weren't at the stage where they were spending the night with the boys under the same roof. It was much too soon. He pushed all thoughts from his mind and concentrated on how her lips felt against his.

Pure heaven.

*

A couple of weeks later, Liza was putting the finishing touches on the crush party. Her cell rang and she picked up without looking at caller ID. "Liza Bradford."

"Ms. Bradford, I understand you are working a gig this weekend at Crescent Lake Winery. Is there any chance you'll be looking for an extra set of hands to assist you?"

She laughed. "Who's calling, please?"

"My name is Andrew Cameron and I do have a little experience with wine."

She stifled another laugh. "And just what is your experience?"

"I can open a bottle and pour, and I have been known to drink a little from time to time."

"It just so happens I have a need for one more

bartender. I can't pay more than the standard rate. But the perks are pretty good."

"Perks? Do tell."

She leaned back in the chair and chuckled. "Kate Price is catering. You'll be able to sample some of the wines, enjoy delicious food, and," she drawled, "at the end of the evening, you get to kiss me good night."

"Then I accept the terms of employment." He chuckled. "Hello, sweetheart. How's your day really going?"

"Busy but good. I'm at the winery now. The harvest is in full swing, so things are buzzing here. Literally. There are bees everywhere."

"Do you have your EpiPen with you?"

"Always in my pocket. I don't have time for any problems; there's way too much to do for that to happen."

"My very own whirlwind."

She glanced at her checklist and said, "So other than looking for a job, what else is going on?"

"I have other news to share."

Liza stopped multitasking when she heard the excitement in his voice. "What's that?"

"My parents are coming in this weekend and they can't wait to meet you and the boys. They're staying with me, so I thought maybe we could have dinner at my place on Sunday night. I know you might be tired from the party on Saturday, but they're leaving Tuesday. Please say yes. I'll handle everything so all you need to do is show up and just be you."

Meeting his parents was a big step, but since he already knew hers, she thought it was only fair. "When do they actually arrive?"

"Thursday, but that's fluid. What do you say? Dinner

Sunday? We'll eat early too, in case the boys need to finish homework or something."

"Great. Can we set a firm time toward the end of the week? And if they do get here Thursday, be sure to let them know about the party. They might enjoy it, and Mom and Dad would love to meet them too."

"My parents are going to love you as much as I do."

"What did you just say?" Did she just hear him correctly? Had he used the *love* word with her. "Drew?"

"Turn around."

She spun around and there he was, leaning against the doorjamb to the tasting room with an ocean of customers between them. Still speaking into the phone, she said, "Hi."

He slid the phone into the back pocket of his faded black jeans. With a slow and easy walk, he was taking his own sweet time about closing the distance between the two of them.

She ended the call and placed her phone on the table. Her breath quickened as he grew closer. "Hello. Have you been here the entire conversation?"

"I was on my way when I dialed and I decided it was time."

"Time for what?" Her pulse revved up.

He cupped her cheek with his hand and brought his mouth to hers, lingering there until she melted into him. "I have something very important I want to tell you." He laughed softly. "My sweet Liza, it's not that. At least not yet."

Had her eyes shown the look of excitement and panic all at the same time when the first thing that sprang to her mind was a proposal? And then she was embarrassed she had even thought of it.

"We'll get to that in due time, but I'm an old-fashioned kind of a guy—well, to a point."

She was sure now they were on the same wavelength. "Drew." Breathless, she said, "You're driving me nuts."

"Liza, I'm in love with you." He looked into her eyes, and she would never forget this moment. "I have loved you since the first time we met."

"You didn't even know me."

He laughed softly. "It was a ka-pow moment." He placed her hand over his heart and his over hers. "My heart knew."

"I love you too."

He brought his mouth down on hers, crushing them together, filled with longing and hope for what was to come next.

A deep voice said, "You guys should get a room."

They broke apart. Liza stayed tucked in Drew's arms.

"Jack, stop picking on your sister." Peyton swatted his arm. "Don't you know when a couple needs some privacy?"

"Heck, this is a business, not a kissing booth."

Peyton popped her hands on her hips. "You kiss me in the tasting room, storage room, pretty much everywhere and whenever the mood strikes."

"That's different."

"No, it's not." She laughed. "You're gonna lose this argument, hubby dear, so just let it go."

Liza and Drew watched as Jack whisked Peyton into his arms. "Drew, my man. You may have a great idea." He dipped his wife and planted a passionate kiss on her lips.

She pushed him away and laughed even harder. "We have work today. There will be time enough for smooching later."

Jack patted her on the butt as she walked to the bar.

"If you're done fooling around, we have a new recruit for the weekend." She looped her arm through Drew's. "Guess who has volunteered to be one of Peyton's pack mules this weekend?"

Peyton clapped her hands. "Thank heavens, but do you know what you signed up for? Wear comfortable shoes. Once the doors open, we'll be on the run until closing."

Drew looked at the three faces watching him.

Liza saw his eyes go wide as she gave his arm a reassuring squeeze. "This will be fun."

Peyton said, "Why don't you come with me and I'll show you around the storage room? We'll be moving a lot of product on Saturday and you can get the lay of the land, so to speak."

"That is a great idea. Peyton will show you the ropes." Liza turned to Jack. "If you have a minute, I want to talk to you about where we're going to put the kids' activities."

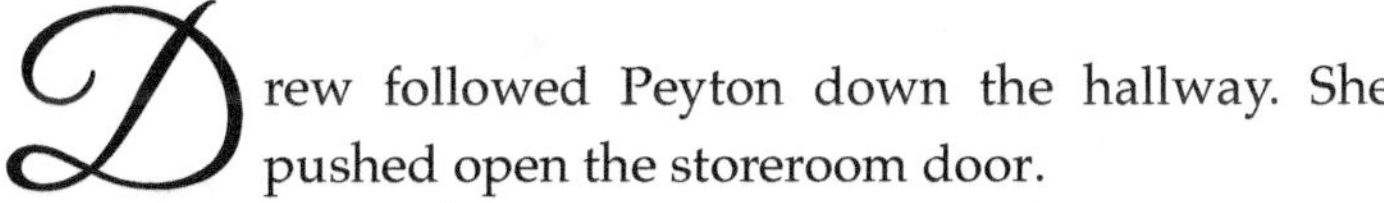

rew followed Peyton down the hallway. She pushed open the storeroom door.

"I'll give you a key for the weekend. We keep this locked at all times."

"Oh, I don't need a key."

Peyton gave him a level look. "Oh, yes, you do. It's only a matter of time now."

"For what?"

"I've seen that look before and by the end of the year, we'll be planning another family wedding."

How the heck did she guess?

"Don't worry. The rest of the family hasn't figured it out yet, but let me be the first to welcome you to the wonderful and wacky world of the Price family." She placed a hand on his arm. "Your secret is safe with me."

All he could think to do was stammer his thanks.

30

It was the end of a busy weekend and Sunday night dinner with Drew sounded like heaven even if Liza was tired and now nervous. She was about to meet his parents. She parked the van in front of Drew's house and noticed her parents' car was already in the driveway. It was nice Drew had invited them too since his parents hadn't gotten into town until the day before. The boys tumbled out of the back, ran up the front steps, and burst into the house. How she wished they'd at least knock before storming in. She'd have to remind them of their manners. Hopefully the rest of the night would go a little better in the etiquette department.

She carried a platter that held a chocolate layer cake with buttercream frosting, one of her specialties. As she walked up the front steps and flashed Drew a smile, he took the cake from her and kissed her upturned lips.

"This looks delicious, but you didn't need to bake. I'm sure you're exhausted after yesterday; I know it took the wind out of my sails."

"I'll be fine. Besides, you're doing the bulk of the

cooking tonight and the boys helped make the cake, so make sure you tell them it's delicious."

He stepped to one side so she could enter the house.

Over her shoulder, she said, "Sorry about the boys busting in like that."

"I'm glad they feel at home." He whispered in her ear, "You look beautiful; the green blouse suits you."

She was dressed in jeans and a cotton blouse with a cardigan sweater. She wanted to look nice but not overly fussy and she was comfortable in case they sat outside on the deck. "Thank you."

"Our parents are in the family room. I set up a game system for the boys in the living room. The big screen is so much better for video games anyway."

She arched a brow. "You're spoiling them."

"I'm having fun." He gave her a puppy dog look that made her laugh.

"Don't get too carried away. I need to have something on their Christmas gift list. Oh, and there is a rule that after Halloween, unless it's your birthday or an essential, no new purchases."

"Does that go for adults too?" He gave her a cheeky grin.

Playfully, she wagged a finger in his direction. "Yes. No one is excluded."

She glanced in the hallway mirror to check her hair and makeup as she took a deep nerve-calming breath. But at least Mom and Dad being here relieved some of the pressure.

From behind her, he looked at her in the reflection. "Are you ready?"

She met his eyes. "As ready as I'll ever be."

"They don't bite."

"Speak for yourself, son."

Liza jumped as an older version of Drew appeared behind her.

"Are you trying to keep Liza all to yourself?"

She turned and extended her hand, but the older man pulled her in for a bear hug.

"Dad, this is Liza Bradford. And sweetheart, this is my father, Andy."

"Nice to meet you, sir."

The corners of his eyes crinkled from a lifetime of smiles. "Skip the sir and just call me Andy." He looped his arm through hers. "I met your boys. They're full of energy."

She cringed. "Please tell me they didn't break anything?"

Andy gave a hearty chuckle. "Not at all. Your parents introduced us and they shook our hands before telling us all about the cake you baked for dessert, right down to licking the bowl."

She laughed. "I can vouch for the batter tasting good. We have a bad habit of eating raw cookie dough and cake batter."

His eyes twinkled. "Son, she's my kind of girl. Let's get out of the hallway and make an entrance."

She felt at ease with Andy; he had a great sense of humor and she guessed a zest for life as well.

Drew led the way, easing her forward.

"Mom, Dad is up to his tricks already."

A tall, thin woman with Drew's eyes got up from the sofa. She walked to Liza, who couldn't help but notice she wore minimal makeup—just enough to enhance her eyes —and light-colored lipstick. Her blond hair was short with brown highlights. She was stunning.

"Liza, I've heard so much about you." She gave her a warm hug.

"Mrs. Cameron, it's nice to meet you."

"Call me Diane." She steered her to the sofa and had Liza sit down next to her.

Liza looked at the other sofa and smiled at her parents. "Hi, Mom. Dad."

"Hi, kiddo." Dad grinned.

She shifted on the sofa and decided to overlook the kiddo comment. "How long have you been here?"

"Maybe a half hour?" Dad looked at Mom for confirmation.

"We have been having a wonderful time getting to know your parents." Andy sat in a leather chair across from them. "They brought several bottles of wine and we've enjoyed sampling."

"Drew, if I had known Mom and Dad were coming earlier, I would have been here too."

Mom waved off her comment. "We were out driving around. You know Dad; he wanted to check on some vines and we were running early. We called Drew to see if we could come by and here we are."

That sounded just like her parents.

Diane said, "Drew told us the event yesterday was a huge success. Andy and I are sorry we missed it."

Mom said, "We hold it every October, and each year is bigger than the last."

Dad held out a bottle of red to pour Liza some. "Cab?"

She nodded. "Please." They were all acting like old friends, which was oddly comforting.

"We will make sure we're here in plenty of time next year so we can attend."

Mom said, "If you'd like to see the winery, we can give you a behind-the-scenes tour before you leave."

Diane glanced at Andy with a twinkle in her eye. "We've been on tastings before, but I'd love to see how it all works behind the scenes."

The parents were definitely hitting it off. In between conversation, Liza realized she didn't hear sounds of a video game. She got off the sofa. "Any idea where the boys are?"

Drew said, "They're down on the dock, feeding the ducks."

She stepped to the wall of glass. The boys were tossing something to the growing gaggle of ducks in front of them.

He followed her to the glass and rested his hand on the small of her back. "They come every year. Maybe it's because I always have duck food for them. It's a long journey to their winter home."

His body was warm next to hers. She could hear the boys laughing and it caused her to smile, realizing they were comfortable at Drew's. "That's sweet, and the boys are enjoying themselves."

"There's a lot of fun stuff to do around here. Winter, we can skate on the lake after it freezes. Do they play ice hockey?"

"No. We never got into that, thank heavens. I would have frozen my toes and fingers off waiting for them at practices."

"Cross-country skiing?"

She liked it as he talked about future plans, and they all sounded like things the boys and she would enjoy. "That would be fun."

He kissed her hair. "Then we'll make it happen."

The boys turned as if they could sense they were being

watched. They waved and beckoned the adults to join them.

Over her shoulder, Liza said, "The boys want us to come down."

Andy said, "Then by all means, let's go feed the ducks. It has been a long time since we've seen them, Diane."

Dad said, "I'll admit this will be the first time I've fed ducks."

"No, it's not." Mom laughed. "Dear, you don't remember? When we started dating, we'd go to the park in town and feed them."

His smile softened. "I do remember." He kissed her cheek. "Just wondering if you did."

The glass wall seemed to magically slide open and the six of them descended the stairs and walked down the long wooden dock.

Dad glanced around. "Drew, this is quite a setup."

"I can't take credit for the location. Dad bought it before I was born."

Andy said, "It was an abandoned summer camp. Diane fell in love with the view. As an anniversary present, we bought it for each other and the rest is history, as they say. After the original buildings were torn down, we built the house. Then Drew took it over and he did a complete renovation and added on to it. He did a fine job."

Liza could hear the pride in Andy's voice and she slipped her hand in Drew's as they brought up the rear.

He whispered in her ear, "They like you."

She swung his hand with hers as they walked. "They just met me."

"Formally, yes, but I told them all about you, and meeting your parents is a glimpse into who you are. You should have seen my mom's eyes light up when the boys ran into the room. After giving your mom a hug and high-fiving your dad, they introduced themselves to my parents. They are really good kids."

"I'm gonna keep them." With a laugh, she said, "I just hope they want to keep me when they become teenagers."

"Are you kidding? They know how lucky they are to have you in their corner. Never doubt that."

She was surprised at the seriousness in his tone. She hip bumped him. "I was kidding." He put his arm around her shoulders and placed a kiss on her temple. A zing raced through her at the simple gesture.

The boys were passing out handfuls of duck food to the mothers first and then to the fathers.

George said, "The best way to do it is like your gonna try to skip a rock and let the food scatter on the water. Then you can watch them dip under the surface and grab it before it sinks."

He took Diane's hand and walked her to the edge of the dock. "Ready?" He flung the seed out and it landed on the top of the water just as he had said. "Your turn."

Diane opened her hand too soon and the feed dropped in front of the dock. She laughed. "I'm not very good at this."

"Try again." Johnny gave her another handful.

It warmed Liza's heart to see her sons with Diane, feeding the ducks. She suspected Diane already knew the best way, but it was very kind of her.

She dropped her voice so they wouldn't be overheard. "Your mom is a good sport."

He whispered in her ear, "She's never fed the ducks before. It means she's taken a shine to the boys."

"The feeling seems to be mutual."

"Hey, Drew," Johnny called. "How much should we feed them?"

"A few more handfuls, then we should go up to the house. Dinner will be ready soon."

"Okay." He took one final handful and tossed it. He was bent over the can and he looked at Liza. "Mom, you didn't get a chance. Come 'ere. I'll show you how."

She walked the last few feet on the dock and held out her hand. "How do I throw it again?"

He filled her hand. "It's easy. Just flick your wrist and let it fly; you've got this."

"Thanks for the vote of confidence." She gave him a quick one-armed hug.

"You can do anything, Mom." He grinned.

She looked back at Drew and flicked her wrist as their eyes met. She felt like she could conquer the world.

31

A few weeks later the early October sun was high in the cloudless sky; the day was almost perfect. A light breeze rustled the bright yellow, red, and orange leaves on the trees. It was a rare Saturday when Liza didn't have an event and today, Anna and Colin had invited her and Drew to play nine holes of golf. Anna was feeling good despite being seven months pregnant and wanted to get out and play a round while she still could. It was the perfect opportunity; Leo and Steph were taking the boys fishing so she could have some time with her handsome hunk. She smiled, thinking of Steph's words, not hers.

Liza looked in the mirror and couldn't help but smile. She looked like a picture in a golf magazine, and she had to wonder if the models in the ads played better than she did, or maybe they didn't play at all. She could get the ball down the fairway, but it didn't look pretty.

She ran down the stairs and scanned each room to make sure it was tidy. A sharp honk of a horn prompted her to glance at her watch. Drew was right on time.

She had grabbed a small tote and put a color-coordinating ballcap in the bag when the door opened and Drew popped his head in the door.

"Good morning, beautiful. Ready to leave?"

"Other than grabbing my clubs, I'm ready."

"I'll get them." When she came within arm's length, he tugged her into his arms. "You look gorgeous in green."

"I can't take credit; I borrowed the outfit from Anna. She said the rules were pretty strict and I couldn't just wear a cute t-shirt and shorts."

He frowned slightly. "Well, you could have worn any shirt as long as it had a collar."

"It's just typical sister stuff; we're always borrowing each other's clothes."

"Can I ask you a personal question?"

"Sure. I have nothing to hide." She couldn't imagine what he might want to know. She didn't have anything to hide from him as it had been from the beginning.

"Are you having any financial concerns?"

"What? No." She laughed. "I'm fine."

"I know you've been having trouble with the van and I've offered to help you get a new vehicle from one of my dealerships, but you haven't taken me up on the offer."

She laid a hand on his arm. "It is really sweet that you want to help, but I'm pretty independent. I've been busy with work, the kids, and everything so when I get some time, I'll get a new vehicle."

He looked unconvinced. "Are you still thinking of getting an SUV like Kate's?"

"Yes, size-wise but not as fancy, a few bells and whis-tles but not fully loaded. I like to keep my money in the bank. I've had my van since before I got pregnant with Johnny. I like to get my money's worth."

He touched her hand. "Promise me. If you ever need anything, don't hesitate to ask. I'd give you the world."

"Thank you but I'm fine." She flicked the overhead light switch off. "We need to get going or they'll think we're not coming. Or worse, Anna will think I've chickened out."

He wore a heart-melting grin. "Just how bad do you golf?"

"You know how they say practice makes perfect?"

He nodded. "I do."

"I've played on a golf course twice and the number of times I've gone to the driving range, you could count on both hands."

He pretended to cringe. "I guess I'll be carrying our team today."

"If we're playing best ball, there are bound to be a few holes where my ball is going to have the bigger advantage." She patted her pockets and then checked her bag. "Oh, wait. I need my cell phone charger."

She dashed back into the house and grabbed it from the counter and rejoined Drew. "I hope you don't mind, but I gave Leo and Steph your cell number. Just in case."

"I'd be upset if you didn't." He held open the door to his SUV.

"Oh, shoot. My clubs." She pointed to the bag resting against the side of the van.

"I've got them. You get in and buckle up."

*D*rew was concerned that she had put on a brave face for him regarding her financial situation. Borrowing clothes from her sister, wanting a new car but putting it off with the excuse she didn't have time. She had been talking about getting a new vehicle for several months; was that really the issue?

He picked up her clubs. They looked like she got them from a secondhand shop. Not that there was anything wrong with that, but he could give her the best of everything if she'd let him. He stored the clubs in the back and got in.

"Where did you get your clubs?"

She beamed. "Aren't they great? I found them at a tag sale and loved they were in that purple bag, which matched the little bit of purple on the club heads."

He smiled. "I didn't know the coordinating color of the clubs and bag was important."

With a laugh, she said, "It's always important to add a dash of color."

He glanced her way, and her smile melted his heart. "You're my bright spot in full color."

She laughed again. "And you're cute."

The rest of the drive was filled with Liza telling him about upcoming events she was working on. Her business was thriving and Dawn was working out. In fact, if it continued to go well, she was going to offer Dawn a full-time job and be able to book more events throughout the year.

"Are you ready to expand?"

With a flash of a wide grin, she said, "I am. I've hired a woman part-time, but I've had to turn down several events since I couldn't be in two places at once. I'm going all in, no guts, no glory."

"There is one thing to be bold, another to rush in before you have some assurances of steady growth."

He swore the temperature in the SUV had dropped to near zero. A frosty silence answered him.

"I happen to be very cautious when it comes to my business, and I am a Price. I have a logical mind and a shrewd eye for the bottom line."

In that instant, he knew he had overstepped. Sufficiently chastised, he took her hand. "I'm sorry. I didn't mean to upset you."

"So far today, you've insinuated I was poor, expressed a lack of enthusiasm for my golf clubs, and now you're trying to put a damper on my business expansion. Is there anything else you think I could do better?" She held up a hand. "Wait. Not borrow my sister's clothes?" She stared out the windshield.

Had he really sounded that insensitive? He wasn't going to have this conversation at fifty miles an hour. He put his blinker on and pulled over into the breakdown lane and parked.

He turned in his seat. "Liza, I'm very sorry. It was not my intention to hurt your feelings or make it seem like I don't think you have a good handle on your business. I tend to want to jump in and fix things for people I care about. Since you're first on my priority list, I want to help you in any way I can."

She looked at him and chewed her bottom lip. "Do me a favor. Wait for me to ask for help before you try and give it to me. I take pride in being fiercely independent. Just ask my dad."

"If I say something stupid again, do *me* a favor and tell me to be quiet."

She leaned over and pulled him close. "You might be sorry you told me that, but you can count on it." She smiled and pecked his lips. "I guess this could constitute our first argument." She made a little checkmark in the air. "Another first behind us."

He cocked his head. "Another?"

She gave him a steady look. "How quickly you forget."

A gleam came into his eye. "Every time is going to be the first time with us."

"If you keep up with the sweet words, I won't be able to stay annoyed with you for long." She gave a small laugh and pointed to the road. "Drive, Mr. Cameron. I also hate being late."

"At your service, Ms. Bradford."

*L*iza slid her putter into her bag like a boss and flashed a cheeky grin at Drew. "And that, my friend, is how it's done."

"I can't believe you've missed all but one putt today, but darlin', it was the most important one. What is your secret?" He slid his sunglasses to the top of his head and then twirled her into his arms. Laughing, she landed against his chest.

"I don't choke under pressure." She batted her eyelashes and looked up, feigning coyness.

He started to tickle her and she squealed. This had been such a fun day once they got past the car ride.

"Hey, you two," Colin yelled from their golf cart. "Stop horsing around. It's time for a cool beverage and a bite to eat."

Drew brushed back her hair. "I had a lot of fun today. This was nice being with you and, of course, hanging with Colin and Anna."

"So," she drawled, "does this mean you want to play again sometime?"

"Absolutely. When you're ready, maybe we can even play a full eighteen holes."

"I'm up for it. However, I think I need more time at the driving range and another few times here." Her gaze swept the course. "Steve and I always talked about taking up golf when the kids got older. He thought it would be a good family thing to do."

"We could bring the boys to the driving range. Get a couple of starter sets and see if they like it."

She blinked tears from her eyes and started to cross the green to the cart. "I'm sorry."

He reached out and stopped her. "You have nothing to be sorry about. I like hearing about Steve. I think we would have been friends."

"He was a great man, an amazing husband, and an even better dad. They broke the mold after him."

"If his sons are any indication, they did." He draped his arm around her shoulders and pulled her to his side. "I want you to feel free to talk about him and your life before we met. Your marriage and family shaped you into the person you are today."

"It really doesn't bother you?" She thought it would make him uncomfortable or at least would be weird.

"Nope, not at all." He stopped and kissed her and then smirked. "Do you know there is a rule on the golf course that whoever sinks the last putt has to buy the first round of drinks?"

With a loud laugh, she said, "Then it's water all the way around."

She jumped into the driver's seat of the cart and patted the passenger side. "I'll drive."

"I don't know if that's such a good idea."

"To be seen being driven by your girlfriend?" She gave him an exaggerated wink.

He stepped into the cart and stretched out his legs to the side of him.

"Not at all. Onward."

She took off as fast as the little cart would go, which wasn't very fast, leaving a trail of laughter in her wake.

32

*I*t had been a week since Liza and Drew had gone golfing. Sitting at the breakfast table, Johnny and George were debating if they should ride bikes, convince Liza to go for a hike, or see what Drew was up to for the day. Thankfully they weren't asking to go fishing again.

"Hey, Mom." George finished the last of his banana pancake. "Is Drew coming for dinner tonight?"

"He has been coming over on Sundays. Why?" Did they have something else they'd rather do?

"I was thinking maybe we could hang out at Uncle Leo's garage this morning and this afternoon, we could go biking. That's if Drew has a bike."

"Why don't you call and invite him?" She was glad to see that her son was thinking of Drew.

She handed him the house phone. She was going to tell him the number when George dialed.

"Hi. It's George." He grinned into the phone. "Do you want to come bike riding with us this afternoon?" He was nodding. "Yup. The bike trail." He looked at her. "Drew wants to know what time we're going."

He was obviously taking charge of the plans since he didn't hand her the phone.

Johnny piped up. "Let's skip the garage and if we help Mom around the house, we can go to the trail sooner."

Now the boys were planning her day. She smothered a laugh.

"Mom, is that okay with you?"

She put her hand out for the receiver. "Yes. You can start by putting your dirty dishes in the dishwasher and letting me talk with Drew."

"See ya later." George handed her the phone.

Johnny and George were in motion at top speed to get the kitchen tidy. Out of the corner of her eye, Liza watched Johnny swipe his arm across the table. A few pancake crumbs fell to the floor. She rolled her eyes and turned away. He could sweep the floor next.

"Good morning," Liza said.

"Hi. I didn't expect George to call me this morning. When we talked last night, I thought we were taking the boys to the movies and then going out for dinner."

"They asked if we could do this instead and I thought it was a really good idea." She took the receiver away from her mouth and whispered, "Take the sheets off your beds next."

They bounded up the stairs.

"Sorry about that," she said. "They actually offered to help me get the housework done."

"What's gotten into them?" He laughed. "Was it so you could get done faster?"

"You got it." She refilled her coffee mug and sat down

at the table. "You don't have to feel obligated to come with us if you had other plans."

"I was supposed to meet with someone about a project I'm working on, but it can wait."

She was curious. Drew was being cryptic, but if there was something he wanted her to know, he'd tell her.

"We could pick you up at eleven and I can pack a lunch."

"Just pack some water and a few snacks. I think since we've had a change in plans, we should get lunch along the trail at The Burger Box."

"The boys would like that." She blew on her coffee before taking a sip. It was so easy making plans with Drew, and he was always up for something with the kids too.

"What would you like?" His voice was smooth and sexy and the question had her mind racing with all kinds of things they couldn't do today.

"Stop." She laughed.

"But it's so much fun. I can picture your cheeks getting a charming shade of pink, extending down your neck. Which, if I was there, I'd start by kissing you behind your ear in that soft, sensitive spot that makes you giggle."

"I don't giggle." He was right; her face had gotten warm.

"Trust me. You do."

"Well, enough teasing. It's not like you're going to have the opportunity to do that anytime soon."

"Is that a challenge?" His voice was light. "Because I'm up for the task."

"Remember the boys have rules." Her voice was light and teasing. Good butterflies bounced around her insides.

The idea of Drew's hands on her body and his lips on hers made her blood hum.

"There are ways around rules. Remember, I was a teenage boy and"—he groaned—"well, I'm not even going to go there. I don't want you locking the boys up until they're twenty."

"Now you're really scaring me."

"Anyway, back to our plans."

She liked how that sounded. "I'll swing by and get you. My rack can easily hold four bikes."

"I'll pick you up. I bought a new bike rack last week for the SUV. It needs a maiden run."

She smiled, suspecting he had bought the rack with her and the boys in mind. "Sounds like a plan. I'll see you later."

He made a kissing sound over the phone. "Can't wait."

She got up from the chair and set the phone in its cradle. Was he going to get bored with always having to get something to accommodate her family? Maybe she should offer to pay for it. With a shake of her head, she dismissed that idea. It would only irk him.

"Hey, Mom? What time are we leaving?"

She hadn't heard Johnny come down the stairs. "Drew's picking us up at eleven, which gives us plenty of time to get the laundry done and beds remade."

He handed her the ball of sheets he was holding, but she didn't take them.

"I think it's time you see how the washing machine works. It's not hard." She turned him in the direction of the laundry room. "And I'm happy to give you a lesson."

With a serious expression, he said, "You're right; I probably should learn. I'll be going to college soon."

Her heart jolted, and then she laughed. "We've got a few years before I drop you off."

✦

Drew pulled into Liza's driveway in a brand-new SUV. It was a cool gray with a dark interior and it had a lot of the bells and whistles a person could want, but he hadn't gone over the top. When he saw this sitting on the lot last week, he had immediately thought of her. Adding the bike rack and a tow package to it had been a good idea, in his opinion. If Liza was up for it, they could get one of those small tent campers and take a weekend here or there with the boys. But that was after they officially became a family. Although he wanted to spend every night with her wrapped in his arms, even just to sleep next to her, well, that needed to wait until they were married. He wanted to set a good example for her sons.

With a light toot on the horn, he got out of the vehicle and waited for the boys and Liza to come outside. For extra effect, he had added a big red bow to the hood right before he turned into the driveway.

As if on cue, the door burst open and the boys ran down the back steps. They were already climbing in the front seats to check it out. When Liza saw him standing next to the vehicle, a look of confusion washed over her face. With slow steps, she walked toward them, frowning.

"Hi."

He kissed her cheek. "Surprise."

"What's this?" She looked at the SUV and frowned as she studied the bow. "Please don't tell me you bought this for me."

Now he was confused. This was not the reaction he

had been expecting. He hoped she'd be thrilled when she saw it, but the look on her face said he had definitely read the situation wrong.

"I did." He put his hand on the hood. "You said you wanted something like Kate's, and this one is. Only in a color you admired once in town, and it's brand new."

"Boys." She snapped her fingers to get their attention. "Go in the house now." Her words were clipped, and that was not a good sign.

"But Mom, this is so cool and you should see how much room we have in the back." Johnny finally looked at her face and the rest of what he was going to say died on his lips. "Come on, George."

Once the boys were behind closed doors, Liza turned. Her lips thinned and her eyes narrowed. "How could you go out and get me a new vehicle? I told you I'd buy one when the time was right. Did you think that I wasn't capable of making a decision like this?"

"You said you've been really busy and when I saw this SUV on the lot, well, I just wanted to help out."

"Helping out is cleaning up the kitchen with me after a meal or carrying in the grocery bags for me. It is not spending fifty plus thousand dollars on a vehicle."

"But Liza." She held up her hand and he stopped at her name. "And for the record, my family swears I'll pinch a penny until it begs for mercy. I'm extremely frugal. I can afford to buy a vehicle or two if I wanted. Time was the real issue."

He cringed. Boy, had he been off the mark. Here he thought he was doing a sweet thing, and instead, all it had done was tick her off royally.

"Sweetheart, I am very sorry. I didn't mean to upset you. I was just trying to do something nice for the woman

I love. I worry the van is on life support and you and the boys will get stranded. Is it so wrong to want to make sure the three of you are safe?"

Her face softened slightly. "No." A smile tipped on one side of her face. "In fact, it's nice." Now she seemed to relent just a bit. "Why don't you sell me on the car, and then I'll buy it from you for what you paid for it and not a penny less."

"That's not necessary."

With a shake of her head, she crossed her arms across her chest. "You have two choices. The SUV can go back or you can sell it to me. I will not change my mind."

He gave her a smile and held out his hands to her. "I paid invoice, so you'll get a good deal."

She took the keys and pecked his lips. "The color is perfect. Now, tell me about these bells and whistles."

"I didn't go over the top, just a few essentials like making sure there were lots of cupholders in the back, third row seat, and plenty of cargo room for the boys' sports equipment." He let out a laugh. "Did I do okay?"

He opened the driver's door and she got behind the wheel.

"Do me a favor?" Her tone was no-nonsense. "The next time you decide to buy me something, ask first. I really don't like anyone to spend money foolishly, especially on me."

"You do realize that takes away the fun of buying you a gift, right?"

She cupped his face with her hand and kissed his lips. "Between my sons, you, and my family, I don't need anything more."

"What about Christmas, birthdays, and all the other

milestone days? Do I have to clear gift buying with you first?"

She pointed a finger at him. "I'm going to have to give you a budget."

He took it and kissed the tip. "When a gift comes from the heart, you can't put rules and restrictions around it. Please allow me to treat you on special occasions only."

She arched a brow and gave him a stern look.

He cocked his head. "What? You're not going to say anything?"

"I figure I can let you off the hook with a compromise, if you insist."

"I can agree for all, *just because I'm thinking of you gifts,* I will keep it reasonable."

"You don't need to buy me anything. I just said I have all I need and nothing I don't."

"If I want to buy you flowers or a coffee or something on the spur of the moment, I don't need to wonder if I'm going to upset you."

She tapped her chin and looked up at the sky before she gave him a huge grin. "I promise not to get upset or annoyed if you do something sweet, like pick me wildflowers or cook dinner or rub my feet after a long day and draw me a bubble bath." She leaned out of the SUV and tapped the door before she kissed him. "But don't get carried away like this again."

"So, as long as I stick with the super personal surprises, we're okay?"

"Yes, we're good and you can expect the same for me from time to time." She gave him a sidelong look, and then her grin slid from one side of her face to the other. "It's the little things in life that count the most." She touched his cheek. "Thank you for picking out this SUV. This model was the one I had my eye on just last month. I guess you do know me."

He kissed the tip of her pert nose. "Better than you realize."

"Come inside and I'll write you a check."

He kissed her again. "I love you, Liza."

She looked into his eyes and kissed him softly. "I love you too."

33

$\mathcal{A}$fter the bike ride Drew, Liza, and the boys went back to his house. While the boys played their video game in the family room, she and Drew had some time alone. They were enjoying a glass of wine while sitting on the deck when she set her glass on the arm of the chair. "Leo and Steph's wedding is in three weeks, and I was wondering if you'd like to go with me, as my date."

His lashes lowered and he looked at her like he was going to kiss her, causing her stomach to flip in a good way. "I would be honored to escort you."

"Well, before you get too carried away, Steph and Leo changed their minds to a more formal affair. Even though it's still small, it's a night wedding and black tie. So you can change your mind if you want." She chewed on the corner of her lip. Steve had never been too keen on wearing a tux for any event. Even when they got married, he would have preferred a basic suit.

"Does this mean you'll be in a gown?" He cocked one brow.

That had piqued his interest and her mouth went dry, knowing she wanted to see him in a tux next to her. "Yes, and the boys are wearing tuxedos too, as they're escorting the bride down the aisle."

He took a sip of his wine while he watched her over the rim of the glass. "I'm curious. How did that come about anyway, them standing in for the father of the bride?"

"It's a great story." She smiled. "Leo was watching the boys for the day since I was working. He went to see Steph's dad, coincidentally about the paint job on your Chevelle. He didn't know Eddie had recently passed away and, in fact, it was the day of his funeral."

His smiled dropped. "How sad for her."

"I think her dad was playing matchmaker, if you catch my drift." She swirled the wine in her glass. "Well, the boys were up to their usual antics and knocked over a display of model cars that Steph's dad had built over the years."

He frowned. "I can guess where this is going."

She held up her hand. "It gets better. When Steph had gotten her driver's license, she and her dad rebuilt a Bronco for her."

"The one she's driving? That's a beaut."

"The same one, but the replica got broken. I'm gonna guess she was ready to write the boys off as little monsters, but in the hubbub, Johnny got hurt and she patched him up. It was then they shocked Leo." She placed a hand over her heart. "George reached in his pocket and handed Steph his allowance to pay for the damages, and then Johnny did the same thing."

He smacked a hand on the arm of his deck chair and

grinned. "That's your boys. I'll bet that made you so proud when you heard what had happened."

She held up a hand. "It's even better than that. She thought the boys were his kids and he was in a relationship. It took a few weeks before that got sorted out. On top of all that, she was only planning on staying for six months to clean up her dad's business affairs and get it running smoothly before she went back to Portland. The rest, as they say, is history."

"Love won and my car helped." He clasped her hand. "You're cold. Would you like to go in?"

"No, it's a beautiful night and I'm enjoying being here with you."

His lips grazed the back of her hand. "You know, in a small way, the boys brought us together too."

"How do you figure?"

"The first time I saw you at Colin and Anna's party, you were with the boys. You had squatted down and were talking to them at eye level. I loved the connection I saw; it was like my relationship with my mom and that was a woman worth getting to know. Why do you think I kept coming to all of Colin's parties?"

"Because you're his best friend."

His head bobbed from side to side. "True, but each time I went, I got to see you. Even though you didn't know I existed at the time, I was hooked."

She moved to sit on his lap. Drew slid his arm around her waist and held her close. She relaxed in his arms.

"Last night over dinner, the boys wanted to know how come we don't have sleepovers like Steph and Leo did before she moved in with him."

In a low, sexy voice, he said, "Really. Now that is interesting."

"I was thinking if you wanted to stay over Saturday night, we could have breakfast together and see how the day goes—" She was interrupted by a heat-filled kiss. Her pulse hammered.

Drew said, "I would love to spend the night, and we can just sleep. Nothing more, just in case."

She placed her cold hands on his cheeks and pulled him to her. "Let's see how the night goes. You just never know." She poured her heart into this one kiss.

"I'm already looking forward to Saturday."

"Me too."

The following day, Liza slipped her brand-new wheels into a parking spot on East Street in Buffalo. She had to run to the stationery store for a client. As she strolled down the street, she hummed a happy little tune. Foot traffic was light and she looked up to check the building numbers; the store should be just a few doors down.

She noticed a Corvette parked on the street up ahead. It had CAM1 on the license plate. It was Drew's. What was he doing here? Maybe she'd bump into him and they could grab a cup of coffee before she went back to work. She slowed as she passed each shop to see if he was inside. She was halfway down the block when she saw them. Her footsteps stilled and she stared at them; Drew and a tall, beautiful brunette came out of the art gallery. They paused on the sidewalk and he wrapped his arms around her and gave her a hug that was anything but casual, and he kissed her on both cheeks. Liza moved closer to the building in hopes they wouldn't see her, upset they were too far away for their voices to carry. The woman kissed him again and he jogged to his car, did a U-turn and, with a short toot of the horn, drove in the opposite direction.

Liza blinked away hot tears as her heart sunk in her chest and her stomach clenched into a knot. Was Drew cheating on her? After all they had said and the future they had implied to each other. Here he was, kissing and hugging a beautiful woman?

The woman had turned to go back inside when she saw Liza. She gave her a concerned smile and began to walk toward her. "Miss, are you alright?"

Her voice had a faint Italian accent, which went with her beauty. The heel of Liza's boot got stuck in the brick walkway. She stumbled and caught herself before she fell.

"Miss." She was now at Liza's side. "Are you ill?"

Liza shook her head. "No. I'm fine. Thank you."

The woman took her arm. "Come. Let me give you a glass of water."

Despite her better judgment, she allowed the woman to lead her into the gallery.

The woman gestured to a chaise. "Please have a seat and take a few deep breaths. I'll get your water."

As she disappeared from sight, Liza's gaze roamed the large spacious room. She crossed the space and studied an oil painting. Somehow, it looked familiar. It was signed *B Ricci.*

"Do you like it?"

Liza jumped. "I'm sorry. I didn't hear you come back."

"You only need to be sorry if you say you don't like it. I'm the artist. Brea Ricci." She extended her hand.

Liza shook it. It clicked. The painting in Drew's foyer was by this woman. She looked back at the painting.

"It's lovely. You're very talented." Liza took the glass

of water and sipped. Drew was involved with this artist, and why not? She was everything Liza wasn't—beautiful, talented, and probably a thousand other things. She handed Brea the glass. "Thank you. I must be going now."

The concern in Brea's eyes seemed to burn her heart. "Are you sure? You're welcome to stay as long as you like."

"You've been very kind, but I must go." Liza hurried to the door and pulled it open. She fled to the safety of her SUV, the one Drew had picked out for her. She felt like such a fool. He was coming over tomorrow and they had plans to spend the weekend together. She groaned. Like that was going to happen now. She turned the ignition and, using hands-free, called Leo.

Before he could even say hello, she said, "I'm stopping at the shop. I'll be there soon."

"Okay," he sputtered.

Next, she called Anna, but it went to voicemail. Her cheeks were growing wet. She left a message. "I have to break it off with Drew. I'm on my way to Leo's. Call me."

*L*eo and Anna were sitting in his office when she strode into the shop office and flung her keys and bag on the desk.

"Drew's cheating on me with a gorgeous artist. They were embracing in the middle of the street." She dropped into the wooden chair on the side of the desk and dropped her head. She was destroyed.

She could smell her sister's perfume as Anna's arms encircled her and the door closed. Leo had left them. She didn't have any more tears left. She had cried herself dry.

"Do you want to talk about why you think Drew is cheating on you?"

She sat up straight and looked across the room to the field of vines across the road. CLW land.

"I saw him with Brea Ricci. Right there. On the sidewalk. In Buffalo. She's beautiful and Italian with a perfect accent. You know, where she could say anything and it would sound sexy." She waved a hand over her outfit. "Look at me. I'm approaching middle age, squishy in some places that she isn't. Why wouldn't he want to be with her?"

"Were they kissing, on the lips?"

She shook her head. "No, on her cheeks, and he hugged her. Like he knew her."

"How do you know her name?"

"When I saw them, he didn't see me. I started to cry and I tripped. She saw me and took me to the art gallery to give me a glass of water. That was when she introduced herself. He has one of her paintings in his house."

Anna handed her a box of tissues. "Dry your face and blow your nose."

She narrowed her eyes and gave Anna a hard look. "Are you taking his side?"

"I'm always on your side, but in this instance, I will tell you that you are so wrong." She pointed to the tissues. "After you dry your eyes, you're going to fix your makeup, as currently you look scary." Anna gave her a smile. "And you're either going to call Drew and straighten this out or you're going to believe me when I tell you that you have *nothing* to worry about."

"How can you be so sure?" Liza wiped her face and the black streaks of mascara were on the tissue. She was going to need a repair job before she saw anyone.

"Colin and Drew have been talking quite a bit lately and I can assure you that man is head over heels in love with you and he would never even think to look at another woman, much less play kissy-face."

"But I saw them."

"You saw them kissing each other on the cheek, which is how it is done in most parts of Europe. If Colin had freaked out every time a man kissed me goodbye on the cheeks, we wouldn't have lasted a week when we lived in France."

"I should trust him?" She tossed what was left of the tissue in the garbage.

"If I had any doubts at all, Leo would be holding me back from knocking Drew into next week." Anna rubbed her belly. "Me and junior would have taken him down." She tweaked Liza's nose just like she had done when they were kids. "I know it's hard to let go and trust that you have found happiness again. It has to be scary to not control every single aspect of your life, but this once, take a leap of faith."

Liza thought for a moment. Was she putting up a wall to protect herself? Anna was usually right as the older sister; it was probably easy to read her baby sister. She could take a leap of faith if for no other reason than she trusted Anna. "Alright. You'd never intentionally let me get hurt." She gave her a snarky smile. "Except when you told me if I went high enough on the swing, I could fly."

Anna laughed. "I was in trouble for a long time for that one."

"Too bad. I broke my wrist at the beginning of the summer that year."

"But the good news was that you had a bright-pink cast."

Liza got up and gave her sister a hug. "Thanks for having my back."

"You'd do the same for me. For the record, you're a long way from middle age and go find your man and give him a kiss that he won't ever forget."

Liza grinned. "I can do that."

"G'night, Mom. G'night, Drew." George and Johnny clomped up the stairs.

Liza cocked an ear as she heard the bathroom water run and then shut off. Two bedroom lights clicked on with the slow glow illuminating the stairwell.

"Now they'll read for a while and fall asleep with the lights on, and I'll turn them off when we go up."

"Does this mean we're finally alone?"

She sat on the sofa next to him, close enough so their legs were touching. The warmth from Drew wrapped around her. "As alone as you can be with two kids in the house."

He pretended to yawn and then draped his arm around her shoulders.

She laughed softly. "That was lame."

"I had to do something to break the tension. You've been wound up since I got here. Is anything wrong?"

"No. Not that I can think of." She was trying to take Anna's suggestion and just trust him, but the vision of him hugging Brea floated through her memory.

"Well, there is something that just crossed your mind. I can tell."

"I'm just tired. With Leo and Steph's wedding coming up, I have a lot on my mind, and I want everything to be perfect for them."

"With you running the show, everything will be." He gave her another long look.

Music was wafting through the sound system. "Do you want to watch a movie?"

"No. I'm liking this moment." He kissed her temple.

She couldn't not ask him and half turned on the cushion, then blurted out, "Do you wish I was more like Brea Ricci?"

"What are you talking about?" His brow furrowed. "And how do you know Brea?"

He wasn't denying it. "I was in Buffalo. Your car was parked on East Street and as I was walking to the stationery store, you came out of her gallery and that's when I saw you with her."

He averted his eyes for a second and she figured he was not going to answer. Was he going to try and avoid the truth?

"You should have called out to me. I would have loved to have introduced you."

She wrung her hands. "Do you have something you want to tell me?" She sounded like a jealous lover. *That is exactly how I'm acting.*

"Sweetheart, I collect her art and she's become a good friend and I stopped to ask her for a donation for the charity auction after the new year."

"There's nothing romantic between you?"

"I promise, she's my friend. You are the most beautiful woman in the world and I only have eyes for you."

The sincerity in his eyes assuaged her worry. "That's a little corny." She let him take her hand and looked at him through lowered lashes. "But I liked it."

"Now that we have that cleared up, I'd like to kiss my girl and show her just how much I love her."

Pushing all thoughts of Brea aside, she slid back on the cushion and said, "Don't make plans for Friday night. I have a surprise for you. No questions, but dress warm."

"Hmm, now that sounds intriguing." He nuzzled her neck.

"Well, I do have a few more surprises for tonight." She eased back into his arms. "By any chance, did you take a nap this afternoon?"

"No." His lips twitched. "Should I have?"

She tipped her head to one side. "Well, we might not get much sleep."

The next morning Liza was in the kitchen when the boys came down the stairs. Their hair was sticking up and George was rubbing sleep from his eyes.

"Johnny said he smelled bacon." He snagged a piece from the plate next to the stove and looked around. "Where's Drew?"

"He walked out to get the paper." She pointed to the table. "Will you guys help set it?"

Johnny picked up the plates and George got the silverware.

The back door opened and Drew came in with a smile. "Hey, boys."

"Hi, Drew." Johnny grinned.

Liza watched their interaction, looking to see if there was any awkwardness, but so far they seemed unaffected by him standing in the middle of the kitchen early on a Sunday morning.

"What should we do today?"

George looked over from the cabinet. "Are you hanging out?"

"I thought I would. Mom and the ladies are going to the dress shop, so I thought we could have some guy time."

They broke out into smiles.

Johnny said, "Cool."

Liza didn't need to worry. Drew had made his own place in the boys' lives.

riday night Drew came down the front steps of his house and opened the passenger door to Liza's SUV. He leaned over and kissed her cheek. "Hello, pretty lady. Am I dressed okay for our Friday night adventure?"

She took note of his turtleneck, sweater, and a jacket.

"Did you bring gloves and a hat?"

"Lady, where are you taking me to? Antarctica?"

"It is late October so it is getting cool out at night." She grinned and cocked her head. "And I'm not answering your questions. You'll just have to wait and see."

He patted his pockets. "Hat and gloves, check and check." He closed the passenger door and she eased out of the driveway.

He looked at the road signs. "We're headed toward farm country."

"Uh-huh." She picked up speed.

"They've cut the fields. So we're not going to the corn maze out there."

She glanced his way with a gleam in her eyes before looking back at the road. "You'll see."

"Come on. You're driving me crazy."

Her voice was light as she concentrated on the road. "Hasn't anyone ever given you a surprise before?"

"Not since I was a kid." He watched her instead of watching the scenery.

"Then you're overdue."

He glanced in the back seat. "A picnic basket. Hmm."

She smiled without looking at him as they passed a billboard for hot air balloon rides. He was going to be surprised. At least, she hoped.

"Are you afraid of heights?" She flipped on her blinker and turned down the gravel road.

"That was fast." He looked around. "There are a lot of people here for our picnic." His eyes opened wider when he saw the activity buzzing around them. "Hot air balloons. I've heard people tailgate at these sunset events." The excitement ratcheted up in his voice.

Her smile widened and she laughed. "I'm still not telling you." She parked and stored her cell phone in her jacket and her keys in an inside pocket. "Ready?"

He opened the back door. "I'll grab the basket."

"Leave it for now." She waited for Drew around the back of the SUV. She took his hand and pointed to the right. "We need to go over there, to the bright orange and yellow balloon with the chevron pattern."

The sun was slipping toward the horizon with streaks of orange and pink-tinged clouds drifting across the sky.

As they crossed the field her heart thudded with excitement. "You didn't say if you had an aversion to heights."

He gave her a quizzical look. "Are we going up?"

She grinned and threw her arms up in the air. "Surprise!"

He swooped her up and twirled her in his arms. "This is awesome!"

"I wanted us to experience the magic of floating through the air as the sun sets. Tonight is about making a special memory for us. The brochure describes the ride as flying into a stained-glass window. We'll land a few miles from here, have a glass of champagne, hop a van, and then have a short drive back. Once we return to the parking lot, we can tailgate and watch the balloons glow."

"How many people are riding with us?"

"Except the crew, it's just you and me." She hugged his arm tight. "I'm going for the ultimate romantic experience."

He drank in the sights and sounds of all the balloons filling and slowly straightening up. "I've never seen anything like this." He was in awe of the colors and the roaring sound of the burners blowing hot air into the towering balloons. Liza's engagement ring was in his pocket, where it had been for days. It might make an appearance tonight; it was a perfect and unexpected setting. "When do we climb aboard?"

She glanced at her watch. "They should be ready for us now."

As they got closer to the balloon, he was struck by the enormity of what they were about to do. She had put a lot of thought into tonight and she was right; this was a once-in-a-lifetime memory.

"Do you have a camera?"

She withdrew a small digital camera from her jacket pocket and smiled. "I do, and we each have our phones too."

A girl approached them. "Are you the Bradford party?"

He wrapped his arm around Liza's waist. "Yes. Are you ready for us?"

She smiled and ushered them to the basket. "Right this way."

Once on board, Liza's laugh was more of a nervous giggle. He wrapped his arms around her from behind and the balloon slowly rose in the sky. He leaned down, kissed her cheek, and whispered in her ear, "Thank you. No one has ever done anything like this for me before."

Her eyes sparkled as she looked up at him. "I'm happy you're having a good time." She pointed to other balloons drifting alongside them. "Look."

He could see some baskets held couples and others, larger groups. He was happy they could share this experience just between the two of them. The operator of the propane gave a tip of his head to Drew and Liza and smiled broadly.

As they floated along, it seemed as if they were aimlessly drifting, but there was a defined plan and Liza had assured him they knew where to set down.

He reached into his pocket and touched the ring, ready to ask her to be his wife, but this was Liza's gift to him. He had his moment planned and tonight was not the right time.

He withdrew his cell phone and nuzzled her neck. "We need to get some pictures before it's too late." He clicked away on his phone, capturing her beauty against the stunning backdrop. Then the girl in the balloon took their picture and Liza took some pictures of him with her camera and phone. All too soon, the balloon was descending like a feather softly floating to the ground. Once the basket was placed, they climbed out.

He pulled her into his arms and looked into her eyes. "Thank you for this amazing night."

"It's not over yet." She pointed to a waiting van. "The grand finale is dinner by the glow of balloon light." She took his hand. "But first, champagne."

He draped his arm around her shoulders and they walked side by side. How did he get so lucky to fall in love with a woman who was kind, generous, and for some strange reason loved him back with all her heart? He couldn't wait for her special surprise.

They approached a group of people and were handed plastic champagne glasses. The bubbles broke the top of the pale-gold beverage. The sunset in front of them was spectacular. He handed Liza his glass and pulled out his camera.

"I want a picture of you with the sunset."

She indulged him with a few photos. She handed back his glass and Drew held it up. "To us. May this be just another wonderful adventure in our amazing lifetime."

She touched her glass to his. "To a wonderful night."

eo and Steph's big day had finally arrived. Liza was combing a cowlick flat on Johnny's head when she glanced at George, who was tugging at the top button on his crisp white shirt.

The back door opened and Drew stepped into her kitchen. "How's it going in here?" He stopped short. His eyes traveled from her curled locks of blond hair down to the toes of her dark-green pumps. "You look… wow."

"Thank you." She wouldn't admit it out loud, but she knew the dark-green sheath dress did show off her curves, as well as give her the illusion of height. The heels didn't hurt, either. Judging by how Drew's eyes were popping out of his sockets, he thought so too.

She nodded to George. "Any chance you can help him with the button and tie?" She glanced at the clock. "We need to leave in five minutes."

He made short work of George's button and the bow tie too. "Leave your jacket on the hanger. You can wear your winter coat and when we get to the church, you can put the jacket on. It'll stay wrinkle free."

"Sure, Drew."

"Can you handle one more tie?" She turned Johnny to face him. "We should have ordered clip-ons for them."

He kissed her over the boy's head. "What would you do if I wasn't here?"

"Double-checked on clip-ons."

"Well, you know how to deflate a man's fragile ego." He chuckled as he adjusted John's tie. "You are good to go."

"Mom, do you have all my stuff?" Johnny asked.

"It's in my black tote bag. Carry it to the car for me?"

"Sure. Meet you guys out there, okay?" Johnny pulled at George's sleeve. "Come on."

Before the door even closed behind them, Liza sighed. "They're so grown-up."

"And they're too smart too. Do you think they know I wanted to get some smooching in before we left?"

"One kiss, and don't mess my makeup or hair." She gave him a wink. "On second thought, the only man worth his salt does mess your lipstick."

He pulled her into his arms and did his best to give her lipstick a good smear. When he let her go, his eyes skimmed over her lips. In a low and husky voice, he said, "You need to fix it."

S trains of music floated out from the open church doors. Liza and the boys were on the church steps after Drew dropped them off and went to park the car. Stephanie was waiting in a small room off the entrance, and when she saw the boys, her smile widened. "There you are."

"Aunt Stephie." They hugged her from each side and smiled up at her. The adoration went both ways.

George said, "You look really pretty."

"A lot different than usual." Johnny's face reddened when he realized what he had said. "I didn't mean that you're not pretty all the time. Just today, you're extra pretty."

"Thanks, guys, and you both look very handsome." She adjusted Johnny's tie. Looking at Liza, she said, "Did you forget their jackets?"

"Drew's bringing them in from the car. We didn't want them to get wrinkled."

They shrugged out of their heavy coats and flung them into the chair where Liza had placed hers. Drew entered the foyer with the hangers.

As soon as the boys donned their jackets, Liza pinned a single white rose to their lapels.

Liza looked at Steph. "Are you ready?"

Her eyes were bright and she nodded. "I am."

"I'll be right back." Liza pushed a little button that would flash a light to the organist to change the music. She ducked back into the room. "I'm going down to make sure everyone is ready at the altar. John, keep an eye out. When I give you a wave, you and George can walk Stephanie down the aisle and give her hand to Uncle Leo."

"Mom, we practiced this last night. We've got this."

Drew kissed her cheek and went to the front of the church to take a seat with the rest of her family. She blew a kiss to Stephanie and then her boys. They looked so handsome in their black tuxedos and sage-green bow ties. From the top of their heads to their shiny-tipped shoes, they seemed to have grown up. She blinked a tear away as she wished Steve could see them, but she knew in her heart he could.

Gary, Stephanie's best person, was waiting to escort Liza down the aisle.

When Liza was standing next to Leo, her eyes locked with Drew's. She could see the love in them. Her heart expanded as her sons kissed Steph's cheeks before they officially gave her hand to Leo. Drew slid over in the pew and made room for them. Her heart sighed with happiness. It was time to watch her twin marry the love of his life.

The reception was in full swing and Dawn had everything under control so Liza could sit and relax with Drew. He took her hand. "Another wonderful event. I don't know where you come up with the ideas to make each wedding or party personal."

"This one was easy by comparison; it's my brother. But it all comes down to listening more and talking less. Besides, I had Dawn's help, which has made the entire event run smooth as peanut butter." She yawned. "How do those kids still have energy to run all over the place? I'm beat."

"Too tired to trip the lights fantastic?" He wanted nothing more than to hold her in his arms, their bodies melding together until it was time to ask her the most important question of his life. He caressed her hand and pulled her to a standing position.

She gave him a tender smile. "And miss the opportunity to dance with you again? Not a chance."

Once on the dance floor, he twirled her into his arms. He slipped one arm around her waist while he held her close and kissed the palm of her other hand. Her head was on his chest as they swayed to slow and seductive music. Her floral perfume filled his senses.

They danced, first one song and then another until the song he had requested played. He slipped her hand into his jacket pocket. She lifted her eyes when her fingers grazed the velvet square box.

"Drew?" A question was in her eyes.

"I can wait." He kissed her face and lips. "If that's what you want."

Tears glistened in her eyes. She looked at Johnny and George and her entire family at the edge of the dance floor, watching them with huge smiles on their faces.

She stopped dancing. "Can I see what's in the box?" She ran her finger down his jawline.

The air was electric. Drew smiled to the boys. He waved them over and they took their place on either side of Liza. Steph and Leo stood behind the boys and he dropped to one knee.

"Liza Price Bradford. From the first moment I saw you, my life changed for the better in more ways than I could ever have imagined." He winked at the boys as his heart thumped in his chest and he popped open the box.

He held up an emerald cut diamond ring and looked deep into Liza's eyes. "Will you continue to change the rest of my life and agree to marry me? And together, with John and George, become a family?"

Liza looked first at Johnny and then George.

"We already said yes, Mom," George announced.

Johnny quickly said, "Say yes, Mom."

Her hand flew to her mouth, and she extended her left hand.

"Is that a yes?" Drew couldn't help but tease her a bit.

"Yes, I'll marry you." She smiled at her sons. "We'll be a family."

Thunderous applause broke out around them. He pulled her into his arms for a kiss, and then the boys joined them in a family hug.

Leo and Steph were the first to rush over and congratulate them, and the rest of the family gathered around.

Dad came over and kissed her cheek and shook Drew's hand. "What took you so long? We've been hanging around, waiting for this monumental moment."

Liza looked from her dad to Drew. "Did everyone know but me?"

Drew held her close to his side. "Yes, everyone knew I wanted to propose to you and before you think we stole any of Leo and Steph's thunder, this was Leo's idea for the two of you to get your happily ever after on the same day."

Her eyes grew wide and she looked at Leo and then Steph. Leo grinned and kissed her cheek. "I told him it was a twin thing."

Drew kissed her cheek. "Do you remember when you ladies went for the final dress fitting?"

Liza gave a knowing nod. "You got everyone together and discussed it."

"Not quite. The toughest conversation I had was with the boys. I was nervous they'd say no."

Her mouth formed a large O. "You asked the boys if you could propose to me?"

"Of course I did. After I got their approval, we had plans to meet at your parents' house with the rest of the men in your life. I wanted to make sure that your family knew what my intentions were, not just for you, but for the boys too."

Tears slipped down Liza's face and he withdrew a soft silk handkerchief.

"That is the sweetest thing I've ever heard."

Dad and Mom ushered everyone to the bar, leaving Liza and the boys with Drew.

"What else did you three talk about?" She arched a brow and looked at her boys, who were grinning from ear to ear.

"If you agree, the boys would like to change their names to Bradford-hyphen-Cameron."

Her eyes grew wide.

"I would be honored to be their second dad, but only if that is really what the three of you want. It won't change how I feel about them."

"Boys? Are you sure that is something that is important to you?"

"Poppi said a slip of paper makes what's in your heart official." George grinned. "At least that's what he told Drew when he asked if he could marry you. And Drew told him that the paper is so the world knows you want to walk through the world as one." He stuck out his thumb to Johnny. "We talked about it and we want the world to know that we are a family, with a paper to prove it. But keeping Dad's name means he's always with us too."

"When did you get to be so grown-up?"

He shrugged. "I dunno."

Liza thought the boys were wiser than some adults she knew.

Drew said, "We don't need to make any decision tonight, but know going forward you, George, and Johnny are my family."

She bobbed her head toward the large group of people at the bar. "We're a package deal. You know that, right?"

"I'm counting on it."

"Don't forget to warn your parents. The Price family is large, loud, nosy as heck, but when the chips are down, these are the people who'll be there for all of us."

He opened his arms and Liza stepped into them, and then he extended them even wider. "Family hug."

George groaned with a grin. "Mom, we're gonna need to explain the ground rules to Drew about hugging and stuff in public."

Drew chuckled. "We're making an exception tonight, okay, guys?"

They joined the hug. "Can we go home after Poppi gets all sappy?"

"Why do you think he's going to get emotional?" They looked at the family waiting for them.

"When he did the toast thing for Uncle Leo and Aunt Steph, his voice got all funny and he dabbed his eyes with a napkin."

Drew ruffled his hair. "Son, this is the stuff that memories are made of, and when it's your turn to get engaged and I give the toast, I'm sure Mom and I will both get choked up."

Liza looked up at him and smiled. "I do like the sound of that."

"What?" He kissed the tip of her nose.

"Our future just fell into place."

The Following Summer

Anna zipped Liza's barely green dress while Stephanie and Tessa watched. Liza adjusted an aquamarine necklace. She had worn it when she married Steve and it was the perfect finishing touch for today. Her wedding day, seven months after Drew had proposed.

Peyton and Kate were checking on the flowers and guests surrounding the gazebo. Mom was dabbing her eyes with a lace handkerchief.

"You're so beautiful, Liza." Steph placed a hand on her small baby bump.

Liza touched her arm. "Remember there are plenty of water dispensers scattered under the tent, so stay hydrated. And I've asked Dawn to keep an eye on everything too."

"With Leo fussing over me, I will. More than likely, my eyeballs will be floating. You'd think I was the first woman ever to have a baby." She laughed. "But don't tell him I said that. I love that he's so excited about our son."

"Have you chosen a name yet?" Mom asked.

"Edward Samuel Price, Eddie for short." She blinked away the tear that threatened to fall. "I hope Sam doesn't mind that we're naming him after my dad."

Mom sailed across the room and hugged her tight. "Not a chance."

Steph hugged Sherry and blinked away her tears. "Hormones."

Mom placed her hand on Steph's cheek. "Can you ladies give Liza and me a few minutes?"

Anna said, "I'll make sure the groom is ready and be back in a few minutes, okay?"

Mom waited until the door was closed. She took Liza's hands. "Are you happy?"

Her heart melted. "Mom, more than I dreamed possible. After Steve died, I never thought I'd fall in love again. Leo and Liza are going to be parents, Anna and Tessa with babies, Don and Kate and Jack and Peyton have wonderful families, and now here I am, getting ready to marry the man who's become my best friend, my lover, and my sons' second father."

"I was thinking the other day how out of everything bad comes good. If your father hadn't had his first heart attack, Don and Kate might not have moved home to Crescent Lake, and that had a ripple effect. Tessa met Max. Jack and Peyton found their way back together. Anna blossomed and fell in love with Colin, who brought Drew into Leo's life, which caused him to meet Steph, but the most important thing, it led Drew to you. My children are living their best lives." She kissed Liza's cheeks. "He's a good and smart man."

"Like in business?" That was an odd thing for her mom to focus on.

"No, sweetheart. He was smart enough to recognize the woman he was destined to love."

She smiled. Her heart was full and Mom was right. "You're such a romantic. But the chain of events really started with Grandpa Donald's heart attack and you marrying Dad."

A light tap on the door interrupted them.

Anna poked her head in. "Are you ladies ready? I think there is a groom getting antsy, and Dad and Leo are ready to give you away."

Liza touched her necklace. It grew warm under her fingertips. It was as if Steve were giving her his approval. "I'm ready."

Drew watched Hannah and Madison drop flower petals along the covered walkway. Anna would be next, and then Liza. John and George stood to his left. The boys beamed. The music changed to their song, and he stepped forward, anxious to see his bride for the first time.

After what seemed like an eternity, he saw her on the arms of Sam and Leo. Her smile radiated pure sunshine and love. They made the short walk down the aisle, stopping where he waited for her.

Her heart-stopping smile put a lump in his throat and he forced himself to swallow. "Hi."

"Hi, yourself."

"You look—" He looked her up and down, at a loss for words.

"You're speechless." She took his hand. "Now that's the best compliment you've ever given me."

He grinned and squeezed her fingers before kissing her hand. "You're ravishing."

With a soft laugh, she said, "You're not so bad yourself."

The pastor cleared his throat. "Shall we begin?"

Her laughter was contagious and Drew started to chuckle, which got the boys laughing too.

"Sorry, Pastor. A family that laughs together loves together." He took a step closer to Liza and kissed her before saying, "We're ready."

The ceremony words they had agonized over were a low hum until Liza recited her vows.

"Drew, I promise to share every high and low with you. You've completed our family in ways I can't begin to put into words. I promise to treasure and rejoice in our love for now and always. And like the canopy of a grapevine, our love will shelter our family as our roots run deep into the fertile soil we stand on."

"Liza, I promise you that I will stand by your side. I will love and care for you and our family each and every day for all time. I will walk through life holding your hand, and I promise I won't let go. Today you have made me the happiest man on earth. Today, I marry my best friend and become a father."

The pastor said, "I pronounce you husband and wife. Please kiss your bride."

Liza tilted her head back for this first very special kiss. Later, she would tell him they would need to add on to his house—their house now. Who knew? They might even have twins. After all, they did run in the family.

The End

If you loved the Price family check out the McKenna Family. These two series are connected to each other with Kate and Don in both series.

Here's a sneak peek at Lost and Found.

"Cari, if you're all set, I'm going to take off, too. Unless you need something, and then I'm happy to hang around." He wasn't in a rush to leave, but he didn't have a good excuse to stay.

"I'm all set. Thanks again, Ray, for everything. You were a big help tonight. I'll see you tomorrow at the shop? Breakfast is on me. After all, it's the least I can do." She gave him a lopsided smile.

"You don't need to buy me breakfast, but thanks. You're my favorite cook." He snapped his fingers for Gifford to follow him. "Good night." As he walked through his kitchen door he looked at Cari. Her shoulders were slumped as she walked into her house.

She found herself inexplicably drawn to what was left of the sunroom. Standing on the threshold, she peered into the gloomy darkness and the long shadows cast by the tree. She could see her piano on the other side of the room. Unsure of its condition, she picked a path over the debris and, to her delight, discovered the old baby grand and her treasured family photos sitting atop it were in pristine condition. The cushions on her overstuffed chair and ottoman were littered with pine needles, but otherwise untouched. Ben had given her the set when Ellie, her youngest daughter, was born. She was amazed at the total destruction on one side while the other perfect.

The ivory keys called to her, waiting for her fingers to lovingly caress them from rich low bass tones to sweet high notes. She studied the photos on display. Frozen moments in time of a full and happy life: a wedding photo with Ben and one with their newborn twins, Kate and Shane. She reached out to study a picture of the twins tucked into a chair and proudly cradling Ellie the day she came home from the hospital. She could still hear Kate tell her that baby Eleanor looked like a pixie, with wispy blond hair and crystal blue eyes, long eyelashes, and deep dimples. She had begged Cari to rename her Pixie Dust. She and Ben had laughed it off, but the nickname stuck.

Cari set the picture down and continued her journey down memory lane until her eyes came to rest on a framed photo. She, Ben, and the kids were grinning, despite the freezing cold. They were gathered around a freshly-cut Christmas tree. It turned out to be their last trip to the tree farm as a family. The smiling faces in the photo weren't prepared for the heartache to come a few months later, when five became four.

She dropped to the bench in front of the keys. Unaware of what she would play, her fingers found a melody. Raw emotions bubbled up from the depths of her soul. Slow and thick with emotion, music began to drift to the heavens.

She played music late into the night as a feeling of peace enveloped her. She glanced up through what used to be the roof. Pinpoints of light dotted the heavens. Shivering in the cool night air, she made a wish on the stars. Turning on the bench, she took one last look around the room. Countless moments—wonderful, bittersweet, and heart-breaking—had all taken place within these walls. She knew it was time for changes that went beyond paint on the walls and new curtains. Rebuilding would be the first step in making a fresh start, but there would need to be significant change. Cari decided to speak with Ray tomorrow. She wondered what could be possible without changing the footprint of the house. Exhaustion invaded her weary bones. New ideas would have to wait until tomorrow. Without a backward glance, she left the room and crawled up the stairs. Sliding between the cool sheets, drained, she fell into a dreamless sleep.

Soft notes wafted across the yard to Ray. He sat in the dark on his patio. The music tugged at his heart. In his mind's eye, he could see tears sliding unnoticed down Cari's cheeks. There had been countless nights when she played for an unseen audience.

Just click to start reading Lost and Found.

MORE BOOKS BY LUCINDA RACE:

LAST CHANCE BEACH

Shamrocks are a Girl's Best Friend March 2022

Orchard Brides Series

An introduction to the Cowboys of River Junction – Coming 2022

Apple Blossoms in Montana

The Sandy Bay Series

Sundaes on Sunday

It's Just Coffee Series 2020

The Matchmaker and The Marine

A Dickens Holiday Romance

Holiday Heart Wishes

Holly Berries and Hockey Pucks

The Journey Home
The Last First Kiss
Ready to Soar
Love in the Looking Glass
Magic in the Rain